INTRODUCING
Charlotte X

Charlotte Hains

SilverWood

Published in 2015 by SilverWood Books

SilverWood Books Ltd
30 Queen Charlotte Street, Bristol, BS1 4HJ
www.silverwoodbooks.co.uk

ISBN 978-1-78132-317-5 (paperback)
ISBN 978-1-78132-318-2 (ebook)

British Library Cataloguing in Publication Data
A CIP catalogue record for this book is available from
the British Library

Set in Sabon, Chedder Jack, and Univers by SilverWood Books
Printed on responsibly sourced paper

CHARLOTTE HAINS left the UK for France after deciding she needed a change, taking on the huge project of renovating a house. In the UK her life consisted of getting up, going to work, coming home, going to bed, and just surviving. She now enjoys French life within the community of the village in which she lives, and feels privileged to be part of it. She describes her French neighbours as fantastic, offering her help in every way they can, and says she might have given up long ago if they hadn't been so understanding.

With her house nearly finished she found herself with long nights and lots of thumb twiddling, reading anything she could get on her iPad. In honesty, she admits it was here that *Fifty Shades of Grey* caught her eye. Unbeknownst to her, her sister was reading it as well. Her sister thought that, because Charlotte has such a creative side, maybe she'd be able to write a book too. As a joke, Charlotte emailed her sister her stories, also written on her iPad. She researched blogs and BDSM sites on the internet, and so *Introducing Charlotte* came alive. Before she knew it, Charlotte had over 150,000 words which she'd sent by email in instalments to her sister, and there was more than enough for a book…or maybe even two!

Contact Charlotte at misschains@gmail.com

For my sister for believing in me

Chapter One

Leaving the hospital that morning, battered and bruised after another violent argument with the bastard, I was preoccupied with what I was going to do. Mainly, how I was going to get my clothes and belongings knowing he would still be there in the flat waiting for me? I was feeling ashamed of myself when two hands suddenly grabbed me and a voice said, "Hey, good looking!"

Looking up, tears in my eyes, I didn't recognize the face through the blur.

"Oh my God, Charlotte!" He paused, looking at the black eye and swollen lip, and put an arm around me. He carefully guided me to the side of the pavement, out of the way of the stream of passing people.

"What the hell happened to you?"

He glanced around the crowded street, then took my hand and led me into a nearby coffee bar. Sitting me down in a quiet corner he looked at me with shock in his eyes. The waitress arrived at the table and he ordered two cups of coffee, and then turned back to me. His expression made it clear that he still didn't believe what he was seeing. I looked down, wanting to hide my shame.

"Has anyone taken a look at that for you?" he asked.

Tears running down my face, I could feel the stinging of

the salt from them on my cheeks. I nodded a yes, hanging my head even lower. This is the first time I had ever let anyone I knew see me battered to a pulp; I'd always hidden it, scared of what people might think of me.

The waitress arrived with the coffees and put them down on the table.

"Anything else, sir?" she asked.

I could feel her eyes burning into me even though I couldn't actually see if she was looking at me or not as my head was bowed.

"No." Anthony's reply was sharply dismissive. The waitress turned away.

"Charlotte!" Anthony put a gentle forefinger under my chin. "Look at me. Tell me who did this to you – and why?"

I looked up, but I couldn't find any words to explain it to him. I was exhausted and scared of what he might think.

"Please, Charlotte!" His tone was both sympathetic and urgent.

I looked at him. He was frowning in concern. Oh my, I thought, I have known you all my life, and we never had secrets from each other. I thought back to the last summer we spent together, laughing and talking about our futures. He was going off to law school, and I was going into nursing. We had such high hopes and ambitions. I remember his parting words to me: "I stand here holding the hands of my dearest friend. I promise you I'll always be here for you, no matter what, when or where. I'll always hold you in my heart. You are the best friend I could ever want or wish for. I'll miss you as I would miss my Mars bars."

That made us both laugh so much at the time. He always had to have a Mars bar every day; he said he needed the energy to keep up with me, but deep down I knew it was because he was addicted to them.

I looked down at his briefcase now, wondering how many Mars bars he would have hiding in there. I bet at least one!

"Hey!" he said softly. "Are you going to talk to me or just ignore me?"

I looked at him, wistfully recalling the happy memories, and wondering when happiness had deserted me. He picked up his coffee and took a gulp, still looking at me with concern. Why couldn't I talk to him? Why was it so hard?

"Are you going to drink the coffee, or would you rather go to my place? Maybe you'd feel more comfortable and able to chat there?"

I found myself staring at him vacantly, more looking straight through him than at him.

He waved to the waitress and she brought the bill. She looked as if she was still smarting from his sharp dismissal of her earlier.

"Keep the change," he said, handing her some money.

Suddenly I wondered why he wasn't at work. No, please don't take time off for me. You really don't need to, I thought. But although my brain had woken up a little, I still struggled to say it out loud. I looked at him and thought of us as children, and a small smile formed inside me. *You know he's safe. You know you can talk to him.* But I didn't want to involve him. For his sake, I told myself. So I said quietly, "You should be at work. I'll be fine now." I tried to transfer that little smile inside of me onto my face in a hope to reassure him.

"Oh no you don't. You're not getting away from me that easily. I don't know what the hell's been going on in your world, seeing as I haven't seen you since..." he paused as his face crinkled and the penny dropped. "Since that guy you're living with came and rudely dragged you out of the bar last year! Has he done this to you? Is he hitting you?" His face filled with anger as he saw my shame, as if he could feel the pain I was in. "The fucking bastard! Come on, we're going back to mine."

He got up from the table, his case in one hand as he reached across to take my arm, and I flinched, shaking.

"Oh my God, I can see I have some work to do. I am not going to hurt you, Charlotte. Come, I promise you'll be safe at mine, trust me." His eyes were warm as he looked down at me. I nodded and got up and we left the café.

Outside we got into a taxi and a short journey later arrived at his. Leading me through the large Regency doorway he took me up to his apartment. Once inside he went through the first door we came to. I heard taps being turned on and water gushing into a bath. Coming back out into the hallway he said, "First things first, kid. You need to try to relax now. Hopefully a nice hot bath will help with relieving the pain from your bruises."

Anthony took off his jacket, one half of an expensive tailor-made suit. He looked very smart, but then he probably had to be now that he was a high-flying London lawyer.

"While you have a bath, I'll fix us something to eat. Take your time. I have some calls to make. I need to make sure my team knows what they're doing, then I'll be free to spend some time with you."

I looked at him quizzically. I didn't know he had a team, or that he had the power to just take time off whenever he wanted to. In fact the last I saw him, he was working for a firm: court work on behalf of companies.

While I lay in the bath I could hear him dishing out orders and straightening out his calendar for the next few days.

Thinking back to the last time I'd seen him, at the bar in Covent Garden, he'd been celebrating having the chance to open his own office, start his own client base. He specialised in company law legislation, or something, and was very good at binding contracts together, as well as twisting his clients out of the small print in contracts. He was always very good with words, and at worming his way out of trouble when he was a kid. He used to twist me round and round in knots just for the fun of it, laughing at my irritation and taking advantage of it. It was very rare for him to lose any debate.

"Hey you!" he called, waking me from my thoughts of us as children. "You always did take ages getting ready, you'll end up all pruney if you stay in the bath much longer!"

I moved, and my body hurt with a pang that reminded me of the bastard. His words came flooding back to me from when he was hitting me again and again, as I lay on the bed curled into a ball, trying to protect myself from his blows: "I'll teach you. You won't talk to any other person unless I say you can. You're a whore. You'll remember this for a very long time to come. You'll do as I say. Do you understand me?" With each word another blow to my body, as I trembled in pain.

Now, just hours afterwards, here I was in Anthony's flat and he wanted me to tell him everything. How could I? If the bastard found out he would bloody kill me! I couldn't tell Anthony. I had to get out, go somewhere away from here. I started to panic, and my body reacted to the increased tension. Fuck, that hurt! Oh Christ, what the hell was I going to do!

At last I managed to get out of the bath, and wrapped the towel hanging on the bathroom door around my fragile body. Even that was painful.

Walking over to the mirror, wiping away condensation with the flat of my hand, I saw for the first time how bad my face looked, covered in black and blue bruises. I couldn't see properly out of one eye, it was so swollen. I couldn't even see properly that the reflection was mine. What the fuck had he done to me this time? I had to get out of this relationship, but how? Where would I go?

There was a knock on the door. It opened slightly. I pulled the towel around my body, tightly hugging it around me as if my life depended on it. Anthony's face peeked round.

"You decent?"

Mmm. As I recall, that never worried him before. He'd seen my body loads of times when we were kids. Although we never had any sort of sexual relationship, our bodies never bothered us.

"I've brought you some of my clothes," he said, handing me a pair of dark blue joggers and a plain white T-shirt. "I thought you might prefer to put these on. Hurry up, I have your fave lunch ready for you." He closed the door and I could hear him walking off down the hallway.

My fave lunch? How would he know what my fave lunch was these days? I hurried to get dried and dressed, not wanting to keep him waiting. I opened the door of the bathroom and stepped outside, looking around cautiously. I walked down the hallway to where I could hear the noise of plates being put down on a table.

"There you are," he said. "Are you feeling a little better after your bath? You always did take a bath when you had things to work out, or if you were worried about something."

I nodded.

"Come. Sit down." He sat down at the table and looked at me. "Please tell me what has happened to you? I've never seen you looking so sad."

I looked down at the sandwich; to my surprise it was cheddar cheese and Marmite. Boy! We ate loads of those when we were kids. I smiled as I remembered our little picnics on the grass. Any bit of grass would do for us to sit on and eat the sandwiches we'd thrown together that morning. I couldn't believe I'd forgotten about them. He really did know what my fave lunch was.

"A smile, finally! That's much better."

I looked up at him. He was smiling back at me.

There was a glass of red wine next to my plate. I didn't recall having red wine when we were kids, and again I smiled. I picked up the glass in a toast to him and he reciprocated.

"Here's to lost childhoods, past and present." He put the glass to his lips and sipped the wine. I did the same.

"Munch up," he said. "Sorry about the lack of grass, by the way."

I looked at him, puzzled.

"You would never eat your sandwiches unless we sat on grass. I do have a green rug in my bedroom if you wish, but I didn't think you'd want to go out looking for a patch of grass right now."

"You're right, I wouldn't. Was I that much of a pain in the arse?" I asked quietly.

"Yes, and it looks like you still are. What sort of mess are you in? I can't help you if you can't tell me, and you know I'll help, whatever it takes."

Still holding my glass of wine, I looked at him, not quite knowing what I should do. To be honest, I didn't even know if I could trust him or any man ever again. My mind was muddled, confused. I'd had years of abuse, and two relationships both ending with me being mentally and physically scarred. I couldn't even trust myself to do the right thing any more. Touching the side of my face where the bruising hurt me, I didn't ever want to forget the pain they brought. I wanted to remember so that I'd never find myself in the same situation again.

"Do they hurt that much? Do you need someone to take a look at them? I can take you to see a doctor."

I shook my head.

"Oh, are we back to not talking again?" He smiled at me. "We have as long as you want. I've cleared my appointments for the next few days and I don't have to go in for the rest of the week. I can work online from here if I have to."

"No!" I said abruptly. "I don't want you taking time off from your work just for me."

"Hey, my choice! And too late now, it's been sorted."

Crap, what was I going to do? I didn't want to get others involved in my screwed-up world. I would sort things out for myself.

"The quicker you start telling me what's been going on the quicker you can rest, and the quicker I get back to work." I could hear a slight hint of a frustrated tone in his voice, but at the same time he was trying hard to keep calm and understanding. "You know I'll get it out of you eventually, so why not just tell me. It can't be that bad, can it?"

I looked at him. This was the hardest thing I had ever had to do in my life, except for giving up work, because the bastard thought that everyone who spoke to me was trying to get into my pants. I had loved my job as a nurse, looking after people, sick people. Nobody was ever too much trouble for me to try to help, to comfort while they were ill. A tear rolled down my face at the thought of everything I'd lost because of one overprotective, insecure, violent man, a bully, and a control freak without even a hint of compassion. What the fuck was I thinking, to take up with such a guy? Why couldn't I see them coming?

I felt so vulnerable sitting with Anthony. He wanted me to spill the beans and tell him everything, but would that change the way he looked at me? Would he feel that

I was some pathetic woman who couldn't control her own destiny? I didn't want his pity.

"Hey." He raised his eyebrows as if to say, *How about it? Come on…let's get this over with.* "What are you so deep in thought about? Nothing can be as bad as all that, surely?"

I glanced at him over the table. Where the hell do I start? I thought.

Then out of nowhere he said, "Shall I start? Stop me if I have this wrong. The night when I last saw you, you were talking with us all in the bar when he burst through the doors. It was crowded, and we couldn't really see who it was. We all turned back and carried on chatting. I was really excited that you could come to my little get-together, as I'd just got the money to start up my own practice, which by the way is going fine, thanks for asking." He smiled again and then continued.

"You were saying that you were hoping for some kind of promotion, that you'd just passed some more exams and were looking into working in mental health in the community when suddenly there he was, standing beside the two of us looking like he'd been running a marathon. I asked him if he'd like a drink and he stood as tall as he could and squared me in the eyes and said no, not even if he was dying of thirst. He then turned to you and said you were going. I tried to tell him you hadn't finished your drink and you said quietly that it was all right. He looked at me with a menacing glare, grabbed your arm and marched you out. I tried to phone you the next day but you didn't answer. I was so worried but I thought that you'd let me know if there was anything wrong. So – your turn, fill in the blanks, Charlotte." Leaning back in his chair, he waited for me to finish where he'd left off.

I took a deep breath. "How do you remember all of that, when I struggle to remember most of what has happened over the last year or so?"

"It's my job to remember details," he said softly.

"Anthony, if I tell you, you might not see me in the same way ever again. I feel so weak and pathetic. I can't seem to do anything right any more."

"What! What do you mean, you're weak? That you can't do anything right anymore? What has he done to you?" Anthony shouted.

I sat back in surprise. I'd never seen Anthony cross before. "Why are you shouting at me? Why are you so angry with me? See, I said you would see me differently and I've hardly said two sentences!"

"Oh, Charlotte, is that what you think? I don't blame you. It's him. I'm angry with him. The way he's conditioned you, making you think you're weak. He's used your big, kind heart against you, and he's taken – no, *stolen* – your mind, and left you feeling useless. Surely your friends at work have noticed?"

I gazed at him. His eyes widened slightly. "Oh no, you didn't give your job up for him, did you? What the hell are you playing at? No, sorry, I didn't mean you…er…"

He was trying so hard not to put the blame on me.

"Look, Charlotte, I'm out of my depth here. I want to cross-examine you but somehow I don't think it's what you need right now. I've sent a message to Lloyd. Do you remember him? He's a GP and has specialised in psychiatry. He'll have a better idea of what to do."

"No, I don't want him!" I said, alarmed. "I've only met Lloyd a few times and I really don't feel comfortable with anyone else knowing, Anthony."

"I can't do this on my own, Charlotte, and Lloyd can

help. It's what he's trained to do. I've asked him to come for a drink this evening. I'm sure he won't mind, and I'm not taking no from you for an answer."

"Oh, but…but…" I tried to protest, but Anthony wasn't having any of it.

"Charlotte, you need some rest, and this is getting us nowhere. Come on, I'll show you to your room." He came around the table to where I sat, moving my chair as I stood up. He then led me into the bedroom and, turning down the bedcover, he sat me on the edge.

"You rest, my best friend in the whole wide world, and I promise I'll help you and keep you safe." He leaned over to give me a peck on the cheek, but I moved my hand up as if to say no, so he moved over to the window and pulled the curtains.

"I'll come and get you when Lloyd arrives," he said, and left the room.

I lay stunned, thinking I couldn't remember the last time anyone was so nice to me, so gentle, making me feel warm and secure.

Chapter Two

The sound of voices woke me, but I couldn't hear what they were saying so I got out of bed. Feeling a little stiff and aching a little as I moved over to the door, I wasn't sure if I should go out or not. Anthony was talking. The tone of his voice sounded as if he was worried. I could only make out a few odd words and nothing that made any sense. I didn't recognise the other voice. I hurried back and sat on the bed (ecks I am so sore). I could hear footsteps coming up the hallway, then a small tap on the door.

"Hey, sweetness, it's Anthony. Are you awake?"

I went over to the door and opened it.

"You're looking better. How do you feel now you've rested?"

"Much better, thanks." I tried giving him a small smile.

"Come on, Lloyd wants to see you. He remembers you from my graduation. He thought you were so funny that day."

We walked down the hallway to the lounge, where Lloyd was sitting.

"Hey, ouch, nasty! I know, I should see the other guy, right?" Lloyd's face buckled, as if the pain I was feeling had reflected onto his face.

Probably an attempt to break the ice. I appreciated it.

Anthony brought a bottle of wine and a carafe of water to the coffee table, where glasses were already waiting.

"Hey, Anthony, before Charlotte has a glass of wine I need to ask her a few questions."

"Yes, sure, OK." Anthony looked a little surprised.

"You don't mind, do you, Charlotte? Lloyd gave me an encouraging smile. "It's just that I want to establish if you need any meds before you have any wine to drink. I can give you some sedatives if you'd like, to help you sleep, but not if you're going to be drinking."

"Yes, I understand," I said quietly.

"Good, OK, let's carry on, and see what we can do to help you. I'm sure you don't need to be told that you need to be completely honest. Nothing you can say will shock me. I won't and don't judge people, unlike some I know." He looked straight at Anthony and grinned. "Sorry, Charlotte, but I can't resist a dig at Anthony whenever I can. We can go to another room or we can stay here and send Anthony to the pictures. I have a fiver somewhere."

He obviously couldn't help joking. It was actually quite refreshing in some ways, hearing normal conversation and carefree laughter. It had been far too long since I'd heard that and I hadn't realised just how much I'd missed it. I replied to Lloyd with a hint of a smile in my voice. "No, it's all right. I think I'll let him stay. But to be honest, I don't know what I want to say right now. I feel like a complete idiot."

Anthony started to growl as if trying to say something. Lloyd raised his hand to quiet him. Turning, he said, "Right, Anthony, I never get to say these words to you, so I'm going to enjoy this. It's really important right now that you shut up. We need Charlotte to say whatever she wants to, when she wants and needs to, and for no one to cross-examine her in any way whatsoever. If she volunteers the information, that's her choice. For now, Anthony, my dear friend, you become a listener and that's all, to be here for when Charlotte wants or needs to talk."

Anthony looked embarrassed. Maybe because that was probably the first time he'd ever been told to shut up, or even to listen. I gave him a look as if to say 'poor old thing', but anyway he agreed with Lloyd.

"Right, Charlotte, you were saying—" Lloyd looked back at me, compassion in his eyes; blue eyes, that once upon a time I might have looked back at with a little glint of lust in my eyes. But who was I kidding! Who would want to know me?

"Um, yes, well, um…"

Where had my words gone? What did I want to say? Oh crap, I couldn't think.

"Charlotte, are you OK?" Lloyd asked.

I said, "No, I'm not. I don't know what to say. I really don't know what to make of any of what has happened to me. It's like I've been in a nightmare or something, and not able to get out. I'm scared, alone, frightened beyond belief, in fact. I don't know what to do or what to say. I don't think I can trust anyone. I don't even think I *want* to trust anyone. I don't know what I am going to do for work, or even if I'll be able to work ever again. I don't even know if I can walk out of the front door ever again." The words just kept flooding out of me. Once I started I couldn't stop, until I paused to draw breath.

"Right, OK, that's a start." Lloyd spoke before I could start again. "Can I just ask you one question?"

I nodded.

"Why do you feel that you can't do anything?"

I thought for a minute or two and then it came to me. "Because he told me. He has, little by little, taken everything away from me – and I hadn't noticed, until now." I looked at him, into those deep blue eyes. "I must sound crazy to you," I whispered. "I'm a crazy madwoman aren't I?"

"Charlotte, I'm pleased to announce you are not a crazy madwoman, or not tonight anyway. I think you'll be just fine. You need rest and time to adjust, and you'll find that your self-confidence and self-esteem will come back. It might take time. If you want, you can have some sessions with me, or you can just wait until I come over for a drink, usually once or twice a week." He grinned like a Cheshire cat. "Lastly, the first life-changing question for you: do you feel in any way that you might need some sedatives?"

My bewilderment must have been obvious, as both of them looked long-faced at me.

"Er, OK, let's put it like this," Lloyd said. "Do you want a glass of wine or do you want water and tablets to help you sleep tonight?"

"Oh, OK, can I have a glass of wine please? I really don't like taking drugs of any kind if I can help it."

"Good girl!" both boys said simultaneously. Lloyd held out a glass and Anthony poured the wine.

I found out later the whole thing had been staged, to try to put me at ease, and to see if I could make a decision for myself: a little lighthearted banter in an attempt to help me open up a bit.

"Right then, a toast," said Anthony. "To new beginnings and to shutting bloody heavy doors that should never have been or again be opened!"

Anthony raised his glass. Lloyd and I followed suit and clinked ours with his. Anthony always was good at saying the right thing. We sat drinking wine and chatting, although most of the chat was recollecting our childhoods, when they were at university together, and some of the things they got up to. While I listened I realised just how much I'd missed out on in life by being with the asshole and then with the bastard. Well, I was never going back there, that was for sure! And somehow I didn't think these two would let me either.

Chapter Three

The curtains shut out most of the light from my window, but when I woke next morning I could see that the sun was shining. I started to move, and – oh shit, that hurt! The whole of my body trembled in pain and I realised that getting up was going to be a long job. I managed to swing my legs out of the bed and then rest for a moment or two until the pain eased a little. Then I placed my hands under the side of my body on the bed and pushed so that I was sort of sitting up. Jeez, it hurt so, so much! It hadn't hurt like this yesterday evening. Suddenly Anthony was at the door, knocking softly.

"Are you OK?"

He must have heard me moan when I sat up.

"Er, yes. Come in if you want," I said through gritted teeth, and Anthony opened the door. I grimaced. Every muscle in my body seemed to twist as I sat up properly. A long "Awww!" of relief. That was the first part done, anyway!

I looked up at Anthony. He looked just as I remembered him during our last summer as kids, before he went to university. He was wearing faded blue jeans and a white T-shirt, and his feet were bare.

"You only just getting out of bed?" His tone was light and teasing.

"Give a girl a chance!" I poked my tongue out at him, trying for the same light tone.

"You never change, do you? You used to say that when we were kids and I would race you!" In his 'let's pretend I'm Charlotte' voice he squeaked, "Awww, give a girl a chance!" Then, switching back to his own voice, "What you really meant to say was 'let me win'."

"Yes, you could have been a gentleman about it," I said.

He laughed. "As if, right! You need to be getting out of that bed. Should I order a crane or will I be able to lift you?"

"If I didn't know you better I'd think you were trying to make a pass at me. I bet that one's in your copy of *101 Chat-up Lines*." We looked at each other and started laughing. Eventually he helped me off the bed and I made it to the bathroom.

Standing in the shower, I felt the hot water bringing relief all over my body. Soon enough most of this will be healed, I thought, and the aches will be nothing but a memory somewhere in the back of my mind, as they always are for me. I got out of the shower and put on the clothes I had on the day before. Anthony's clothes, as I didn't have any others. I went to the kitchen where Anthony was getting some breakfast ready for us.

"Hungry?" he asked.

I realised that I was starving. I couldn't remember the last time I'd eaten. The cheese and marmite sandwich yesterday had just sat on the plate as I stared at it.

"Yes," I said.

"Bagels and cream cheese do you? They always go down well with fresh coffee and orange juice."

Then as if by magic I could smell the fresh coffee on the stove.

"That's new!" I said, pointing to the cooker.

"Yes, and so is the kitchen that you haven't noticed either!"

I looked around. He had a newly fitted kitchen, with a centre island which had a sink and fridge built in underneath it, and a hanging rack suspended overhead with jugs, pots, pans, and some bunches of dried herbs hanging from hooks.

"Neat idea," I said, looking up, taking in all the things hanging from the rack.

The rest of the kitchen involved units with what looked like oak doors, some with leaded glass and some that were solid. I peered closer. They looked old.

"I had all this made just after my grandparents died. The doors are from the pharmacy they owned. Remember the old shop they bought? Or possibly not, actually, seeing we were only about three years old at the time," he chuckled. "Anyway, they left me everything in their will, so I decided to have these put in to remind me of them."

"I remember," I said. "The shop was full of 'you name it, they had it' type things." I smiled fondly at the memory of spending hours in that shop just looking at all the different curiosities it offered. "Wasn't the name of the shop Curiosity Pharmacy? And the slogan was 'you will find everything you need to lift your spirits'?" We both laughed.

"That's better," he said. "You seem much brighter today. Lloyd said a good drink and rest would see you right, and he was right. He normally is, although I don't like telling him that."

The coffee finished spitting and jumping and Anthony picked up the pot and brought it to the breakfast bar. We sat on the stools, remembering them in the shop. Big oak stools with high backs. His grandparents always sat on them.

Sitting at the bar Anthony looked at my face and stroked softly down the bruised cheek.

"That looks better. The swelling has gone down more than I thought it would do."

"Do you think?"

"Oh my, yes. I bet by next week it will almost be gone."

He poured out the coffee and handed me a bagel, and we sat eating. When we had finished, he said, "We have to sort out some clothes for you. I guess you don't want to go back to your place to pick some up?" My horror must have been clear because he shook his head. "Of course you don't."

I didn't need to answer.

"OK," he said. "I'll ring one of my friends and get her to bring you some clothes over. Did you want to go shopping or shall I just tell her to buy whatever she thinks will work?"

"I don't want to go shopping, and I'm not really sure I want a lot as I don't have any money to pay for them."

"Don't worry about that, I'll sort it out. You don't need to worry about anything. Give it a few weeks and then we can see what you want to do, and what options you have," He smiled reassuringly and picking up his phone, he made a call.

"Nats, darling! How you doing? Good, good. Look, I'll cut to the chase. I need a favour from you. Would you be able to bring me over some clothes? I have an old friend here and she has nothing to wear. Long story." He paused for a moment, and then said, "OK, I'll make a fresh pot of coffee. Till then..." He put his phone down on the counter. Picking up the coffee pot he said, "She's just around the corner. She's going to call in and see us first."

"Oh no! I'm not sure I'm ready for meeting people yet." I could feel the panic rushing through every part of my body. As I tensed the pain increased.

"Now stop! You'll be fine. She's really nice and I'm sure

she'll be able to help you. She's a beautician and hairstylist. There's nothing she can't do with hair."

I chuckled at that. "How would you know? You're as bald as the day you were born."

Anthony had premature baldness. By the time he was twenty-one his hair had receded so much he decided he'd shave it all off, and I had to admit he looked rather sexy.

"Ah, the intercom." He trotted off down the hallway. "Hi, Hon, come on up. I'll open the door for you." He unlatched the door and then returned to the kitchen. Getting another cup out of the dresser, he poured some coffee into it just as Nats walked through the door shouting, "It's only me," with exaggeration on the 'me'.

She caught sight of my face. "Oh my, er...what are we going to do with this?" As she looked closer I turned my face away from her.

"Oh no you don't, lady! You sit with your head held high. Don't you turn your face away from anyone!" she said.

I was so taken aback that I turned back toward her.

"The handiwork of someone you know, Anthony?" She looked straight at him.

"No, I don't know anyone who would do such a thing! Well, not in my social life that is. I've defended some right nutcases in my time, but her boyfriend wasn't one of them."

"Soon to be ex, I hope, honey? You're much too pretty to be black and blue."

"That's Charlotte's choice, Nats, not ours." Anthony said.

"Charlotte, it's nice to meet you. I'm Nats, as you'll have gathered! Now, introductions done, let's see what we can do for a short fix. I have all sorts that can cover this up."

"Nice to meet you, Nats, but I really don't want to bother you and take you out of your work," I said timidly.

"No bother, I've got nothing to do today until this

evening. That reminds me, Anthony, are you going tonight? Kat asked me to ask you."

"No, I don't think so. I was going to ring Kat later this morning to have a word."

"Why are you not going out, and who is Kat? A girl-friend? I don't want to get in the way of anything you have planned," I said, looking over at him.

He was looking at Nats with an odd expression, as if she'd let the cat out of the bag.

She laughed. "Oops, OK, sorry."

I looked at her, and then back at Anthony. "Oh my God, you *do* have a girlfriend? Why didn't you tell me?"

"Firstly, she isn't my girlfriend. Secondly, I am not going out tonight. And thirdly, you are not in my way in any sense whatsoever." He looked grumpy.

I glanced at Nats as if to say, 'Come on, tell me, is this Kat his girlfriend or not?' but she didn't say anything. She picked up her car keys and said, "Just a minute, I'll get my things out of the car, and then I'm fixing you up." She scurried off.

I raised an eyebrow at Anthony, then shrieked "Ow! Fuck!" The pain just from raising my eyebrow was surprisingly intense.

He laughed. "That will teach you to be bloody nosey, and no, I don't have a girlfriend. Kat's a friend who doubles with me when I go out, but she'll find someone else to go with, trust me. Not a problem."

Moments later Nats burst back in, now with three big bags in her hands. "OK, let's get this show going." She put the bags on the breakfast bar and started to unpack them.

"Right, Anthony, off you go. Leave us girls to it."

"Er, hey—" he tried to protest. Poor Anthony. First Lloyd and now Nats telling him what to do.

"Go on, scram, this is girly stuff. Get gone." With a mock wounded look on his face he left us.

"Not sure I can cover these bruises completely," said Nats, "but let's see what we can do." With two fingers under my chin she lifted my head up toward the light. "Let's have a look at your hair." Scooping hold of my hair she let it fall back through her fingers.

"I'm really not sure I want you to do anything," I said. "I'm not really in the mood for this, to be honest."

Ignoring me, Nats said gently but forcefully, "OK, let's put on a nice soothing face pack first, I think." She went over to the fridge and opened the door. "Knowing him, he'll have just the job in here."

I looked at her, not even knowing what she meant. First she talked about a soothing face pack, and then she was looking in the fridge?

"Here we are." She took out a cucumber and an avocado. "This will do the job. Your face will be good enough to eat!" she said, laughing.

I really didn't know what to think. As I watched, she found the food blender, cut the avocado and took out the stone, then scooped out the inside. She chopped up the cucumber and, dropping everything into the blender, blended it for about thirty seconds.

"Done! Now for the secret ingredient."

She went over to where she'd emptied her bags and picked up a tube of Preparation H hemorrhoid cream. What the hell is she going to do with that? I thought to myself, my eyes widening. She squeezed a good amount into the green mush and blended for another twenty seconds or so. Seeing me staring, she shouted over the noise of the blender, "I do love to see people's faces when I do this. It's so funny! No, this isn't for eating!"

My face must have been a picture of confusion, as I really didn't know what she would do next.

"This is for your face. Hopefully it's nice and cold and will help soothe the pain from your bruising. The Prep H cream will hopefully help with the swelling. It's excellent for bags under the eyes and such like. I'm hoping it will reduce your lumps and bumps a little." Bringing the bowl of mixture to the coffee bar where I sat, she grabbed a scrunchie from the table to tie my hair out of the way, and then plunging her hands into the mixture she very carefully patted the green slime onto my face.

"Right, coffee time I think, and I'd better take one in for Anthony. Don't want him coming out here and seeing you like that, do we?" She winked and went over to the sink.

She had very long eyelashes. I thought they must be false. Her make-up was what you would expect of a beautician: she wore a lot, expertly applied. She looked like she'd been tangoed with spray tan, although not as orange as some. As she stood at the sink washing her hands, her hair long, caramel-coloured curls cascaded down her back. It looked lovely. With that and her slim figure she was very attractive. She made the coffee and took a cup to Anthony.

Alone at last, I sat on the stool, eyes closed, thinking. I suddenly realised my face was tingling slightly and the mixture felt very cold, but she was right, it did feel soothing.

Half an hour or so later Nats returned to the kitchen.

"Right, let's remove this mess from your face and admire the results." She grabbed a handful of tissues and started to wipe carefully around my face. The relaxing sensation that I had started to feel the pain came back as she wiped the mixture of my face. God, was this ever going to stop? Every sweep of the tissue felt like a hot towel being pressed into my skin.

When it was all off, Nats walked round in front of me. "Let's look at you."

I tilted my head so I was looking deep into her eyes. They were the deepest shade of lavender blue. I squinted as I looked closer. I had never seen anyone with that colour eyes before. Were my eyes playing tricks because they were swollen? As I squinted I suddenly realised that my eye actually didn't seem so swollen now as it had done.

"It's OK, they change colour."

My eyes opened wide and my head jerked back in amazement.

"*What*?"

"That got you! You spoke!" she laughed. "It gets everyone." Smiling, she stood up from her semi-crouching pose. "They're contacts."

"Oh, OK, that's good, I was beginning to think you were a witch or something, with your magic potion-making and all."

"You ain't seen nothing yet."

She picked up a mirror from the table and held it in front of my face. To my amazement the swelling didn't look half so bad. She picked up the Prep H cream and put a little more around the eyes.

"This will help to take the swelling down a bit more, and I think we'll put some more around the lips as well. It's a sexy look to have big lips, but that is just a bit ridiculous." She had such a gentle touch when she applied the cream. "Right, next stop hair. Nothing like a new hair-do to make us girlies feel like we're on top of the world, especially when we're changing our lives around, don't you think?"

"I suppose so," I said hesitantly.

"So, do you want to talk, you know, girl to girl, bit of hairdressing chit-chat?"

I shrugged my shoulders, not knowing what to say. I didn't know her; she didn't know me, why should I talk to her?

"Oh come on, there's nothing like it for getting things off your chest." She started to spray a fine mist of water on my hair, teasing it with her fingers. "It's been some time since you've done anything with this mop!" she said, half mocking, but half-serious too.

I cast my mind back, trying to think how long it had been since I last went to the hairdresser. I couldn't remember. For about the last eight months I'd hardly been out at all. It was easier to stay in than to have the interrogation on my return: where had I been and who had I seen?

Nats started combing, then cutting. Snip, snip. Her scissors moved easily and professionally through my hair.

"You know, you might not think it, but you have lots of friends who you haven't even met yet."

"What do you mean?"

"You have all of Anthony's friends, starting with me. We'll all stand by you no matter what you want to do, and help you sort yourself out. We don't judge people. We're all what we are and we all respect each other for that, you know?"

What did she mean? I thought to myself. How could people be my friends if they didn't know me? How could I be friends with them if I didn't know them?

"It's OK, you know. You'll get used to having people around you who care, and today is my treat for you: a full makeover, with clothes. You'll feel like a different woman, you wait and see. I know you're probably thinking you just want to be left alone, but deep down you're running scared. You want to hide, shut yourself away, and that's natural, but you really don't have to."

Throughout all of this she was snipping away with the scissors. How could she talk so much and cut hair at the same time? She moved around in front of me. "Right, let's look at this."

Tilting my head first one way, then the other, she started snipping away again. Oh my God, so much hair was coming off! I watched it fall to the ground.

"Right, that should do it, let's get some body into your hair now, and maybe a little attitude too, I think."

She plugged in her hairdryer, then picked up some hair mousse, sprayed a huge lump of it into her hand, and started to work it through my hair, concentrating on the ends. Then picking up the brush and hairdryer she began to dry my hair. When she finished she plugged the straighteners into the socket next to the hairdryer.

"They'll take a few minutes to heat up, so face time again while we're waiting. Let's get this hair up on your head so I can see what I'm doing here."

Pinning my hair on the top of my head with a big springy clip, she put cream on my face, then some concealer, then blusher.

"There, I think that should do it. We don't want to over-work it or you'll look just as bad; nothing worse than trying to disguise something with too much make-up." She winked at me again. "Right, straighteners, but first I'll put the coffee on so we can have a drink afterwards." She set the coffee going then fussed over my hair for an age until suddenly she said, "Done. Want to look?"

She walked round in front of me, smiling.

"A job well done, even if I do say so myself. Look."

She handed me the mirror. I looked in it and for the second time in two days someone else looked back at me from the reflection. My blonde hair looked wild but in a controlled way, and seemed to curl around my face, hiding the worst of the bruising. The Prep H cream took down a lot of the swelling. The make-up had been blended in such a way as to take the harshness out of the bruises. She truly was an artist.

Tears sprang into my eyes, that seemed bluer from the way that Nats had chosen eyeshadow in delicate pink with a blue tinge. My face looked sculptured with blusher, again with pink that highlighted my cheek bones, although I think the swelling was also helping here, a bit like Botox! Finally, a clever shade of lipstick helped blend the uneven look of the swelling. It had been so long, too long, since I'd looked so good; even with my face black and blue I looked good.

"Hey, don't cry, we'll have you back to normal in no time at all." She gestured in the air with her fingers at the word 'normal'.

"I… I just don't know what to say. It's fantastic. Thank you."

"This is the start of the new you. I'll leave you the make-up so you can put it on each morning as you wish. Now for coffee. Anthony, coffee!" she called to him.

Anthony appeared at the kitchen door. He looked at me and did a double take.

"Oh my God, it *is* you! I was starting to think I'd picked up a stranger in the street yesterday." He leant on the frame of the door, staring for a minute or two, and then went over to a big cupboard. From it he grabbed a broom and a dustpan and brush, and then swept up the hair on the floor and put it in the bin.

"That's better. You are tidy and so is my kitchen." He gave me a cheeky grin. He'd always been a neat freak – everything in its place and a place for everything – and by the looks of it he still was. Nats brought a coffee to the bar for us all and we sat down.

"I feel lost for words," I said. "I don't know what to say, or how to say it. To be honest, I feel as if I'm at long last waking up to find that I don't even know who I am any more. Does that sound strange?"

Anthony looked at Nats and said, "Is this another girly moment on its way?" with an air of being slightly out of his depth.

"Oh, Anthony, you don't have to go anywhere. You have helped me so much just by being here, but this is my fight too, and Nats chatting all morning, and what she has done for me, has shown me that I don't want to talk about the past. I want to leave it right there. In the past," I said, emphasizing the last words. "I want the bastard to stay the hell out of my face."

"Are you going to the police?" Nats asked.

"No, I don't want to. I won't be able to go through with it. I've given it some thought, but I just really don't think I can go through all the ins and outs of what's happened, and to be truthful I don't want to relive it all."

"How are you going to keep him away from you?" Nats asked, puzzled.

"Leave that to me," said Anthony. "I need to know what you have there and what you want back, and I'll send my mate from CID to scare the living daylights out of him, and at the same time to collect anything you want, if you make a list."

I didn't understand. I didn't want the police, and now Anthony wanted to get CID involved?

"No, Anthony, no police!" I begged.

"No, you don't understand. He'll go as if it's official and just frighten the creep. I've already spoken to my mate about it. He says he'll make sure he won't bother you again if that's what you want. You haven't got to say anything. Just leave it to him. Write a list of everything you want back."

"I don't have anything there. I have most of my valuables at Mum's. I took it all there when she was on holiday some time ago, when I first thought about leaving him but couldn't go through with it. I was just so scared. I wish now that I had."

"OK, time for a little visit from our friends. Don't worry, he'll never bother you again." He picked up his phone and looked at me. "You sure about this? There's no going back. Once it's done it's done."

"Yes," I said. It was now or never, and I didn't want to go back.

He made his phone call. "OK, he's all yours," and hung up.

Anthony was right. I never saw him again. I don't know what happened or what was said but someone somewhere closed a chapter, for which I'll always be grateful.

Chapter Four

Time flew past over the next few weeks or so. Anthony bought me a new wardrobe of clothes, lovely designer outfits, and he insisted I live at his. The bruises had all gone and I felt like a million dollars. Life got better every day, although I still had some hang-ups I just couldn't shake. I felt insecure around all men except Anthony, and I didn't seem to be able to make decisions for myself. I had to run everything past Anthony first. My self-esteem had taken a big hit.

I had been for some interviews, but if there was a man amongst the interviewers I couldn't answer him with confidence. It was so difficult – I'd only been out of the flat three times in five weeks – and I didn't really know why. I thought maybe I should go and see Lloyd and have a few sessions with him, but I didn't like to ask. Perhaps I could ask him next time he came if he could fit me in for a little chat?

Anthony went out a lot, and if he wasn't out he was working hard. I cooked meals and cleaned the flat for him, although there was no need as he had a housekeeper who came most days. Nats came over a few times and she did some amazing things with make-up for me that I never thought possible. She wanted to give me a spray tan but I wasn't sure about that one. Between her and Anthony they made me look, and feel, drop-dead gorgeous, if I did say so myself.

"Hey, Charlotte, what you up to?" Anthony called out as he came through the flat's front door.

"Oh, nothing much, same old."

"We're going out tonight and you're coming. I'm not taking no for an answer!"

"Where are we going?"

"Just out with Lloyd for something to eat, so I'm afraid you'll have to put up with both of us. Reckon you're up to the challenge?" He laughed as he walked into the lounge.

"What time are we going?"

"Soon. I just need to shower and put jeans on. I'm not going out like this, that's for sure." Anthony was dressed in a very dark navy, almost black, suit with a fine pinstripe, a white shirt unbuttoned at the collar and a tie, which was also navy, loosened around his collar. It all fitted him very well indeed. He rushed through the lounge to his bedroom to change as I got up to go and sort myself out too.

Once ready, we made our way to a bar in Covent Garden – not the same one that the bastard dragged me out of, thank God. I was relieved, thinking that if Anthony had told me that Covent Garden was on the cards I probably wouldn't have come at all.

Inside, Lloyd was waiting, propping up the bar. Seeing him dressed in faded blue jeans and a white T-shirt I looked at the two of them and laughed. "You look like a pair of book-ends." They were dressed exactly the same: Tweedledee and Tweedledum sprang to mind, although Lloyd and Anthony were considerably leaner.

"Pleased to see we provide you with amusement, Charlotte," Lloyd said with a grin.

I realised I was bantering with Lloyd and bowed my head as I felt myself go red.

"Shall we eat? I'm starving!" Lloyd said, as he walked

over to a booth table. "This table's out of the way, so we can chat more easily."

We sat down, and a waiter came over to give us menus.

"Your usual tonight?" he asked as he hovered over us.

Lloyd said, "Share a big plate of everything on the menu, or do you want to go it alone?"

I looked at Anthony who replied, "A plate, kind sir, will do me fine."

"And I'll give it a go too." I looked over at Lloyd.

"Yes, my dearest waiter, the usual will suffice."

To my surprise the waiter, Lloyd and Anthony fell about laughing.

"What's the joke? Have I missed something? And what's with all this 'kind sir'?"

"It's a long story and not one for this evening," Lloyd said, smiling.

"I assume you both know the waiter?"

"Yes, he's studying to be a lawyer and works here for pocket money. To cut a long story short, it was the students' rag week a while ago and he dressed up as a noble lord from days gone by. He was very drunk and did some very silly things, so every so often we like to remind him. We can't help it," Lloyd explained. "Anyway, enough. I want to know how you're feeling now. It's been a while since I've seen you. I can tell your face is better, and you look lovely. Anthony and Nats have obviously been looking after you well."

"Yes, they have, Lloyd, and yes I am much better, thanks." I hesitated. I wanted to say how I was feeling about men but didn't know how to put it so as not to sound stupid.

"Come on, don't be shy. Just say what you're thinking."

I looked at Lloyd. "I don't know what it is, really, or indeed if it's anything at all, but I have this strange hang-up over communicating with men. I feel very uneasy when

I'm in the same space as them. For instance, I've had some interviews over the last few weeks, and whenever any of the interviewers are men I can hardly talk to them. I feel uncomfortable. I know it's stupid as I feel all right with Anthony and you, and I just can't understand why I feel so insecure."

Lloyd thought for a moment. "You've had a lot to deal with, and the feelings you're having are normal. I think, more than anything, it's a trust issue. Trust is a very important part of any relationship, even the one we have with ourselves. Trust is what keeps us safe."

"I don't understand."

"OK. You've repeatedly been very badly hurt by a man, yes? But yet you are comfortable in the company of Anthony. So why do you feel that Anthony's OK? Why are you comfortable with him?"

"Because he's my oldest friend." I replied easily and truthfully.

"That's as may be, but would it be fair to say you feel safe and secure with him?"

Before I could answer, the waiter returned with plates and cutlery for the three of us, which he placed on the table. Anthony thanked him, and he nodded and left us. This gave me time to think before answering Lloyd.

"I don't think I fully understand what you're saying, Lloyd, but yes, I suppose I do feel safe with Anthony."

"Now we're getting somewhere. OK, let's say you were out walking, and you had to get across a river, a small stream with a plank of wood over it. Would you walk over it if it was the only way home you had?"

"Yes."

"What if the plank broke when you were nearly across the river and you fell in? If you then came to another river with a similar piece of wood, would you cross that river?"

"Yes, I suppose so," I said, hesitating slightly.

"Why do you hesitate?" Lloyd asked.

"I would have to test the wood first to make sure it seemed secure."

"Ah, so you wouldn't trust it to be safe, then?"

"I wouldn't assume it was safe, no."

"That is why your brain is not letting you assume that all men are safe. Because your subconscious doesn't trust them."

"OK, I see that now, I think."

"Look, we put trust in everything we do. Without trust we really wouldn't survive. We trust ourselves to keep safe when we cross the road. We trust others to drive safely and not to knock us down."

The waiter arrived with a big platter and set it down on the table. Lloyd said, laughing, "Just as we trust the chef and the waiter not to have spat in the food that he's just about to serve us."

"How do you know I haven't?" asked the waiter. "After all, you two deserve it, with the way you both tease me…on this occasion, though, I haven't. The lovely lady has saved your lives."

We all laughed and the waiter gave me a cheeky wink before he turned away. I felt myself blush. The platter was dressed with a large assortment of starters, garnished with a healthy serving of green salad.

"Tuck in!" Lloyd said with his fork already poised.

While we ate, the conversation turned to more casual chatter about work and schedules over the next few weeks, with Anthony having the heaviest workload, being in court for most of the time and with meetings most evenings. Lloyd worked a steady nine-to-five with a few private patients in the evenings, most of which paid him handsomely for out-of-hours consultations so he didn't seem to mind. I felt a little out of the conversation as I didn't have a job.

After we finished eating, Lloyd sat back in his chair and rubbed his belly. "That's better, full to bursting!" Picking up his glass of wine he turned to me and said, "Where did we get to, Charlotte? Ah yes, trust. I am a great believer that without trust you can't have a relationship of any kind, and you most certainly can't have love."

"I don't agree," I said, ready for a fight.

"Right, the bastard that beat you. You obviously loved him once, but he or you lost that love when he started to beat you, and that's why you left him. You didn't leave him because you loved him – you left him because you didn't trust him anymore. Do you still love him, or do you just think you still love him?"

I sat and thought about this for a minute or two, and then realised what he was saying was right. I didn't love him and I didn't even think I loved him in the beginning. In fact, he was the one who told me *I* loved *him*. It was only a few months after we met that I moved in with him, and one month after that when he first hit me. Why didn't I leave then, before it got too bad?

"OK, I can't argue with that. I didn't love him and I most certainly didn't trust him, but just because what you say works for me, it might not work for everyone."

"That remains to be seen, Charlotte. Anyway it's you we're concentrating on right now, and you we're trying to help. It doesn't matter what might or might not work for anyone else. If you came to me as a paying client, maybe I would handle things a little differently, but you're not a client, you're a friend, and this is just food for thought. Suggestions."

"So what you're saying, then, is that I don't trust men I don't know."

"Yes, well done. Now think...think about everything we've talked about and I'm sure you'll unscramble much more of what's going on inside your brain, but that's enough for tonight. No more talking of work. Let's enjoy the evening."

Holding up the empty bottle of wine, he gestured to the waiter that we'd finished and would like another. Moments later, the waiter arrived with another bottle of red.

"Is this going to be a long night?" Anthony asked.

"Yeah, why not?" Lloyd picked up the bottle and poured some wine first into my glass, then into Anthony's and lastly into his. Picking up his own, he said, "Here's to all the nights to come with good food, good wine and, last but not least, good company." He looked at me across the table. My cheeks started to burn red. I broke from the gaze and looked down.

A familiar voice interrupted us "Lloyd, Anthony, Charlotte! Didn't see you in the corner there."

"Nats darling, sit down have a glass or two with us." Anthony waved to the waiter for another glass, as Nats sat next to Lloyd.

"Looking gorgeous as ever, Nats," Lloyd said.

"I must agree with him, Nats," Anthony added.

"Enough with you two already, let me talk to Charlotte. Charlotte, you look stunning! Who would have thought your face would have healed so well and so quickly?" Stretching over the table she took hold of one of my hands and clasped it. I looked at her hands holding mine. Her nails were perfectly shaped and immaculately painted.

"Oh my, your nails are so beautiful. I can never do mine to look like that."

"You can now, dear. Come to my salon tomorrow and I'll get someone to do them for you, and while you're there I need to talk with you about an idea I have, for which

I think you'd be just perfect." She winked, and I noticed her eyelashes sparkling as she did so.

Intrigued, I agreed and we set a time of 11.30am at the salon. She raised her glass and toasted, "To new friendships and things to come…"

We clinked her glass.

"Right, boys, I think the others are maybe going to The Room. Are you up for it?" Nats said.

"It's a bit awkward, as we have Charlotte with us, and to be fair we are out with her," Anthony said, his mouth turning down.

"What's The Room?" I asked. All three of them turned and looked at me.

"It's a club just around the corner, but it's a little different to the type of club you're used to, and to be honest I don't think you'd be up for it just yet anyway, even if it was your type of thing," Anthony said, looking tense.

"OK, no worries. You two go, and on the way put me into a taxi and I'll go home. I'm starting to feel tired anyway. It's been a fantastic evening, but my bed is calling me. I'll be OK."

"Are you sure, Charlotte?" Lloyd said, with a little excitement in his voice.

"Yes, I'm positive. Go and be happy and enjoy yourselves. You don't need to babysit me."

"Right, that's settled then. You two are coming to The Room and Charlotte is going home in a taxi. Drink up and let's get gone." Nats picked up her glass and downed it, and the boys did the same.

Outside they hailed me a taxi, and as the car sped off they waved until it and I were almost out of sight.

Chapter Five

Next morning, when I woke, the apartment was very quiet. No sound of Anthony rushing around getting ready to go out or to start work, and I couldn't hear the coffeepot spitting and hissing. Maybe he didn't come home last night, or maybe he was hung-over, the latter being more likely, and good for him, I thought as I walked down the hall to the bathroom. I quickly showered as I was due at Nats' salon soon and I didn't want to be late. I did my make-up and put on a nice little red dress that Anthony had brought home for me a few days ago. I grabbed a pair of red heels and headed to the kitchen for a quick glass of orange juice before I went out.

There was still no sign of Anthony, but it was Saturday and even he was allowed to have a day off occasionally. I finished my juice and crept out of the door, closing it as quietly as I could. Outside I got a taxi to the salon. The streets were busy with people shopping, the sun was shining and in general the world seemed pretty happy. As I arrived at the salon Nats was waiting for me outside and came over to the taxi to open the door.

"How are you?" she asked as I got out.

"Fine, thank you, and you? I see you're up, bright and breezy this morning. Anthony wasn't about when I left the flat."

"No, he stayed over at a friend's. He asked me to let you

know when I saw you. As for me, I never seem to suffer the effects the morning after the night before."

"I'm glad he's having a life outside of work and me," I said as we entered the salon. I looked round in astonishment. I had never seen so many beautiful women in my life, all here to have their face, hair, hands or nails done, or a combination of whatever else was on the menu at a place like this...looking around, the dress in which I felt so stylish when I first put it on this morning now felt distinctly shabby.

"This way, come, we'll go to my office where we can have a cup of coffee and a chat before you get your nails done." As we walked through to the back of the busy salon, Nats tried her hardest not to get into conversation with anyone, which proved close to impossible as everyone wanted to talk with her. She opened a door, stepped through and beckoned me after her.

"Quick, let's shut this door before they all try to follow us." Complete silence descended as she closed the door. "That's better. Thank goodness for soundproofing! Now I can hear myself think!"

She went over to a coffee pot and poured two cups of coffee. Handing me one, she said, "Here, sit, let's talk. OK, where to start? I've just sacked yet another waste of space, which is an issue for me because my salons have taken off big time, and I need a person to work alongside me. But, so far anyway, getting the right person seems impossible: the people I've taken on are either lazy or just don't have a clue. They might be good at paperwork but unfortunately they're useless at running the salons, of which I have four by the way. I need someone who can do paperwork and can organise and order stock at the right time and not run out of anything. I need someone with people skills who doesn't ignore my customers. Is that too much to ask for?"

Why was she pouring her heart out to me? Surely she had friends she could talk things over with. Friends who were probably way more qualified than I was as well.

"Charlotte, you are just what I want."

Amazed, I stared at her. "What do you mean I'm just what you want?"

"I need someone I can trust, someone who will work hard and get on with the job. I'm sure you can handle it."

"What? I'm a nurse. I haven't a clue about running a salon. Come to think of it, I haven't a clue about anything to do with beauty! How can I help?"

"You don't have to know anything about beauty. I'll train you. The skills you have from being a nurse will help you. I assume you had to do paperwork and I assume you are excellent with people. You'll naturally know how to pamper people, and that's what most of them want. They come here to feel special and to be spoilt."

"I'm a nurse!" I protested.

"I know you're a nurse, but think about it. You've changed your life; you've been looking for a job but are finding it hard to get what you want...so maybe you should look elsewhere. Maybe you should reinvent yourself. A whole lifestyle change. Here, you'd be with people who need care – in a very different way to nursing, I know, and most of them are very shallow but they still need some TLC, you know. And, as I've said, I'll train you in all aspects of how the salons are run. So how about it? Even if you just do it for a while until you get a job somewhere else, it'll give you your own independence, don't you think?"

I thought about what she'd just said about lifestyle change. Maybe I might like it. Maybe it was what I needed. Looking at her, my mouth seemed to take over and before I knew it I'd agreed to take the job.

"That's fantastic. I thought you would. You'll work from eight till five most days. Occasionally you'll be required to start a little earlier and finish a little later, depending on how business progresses and what the rotas look like. I pay well, however. First things first though. You need some nails. Can't have my new manager without sculptured nails, can we!"

She led me back outside and down a corridor to another room.

"This is the nail bar where everyone gets their nails done. If you notice, there are several doors, all of which lead to a different treatment room. We offer everything: waxing, nails, massage, tanning, spa and sauna, and hair at the front of the salon. Each room has its own coffee machine and water dispenser." Entering the nail bar, she introduced the girl who was going to do my nails.

"Jane, this is Charlotte. Charlotte, Jane. Charlotte needs the full works doing to her nails, and I think we should have lots of glitz too. Make sure you treat her right as she's going to be your new boss!" Nats laughs.

"Oh, Nats, you're such a tease! As if I wouldn't treat everyone the same. Hi, Charlotte, glad to meet you, hon. Please sit down here." Jane gestured to a seat on the other side of the table.

"Thank you, Jane, nice to meet you too," I smiled.

"Right, Charlotte. I have to go and do some work. Come and find me when you're finished and we'll do lunch," Nats left us.

"There she goes, never having a minute since she sacked the last manager. Mind you, I would have sacked her too if I'd found her with her hands in the till," Jane said, without looking at me. "Now keep your hands in here for me for a few minutes, and I'll get you a coffee." She lifted my hands and placed them into two little pots with spacers for each finger.

Then, getting up, she went to the coffee machine. I looked around her table. An assortment of brushes, a magnifying-glass lamp, a pot of nail files, some white powder and a collection of lotions and creams. I looked over at Jane by the coffee machine, talking with one of the other girls. Oh my God, it would be all over London before she had even done my first nail. They both glanced round and looked at me shyly over their shoulders. I turned away, pretending I hadn't seen them. There were some other girls all sitting at their tables with their customers, all busy filing, polishing, buffing. All the girls were dressed very smartly in black uniforms: a tunic with trousers, all piped with a pink trim. There was a laundry basket in the corner by the door, filled with dirty towels that were starting to overflow. They must have had a busy morning, I thought, as Jane brought my coffee over.

"Here you go." Putting the coffee down on the table, she sat down and reached for my hands, removing them from the bowls, She wrapped them in a small pink towel. "Let me dry your hands, and have a look at your nails." She rubbed them through the towel. "There you go, nice clean dry hands." Inspecting my nails closely, she said, "You've never had nails on before, have you?"

"No, I haven't."

"They are so short. Why do you keep them so short?"

"I'm a nurse. Well, I was a nurse. I've never thought about having anything done to my nails before."

"You're a nurse?" She looked up at me in amazement.

"Yes, I am." I raised one eyebrow as if to say so what.

"I thought you were going to be managing the salons with Nats, or is that one of Nats' little jokes? She does that to us sometimes."

"No, no little joke, I am going to be managing the salons with Nats. I'm having a lifestyle change," I said proudly and with as much confidence as I could muster.

She started preparing my nails, filing them down. As she did so she explained every little stage, which I was grateful for because it meant she couldn't quiz me too much. When she had finished she got me another cup of coffee and then rejoined me.

"I am now going to give you nice new long nails," she said, picking up a tray that was divided into compartments and filled with what looked like tops of fingernails of all different sizes.

"Here we go. These are the tips. I'm going to glue them onto your nails and then I'll paint acrylic over the top to make them look like they're part of your own nails." She set to work.

"How do you know Nats?" she asked.

"Oh, she's a friend of Anthony, a friend of mine."

Her face lit up when I mentioned Anthony's name. "Anthony the lawyer?"

"Yes, do you know him?"

"Oh yes, he comes in for treatments sometimes."

"What, Anthony?"

"Yes," she laughed, "we have quite a few men come in for manicures and such like. They like to be pampered too, you know, and it's becoming the fashion for men to take care of their skin and nails, just like us women."

I never would have thought Anthony would be all girly about the way he looked after his skin and nails. With most men I knew it was a wash, shave, a splash of something overpowering, and a haircut on the way to the pub on a Saturday morning.

"We have to be very discreet here, as a lot of men don't want everyone knowing what they have done, and a lot of our customers are famous and don't want the world knowing the treatments they have here. To give Nats her due, she runs a very tight ship where the customers are concerned. Did you notice that the salon's windows are mainly covered with big posters of hairstyles and such like? That's so no one can see in. Anyone who works for Nats has to sign a confidentiality contract before they start work, so they can't tell on any of the customers. It's Anthony who sorts the contracts out for her. On the plus side, though, we all get paid very well and we have fantastic customers, and sometimes we even get passes for shows and things."

"So you like working here then?"

"Yes, it's fantastic. Every day is different."

She picked up a brush and put a little powder into a small glass dish, then opened a little pot of liquid and dipped the brush into it.

"This is the acrylic. I paint this on. Watch how your nails are transformed."

I watched as she painted the acrylic onto my nails, and to my amazement in no time at all I had a long nail. I had never had a long nail before in my life. Within a few minutes Jane finished all of my nails and started buffing them. She then filed again until they were all perfectly shaped.

"Right, now for the colours and designs. What do you fancy?"

"Oh, I'll leave it up to you. I haven't a clue and you have done such a good job so far."

"OK, well, glitz was the brief from Nats, so I think red and gold with crystals."

She sat painting, and I looked at the other girls all still working away. Looking at the clock it had gone twelve, and I wondered when the girls got a chance to have lunch, if they did.

"Do none of you have lunch?" I asked Jane.

"Yes, but on Saturdays we're always fully booked, so we don't take a quiet lunch. When I went and made you your second cup of coffee I ate a banana just to keep me going, and later I'll have a sandwich. We have them brought in from the sandwich bar up the street. We'll all have five minutes when we can go and eat them in the staff room, but I'll not get there until about three today as I have extra customers this morning."

"Oh I'm sorry, have I put you behind?"

"No, not really. If it wasn't you it would be someone else. It's always the same on Saturdays, but we have both Sunday and Monday off, so we get a rest then. If we have customers who want to book on a Monday we get paid double, so it's a bonus for us. Nats is good like that. She always makes sure we're looked after."

"Does that happen a lot, working on your days off?"

"She has one of the salons open on a Monday mainly for her customers who don't want to be treated by anyone else. If we have someone who books on a Monday they have to go to the salon which is open and we meet them there."

"Oh, I see."

"Right, finished. Don't touch anything for at least five minutes to give them time to dry."

I looked down at my nails. They looked fantastic; long and bright red, with gold tips and little diamonds separating the tips from the rest of the nail. I thanked her and, leaving the nail bar, I went to find Nats.

Back in the salon Nats was behind the desk talking with a client and saying how fantastic she looked, thanking her for coming, and saying they'd see her next week at the same time. Nats wrote something down in a large book.

"Charlotte, hi! How was it? Let's have a look at what your hands look like with nails." I held them out and she inspected them. "She's done a very good job. They look beautiful. Long nails suit you. Now, let's go get that lunch." We went back to her office where she had an assortment of sandwiches and cakes. Anthony was sitting on the sofa.

"Anthony, what are you doing here?"

"I got a call about two hours ago telling me that Nats has a new employee and she needs me to go through the contract as they're starting on Monday morning."

"Oh, would that contract be for me, then?" I asked eagerly.

"What! You're going to work with Nats in her salons?"

"You seem shocked, Anthony."

"Yes, a little. What about your nursing, Charlotte?"

"Well, as Nats has so rightly put it, what have I got to lose? I have no job and no money. Even if I do this until I get a nursing job, it's something."

"Makes sense, I suppose."

"Get eating, you two," Nats said.

We started on the sandwiches, which to me seemed impossible to eat as my nails were all over the place and I didn't seem to be able to pick anything up.

"You'll get the hang of it," Nats said, laughing, as I dropped everything out of a sandwich while I grappled with it.

"Oh God, why can't I use my hands?" I said, frustrated.

Anthony laughed. "You are employing this incompetent woman because...why again?" he teased, barely hiding the sniggers.

"Now don't, Anthony, she'll be fine. It's just all quite strange for her, and I guess she's never had nails like this before. She'll work them out." Nats was unable to take her eyes off my clumsy awkward hands. They both sat watching me, eating their sandwiches while my sandwich was like something alive as I struggled to grasp hold of it. Oh pants, there went tomato all down my dress! I was beginning to wonder what the hell I was thinking of, agreeing to this job with Nats when I couldn't even manage to control salon nails.

"Right, Charlotte," Anthony said, "after you've finished feeding your clothes I have a contract for you to read and sign. Don't worry, there's nothing in it that will hurt you unless you do something you aren't supposed to. Principally, you may not talk about anything or anyone you see here in the salons. Otherwise it's pretty standard stuff. Anything you don't understand, just ask me."

He passed me the contract, and I put what was left of my sandwich down on the coffee table. As I scanned the paperwork, flicking clumsily through the pages, Anthony and Nats sat watching, trying not to laugh.

"Glad to be the provider of entertainment," I said, dryly.

"Oh Charlotte, you'll be fine, trust me. In a few days you'll be so used to them it'll be like you've always had them."

I finished reading and signed the contract.

"Good. Excellent. Charlotte, I'll see you on Monday, here in my office for your first day's training. I have a few customers arriving in the morning but apart from that no one else will be here and we can get stuck right in."

"I look forward to it, Nats. In fact I can't wait – something to do at long last! I've been out of work for too long, I think."

We finished our lunch, said our goodbyes to Nats and made our way back to the apartment. Anthony got out two glasses and a bottle of wine.

"Will you and your nails be ok with my wine glasses or do you want a beaker?" he grinned at me. And then, "Sit, I want to talk to you."

"Why so serious suddenly, Anthony?" I asked.

"Because you going to work for Nats is serious, and I just want to make sure you know what you're letting yourself in for. Nats is a very strong-minded woman when she wants to be, and I'm worried that you'll not cope well with her. Also, the job is so different to what you're used to: her customers all think they're special and are very needy. They break a nail and the world comes to an end. I worry that you'll feel out of your depth. You're used to people who need care because they're sick and need to get better, not because they need a nail repaired. I think it may well annoy the hell out of you." He poured the wine and handed me a glass.

"I have thought about them, pampered pussies that they are! But really I think I'll be OK with them. I just have to understand that in their world something like a broken nail is considered a major catastrophe and enough to make them feel ill."

"Pampered pussies! Where the hell did that come from?" he said, chuckling.

"Well, I'll need to call them something outside of work, as I can't use their real name, so I figured pampered pussies sounded about right."

"Absolutely, it's an appropriate description of most of them. OK, well as long as you're sure about this job? Don't think you need a job just to please or prove anything to me. I've told you there's no need to hurry, and I really truly mean that."

"I know, but I need something to do. I need to be in the real world, mixing with people and trying to get some normality back into my life, and this is the start. It actually feels as if a large weight has been lifted off me, like there isn't any pressure because no one's expecting me to know how to do everything straight away, so yes, why not." I raised my

glass to him. "To my new life as a pampered pussies sitter."
He laughed as he clinked my glass, saying "To pampered
pussies. May they be kind to you..."

Chapter Six

The next week passed very quickly as Nats showed me and taught me everything I needed to learn. I didn't think I'd ever remember it all, but she was very kind and understanding with me. She also took me out shopping, buying me clothes and shoes for work, and she assigned a beautician to me, responsible each morning for doing my make-up until I got used to doing it myself, as until now I hadn't worn much make-up and hadn't a clue what to do with most of it. I got used to my nails, although for the first few days I had to get Anthony to help me with buttons and zips, which of course he found highly entertaining. I met all of the staff in all the salons, and they were lovely, although most could only be described as airheads. All the salons had the same layout so that customers felt familiar with the different treatment rooms regardless of which salon they visited. The staff moved around quite a bit too, and to be honest we'd get confused if the layout was different in each. This week I had Saturday, Sunday and Monday off, as Nats thought I'd be out of my depth on a Saturday at the moment and she didn't want to scare me, and on Monday she had someone at the salon whom she felt wouldn't want anyone else there. On Tuesday morning there was a staff meeting with all the managers from each salon. Now, though, it was Friday and I'd just arrived back home.

As I entered the flat, I shouted for Anthony to see if he was in.

"Through here. I have a glass of wine waiting for you." I walked through to the lounge and slumped in the black leather armchair. Anthony handed me the glass.

"How was your first week then?" he asked.

"Fan-bloody-tastic."

"I must admit you've blossomed this week. I've already seen you grow in confidence. I think you were right to take this job. It's done so much for you in just a short space of time."

"Do you think? I'm not one hundred percent OK with it yet. I get so flustered when talking to some people, especially shirty men. Nats has had to save me from them a few times. The men are worse than the ladies. We had one man come in for a wax, and he didn't want to pay because it hurt. What the hell did he expect? Well when he came out he started shouting at me, saying I should have told him what waxing entailed, and I just stood there with my mouth open, wanting to curl up and hide, but Nats immediately dealt with him and told him he would pay, and that if he wanted to visit us again he would be most welcome but that if he ever spoke to any of her staff like that again she would have him thrown out, wax strips still attached or not. Apparently he had given the girl who was waxing him a hard time too. I'm worried that if I can't handle myself and be more assertive Nats won't keep me. I wish I could get this fear that I have about men out of my head. I don't know how Nats does it. She's so good at keeping control of every situation."

"Yes, she is, she'll take no nonsense whatsoever. She told me about that man and your reaction, and I've spoken to Lloyd for you. I hope you don't mind but he's coming over tonight. I'm off out so you and he can talk. He has a plan, I think."

"Oh, OK. To be honest, I don't know if I'm really up for one of his talks tonight."

"Ah, there's the buzzer. Good, that will be Lloyd now. I'll let him in on my way out. Have fun!"

Lloyd entered the flat in high spirits, laughing at something. Maybe Anthony said something as they passed on the stairs.

"Hi, Charlotte!" he called. "May I grab a glass of some of Anthony's excellent wine?"

"Hi," I called back. "Yes, I guess so, if you'd like. I have some already."

He appeared at the door and stopped in mid track.

"WOW! You look drop-dead gorgeous! Well, Nats has most certainly sorted you out."

He came and sat on the sofa opposite and studied me.

"Well, er, sorry, Charlotte, but you've taken me by surprise. I never in a million years thought that...well, anyway, let's start again, shall we? Hello!" He poured a glass of wine for himself and topped my glass up. I suddenly realised that I'd never been alone with him before now. My heart started to race as a hot flush worked its way over my body, followed by a feeling of panic.

"Slow down, Charlotte, what's wrong? Take some deep breaths."

I closed my eyes and breathed slow and deep, pretending he wasn't there.

"That's it, good. Now, why are you panicking?"

"I'm not, it's... I think I'm just... It's been a hard week at work, that's all. Maybe I'm tired or something." I didn't want to admit I was panicking or say it was because I was on my own with him. I opened my eyes slowly and looked at him. He was crouching down by my side, looking at me. I could see in his face a look of concern, even dread, that I might not be comfortable with him here on my own.

"Charlotte, do you trust me? I am not going to touch you. I am not going to do anything that you don't want me to do. I am here as your friend, and I thought we'd already agreed that you need to be completely honest with me." He got up and went back to the sofa. "Take a sip of wine and steady your nerves a little."

I did as he said.

"Charlotte, I am so sorry," he went on. "I never realised this thing with men went quite as deep as it clearly does. Nats had a word with both me and Anthony, saying she was worried and that maybe I needed to have a chat with you. I was hoping that you'd be able to sort this out for yourself, but maybe you need a little more help with unscrambling things?"

He was right. I was unable to handle difficult situations with men I wasn't sure of or didn't know. Tears began to roll down my face.

"What am I going to do? Is Nats going to fire me?"

"No, not at all. It's OK we can fix this. We just need to work on it a bit more. I have a few tricks we can use, but first you need to calm down and be comfortable with me, because you need to be able to work with me on this, OK?"

He chatted with me about something and nothing, and with every word I began to feel more relaxed with him, although he did most of the talking. We drank two bottles of Anthony's wine, and then decided to call up for a pizza. After we'd eaten we opened up yet another red and went on talking. By now I was feeling quite comfortable in his company. Then out of the blue he sprang a question on me.

"Why don't you trust me?"

"That's a little strong, Lloyd, I do trust you."

"No, you don't. I could see from the way you went into panic mode when you realised you were here on your own with me."

"I'm sorry, but I don't know how to answer you. I wish I did. Maybe then I could sort it out."

"I have never hurt you, I have never done anything to hurt you, so why wouldn't you trust me?"

"Lloyd, why are you so harsh with me?"

"I want to know. I need to know."

"It's because I can't see past you as a man. My brain just says that you are a man and therefore you must be a bastard, the same as him, and I can't get over that. I just find it impossible to talk with men. I don't know why. My mouth goes dry and my brain stops me from forming sentences. I wish I could better control my mind, but I can't." I started to cry. It was the first time I'd even admitted to myself that I had such a problem, and that it was getting worse, not better.

"OK, don't cry. I knew we'd work out what the problem was and now we have, and I have something we can work onto help fix it." He spoke more gently.

"Why did you have to do that? Why did you change the way you talked to me? It frightened me."

"I'm sorry, but if I'm going to help you I needed you to tell me what the problem was, so that you genuinely know it's how you feel and not something I have invented for you."

"So what, I have a syndrome, or something?"

"No, not at all. We can fix you. We need to boost your confidence over talking to men. You've done such a good job in reinventing yourself on the outside, and we now need to work on the inside, and that's my job. You've already made so much progress tonight by admitting to yourself that you can't see past men as being more than just men, that as far as your brain is concerned we're all the same – and I don't like being classed as a woman-hater, so I'm going to have to sort you out," he grinned. "First, we need to introduce you to some men, I think."

"Er, wha...?"

"Calm down, don't panic. This is easy, trust me." He picked up the phone as he said, "I use this line for a few of my clients, most of whom have problems with talking about sex or using words of a sexual nature."

"What, you want me to talk on the phone to complete strangers?"

"Yup, that's about it. This is easy. It's a recording; you don't actually have to talk to anyone in person, you just leave a message and you listen to other peoples' messages. You don't even have to answer them, but what it will show you is that men can talk to you and not hurt you, and it will hopefully give you confidence to talk to them in a safe environment."

"Hold on a minute! I don't think this is right. What sort of therapy are you giving me?"

"Look, I know this is radical but trust me, by the end of tonight I'll have you laughing about all this." He handed me the phone and said, "Give a name, any name."

"Sarah," I said into the phone.

"Right, now listen to all the men on the messages, and just push the buttons when it tells you to."

"You have a message," a voice says. "Press one to hear the message, two to delete."

I pressed 1. "Oh my God, you perv!" I said out loud.

"Why, what did he say?" Lloyd asked.

"He wanted to fuck me in the kitchen!" I pressed two.

"You have a message," the phone said. I pressed one.

"Hi, my name is Paul."

62

"Press one to reply or two to delete," said the phone. I pressed two.

For about fifteen minutes I sat listening and pressing one followed by two as men – men whom I had never even met – told me what they wanted to do to me, how and where, until I hung up.

"What do you think now about men?" Lloyd asked

"Apart from them all being pervs and needing their mouths washed out with bleach, not a lot."

"Could they hurt you?"

"No of course not. They're just a message." I tilted my head to one side

"Do you think they were all the same?" Lloyd tilted his head to mirror image mine. What is he doing? I thought to myself. Where is he going with this? I was always trying to get one step ahead of him.

"No, they weren't all the same."

"Why do you think that was, then?"

"Maybe because every message was different. What they wanted was different, but they are all still pervs."

"Pervs they may be but that's a different debate. The most important thing you found out, though, was that they were all different and not one of them could hurt you with words, could they."

"Noo…" I hesitated and look downwards.

"Why do you hesitate?"

"Because if I had a different attitude that little experiment could have gone so wrong." I look back up at Lloyd

"In what way?"

Oh here we go, I thought, he wants the ins and outs of it all. He is as bad as Anthony. "Because if I was a prude or someone shy I would have had a nervous breakdown listening to them." I frown at Lloyd.

"You are not a prude, and, most importantly, you didn't have a nervous breakdown, did you? As I said, I know it's not the norm but this type of thing does work with the right people. I knew you would be OK with it." He sips his wine.

"I might not have been."

"That's beside the point. You have had men offering to do whatever their little imagination has thought up for you, but you haven't panicked, you haven't gone into meltdown, so that's one step forward. Well done you. Now all you have to do is work on it." He leant forward, picked up the bottle of wine and poured some more into my glass.

"How do I work on that? Men wanting to fuck me on the kitchen table and I go out and find one, bring him home and strip in the kitchen?" I start feeling uncomfortable, as I turn sideways in the chair, crossing my legs as I did so.

"Charlotte, if that's what you want to do so be it. Who am I to judge? But first, can I suggest that every time you see a man or talk to a man, just imagine he's a recording. He isn't going to hurt you. And quite honestly what they were saying is immaterial."

"I'm glad you found it immaterial," I snapped. "I found it invasive, men wanting to fuck me. I don't even know what they looked like, for fuck's sake!"

"Is that what's bothering you? The fact that people wanted to have sex with you and you didn't know what they looked like?"

Oh crap, now I'd opened a can of worms. I hadn't seen that coming.

"No, not really, but I've never been in this situation before. It's not one I ever imagined being in, either."

"I can understand that, but do you think that when a man looks at you he doesn't think about fucking you?"

"What are you saying?"

"I can tell you that most men will fantasize over any woman that they see. When drunk they just see something to have sex with. Usually on Friday and Saturday nights most men are out to see if they can get laid."

"Oh well, in that case you'd best be off. It's Friday night and the lady's not for laying."

"Huh, and you think I want to fuck you, then?" Crossing his arms as if to say no, this man isn't for laying either, lady.

"Er, no, that's not what I mean at all. I just thought that..." I rolled my eyes upwards in sheer frustration; he is tying me up in knots.

"Charlotte, Charlotte, it's OK! I'm teasing!" Lloyd said, before I could get another word out.

"I know what you meant – that I should be out getting drunk and looking for a bit of skirt or something." He un-crosses his arms and relaxes once again.

"Yes, exactly that, but I've noticed that you and Anthony don't really have girlfriends, just girls that are friends. Is there something that you want to tell me? After all, you and Anthony have some sort of secret, don't you?" I blurted out.

He moved back in the sofa, startled by what I'd just asked him. Ha, I thought, got you! My turn now to have you running over the coals!

"Charlotte, I don't quite know what you mean by that. Please do expand a little."

Oh crap, it wasn't supposed to go quite like this. He was just supposed to tell me about the club they went to last week, what all the secrecy behind it was, but he wasn't going to let on. Bugger. I didn't know what to say; he'd thrown my mind into meltdown. I tried to think of something smart to say.

"I know Anthony very well, but I don't know anything about you, so I think what I was trying to find out is something about you."

Phew. Did I get away with it? I looked at him and he was looking at me deeply. What was he thinking now? Oh God, I was no good at this, I'd never been any good at pre-empting what people were thinking. Oh shit, please say something, I thought, I've run out of words again.

"I'm still not quite sure what you're asking. Do you want to know about me, or me and Anthony?"

He and Anthony? What did he mean, he and Anthony? Were they gay? Was Anthony gay? Never. He would have told me. My chin hit the floor and Lloyd laughed.

"Got you! You thought I was inferring that Anthony and I are gay."

"Are you not?" I said, relieved that they might not be, but he hadn't said they were and he hadn't really said they weren't… "The way you two carry on with secret clubs and things, I wouldn't be surprised at all," I added quickly, to see what response I would get. I kept eye contact with him and his face didn't even change, not one little bit. Bother. That didn't even faze him.

"Right, madam, just to satisfy your curiosity I'll tell you. I am not gay, you've got the wrong end of a very long stick, I think, but you are right that Anthony and I are very secretive about our personal lives. It's not that we're keeping anything from you it's just that…well, we don't think that at this moment it's appropriate to tell you, but rest assured we'll tell you, all in good time."

"What are you on about? All you've done is baffle me."

"Look, it's easy. We have very healthy appetites for the opposite sex but in a slightly different way. We have other relationships that are also healthy, and for now that's all you need to know. I'm here tonight trying to help you get over your thing with men, not to talk about Anthony and me," he smiled.

"OK, I don't understand, but I've always respected Anthony's space and I'll carry on doing so, and now it looks like I have two men best friends so I'll respect your space too..."

"Thank you, Charlotte, I'll take that as a compliment. So everything I've put you through, even with the phone and all, has made you see me in a different light as I am now one of your best friends." He grinned at me.

"The phone thing went a little too far, I think, but you did prove a point that not all men can or will hurt me, so maybe my subconscious will get it too. We'll see. I don't like the feeling of not being able to control my feelings around men." I fidget as if something had walked over my grave, making every hair on my body stand on end.

"Do you like being in control?"

"Yes, doesn't everyone like being in control of their emotions? This thing with men that I have is driving me mad, because I feel that my mind takes over and I can't stop panicking, and then I go down that imaginary slope, then the panic. I never used to feel like this, I used to be quite level-headed, I think." I grabbed the cushion from behind me and cuddled it close to me, I was never going to let a man condition me like that again, but the worse thing is that they had taken every emotion away from me. No...never again.

"That's very interesting, but Charlotte, with the two relationships you've had, they were the ones in control. The last guy had ultimate control over you. You have in fact not had any control over yourself for a very long time. He made all the decisions – he made you give up work, he made you do what he wanted when he wanted it, and you had no control whatsoever. Now you say that your mind and subconscious has taken over." He looked down at the cushion I was clutching for grim death.

"Yes, I think it has."

"Charlotte, you've taken control back from him physically, and now it's time for you to take control mentally, because that's what it is. He wouldn't let you talk to other men, and he's still controlling that. He would hit you, manipulate and condition you, to make you think that all men are the same. Well, prove him wrong and start, right now, getting control. Don't let him win."

"I've never thought of it like that before," I said slowly, "but you're right, he is still controlling my mind and I should be doing that for myself. I should be able to see past the rubbish he has planted and start taking control of my own mind."

"There you go – phone-chat lines work again."

"How have they helped me?" I didn't understand.

"Because you're starting to see what us men are about. Basically we are all pervs, or should that be pricks on legs, and the sex phone-chat did it." He laughed. "I told Anthony and Nats this would work."

"What do you mean? You don't use sex chat lines in therapy? It was all a joke?"

"No, I don't use sex lines in therapy. It was just a way to get you opening up more. A fun prank. Just to put you at ease, and it worked. You've sorted such a lot out in your head tonight and you've done it for yourself. That's just what you should be doing, mind you. At the same time, it was very entertaining. Your face when you were on the phone was so funny. How I stopped myself from laughing, I just don't know."

"You didn't hear what they were saying, things like… oooh yeah, babes, I bet you look good bent over with my cock up your arse. For God's sake! How would he know, not that he would ever get the chance." I started to giggle then laughed aloud as I thought of all the bizarre things I had heard on the phone. "That doesn't excuse you using me and my mind as a guinea-pig, does it? Just because I'm laughing." I leaned forward placing the cushion; I sipped the last of my wine in the glass, and then placed the empty glass next to the cushion on the table.

"See? I also told you that you'd be laughing about it before the end of the evening."

"You bastard! How am I ever going to trust you again after that stunt?" I gave him a mock glare.

"Trust! Did you say trust? At which part of the evening did you start trusting me? Because I missed it." He looked at the cushion and then back at me. He was, in a strange way, right; I was getting more relaxed and trusting, yes, a little more trusting, of Lloyd. I am starting to feel quite comfortable in his company.

"I must have trusted you when I started listening to Pervy Man No. 4! Oh yeah, baby its good, good, pant pant pant, yup! I think that was the one that made me trust you – why else would I have carried on with it for another ten minutes if I didn't trust you?" We broke into laughter again, but I thought that the wine that we had drunk also had something to do with the lightheartedness of it all.

"Oh Charlotte, you sure are a good sport!" Lloyd poured yet more wine into my glass.

I watched him, twiddling my hair with my fingers, but I forgot I had those bloody nails on. I couldn't get my hand out of my hair. Shit! A blush rushed to my face as he handed me the glass. I said, "If I didn't know better I would think you're trying to get my new fingernails drunk, and do you know what…?"

"No, what?"

"I think it's worked. They've attached themselves to my

hair and they're stuck!" I smiled with all my teeth, as if to say 'help'. He put the glass down on the coffee table and came around to where I was sitting.

"Let me look at your drunk fingernails. I've never seen drunk nails before." Trying to be serious for a moment but not quite pulling it off, he leant over me and tried to move my hand but it wouldn't budge. "Oh dear, we do have a problem here. I could cut them out."

"Oh my God, Nats would kill me! She just wouldn't like that at all!"

"OK, let me have another look. Er, well... I know. I have it! Use your other hand to hold your glass then you can drink your wine. That will do the trick," he laughed.

"I need to get free." I dropped my bottom lip, looking at him all coy.

"OK!"

We were laughing so much while he was trying to get my nails out of my hair that we didn't hear Anthony and Nats arrive. When they entered the lounge, Anthony startled us, making Lloyd fall onto my lap in a very haphazard way.

Lloyd whispered into my ear "See how much you trust me now? A few hours ago you wouldn't let me anywhere near you" he looked at me and for a moment I forgot the other two were there.

"What are you two up to? You're supposed to be giving Charlotte a talking-to, not...not... Well getting her drunk is all part of what plan, Lloyd? How does that help?" Anthony said abruptly – but was that a little protectiveness I could hear as well?

"Look, she has her hand stuck in her hair, and I was just trying to release her drunk finger nails. Nats, come over here quick, before I make a right mess of it!" Lloyd said.

"Oh for God's sake! What the hell have you done here?

70

How have you managed to do this?" Nats asked, trying to untangle me.

"It's Lloyd, he got my new fingernails drunk, and now they've attached themselves to my hair somehow!"

Anthony and Nats fell about laughing.

"I assume you've both had a good night, judging by the amount of red wine bottles there are on the table?" Anthony collected the empties.

"Yes, we have. All went according to plan as well. That's a drink you and Nats owe me," Lloyd said smugly.

"I think I've bought you more than one drink this evening," Anthony shot back.

"Here's your hand back, Charlotte. Don't let your nails get in your hair like that again." Nats put my hand back on the arm of the chair. Anthony returned from taking the empties to the kitchen, with yet another bottle of red and two more glasses, "You two don't mind if Nats and I join you, do you?" he asked sarcastically, sitting down next to Lloyd on the sofa and pouring the wine for him and Nats. Lloyd leaned over to pass me my wine.

"Stop!"

Anthony sounded so alarming that we all turned to look at him, but he just said, "I'm not sure that drunk nails should be in control of my best red." Everyone laughed and I took the glass very carefully, trying to keep my nails under control.

"Here's to your first week working with me." Nats raised her glass. "I must say, though, Charlotte, you've done better than I thought you would."

Oh no, I thought, don't chink glasses for God's sake. I won't be able to do that; it's hard enough controlling nails without chinking too, but everyone just raised their glass. I sighed with relief.

Anthony said that they had been to Nats's sorting out paperwork for business ventures they were both involved in, then they'd had dinner down the road.

Lloyd told them how amusing he thought I was on the sex phone line, as I pulled sulky faces across the room at him to show my displeasure at some of the details he went into, but maybe it was because Lloyd and I were so drunk by now, it just made it all the funnier.

Again, Anthony seemed to be a little displeased with Lloyd over the phone sex and was a little protective toward me saying, "Do you really think that smut was the right way to go? Lloyd, why not go the whole hog and buy her some top shelf mags! No please don't answer that Lloyd. I don't think your head is really in the right place for any sort of answer that would make any sort of sense right now!"

Chapter Seven

The weeks passed. The hang-ups I had with men seemed to pale into insignificance. Unless a man raised his voice or was extremely threatening toward me, I could cope with being in their presence. Work was going well and Nats and I bounced off each other. The other staff got used to me not knowing anything about the beauty trade and some even became my mentors, explaining what the various aids to beauty were, and how and when they were used. In fact it would be fair to say that the staff respected me for not knowing, and no one resented me being there at all, which was what I had expected would happen.

Anthony and Lloyd were two crazy individuals. I never knew what they were going to do next, trying to see which one could embarrass me the most, but their little jokes and pranks did wonders for me, as they boosted my confidence no end.

It was Tuesday, and I had a meeting first thing with all the staff. Nats was going to announce that I would be staying. I had been at work for about an hour setting up the office ready for our bitch and tell session, as I called it, when Nats walked in with a bag of cakes.

"Here, put these on a plate. We must celebrate today, as you're staying with us. It's such good news! I can finally relax, knowing that my right-hand woman is going to stay with me. Not only that, but we've become such good friends."

"Oh, Nats, thank you! It was so nice of you to offer me the job in the first place, and you put so much faith in the fact that you thought I could do the job that I had to give it my best shot, and you were so right, it was what I needed. A complete change. I love the job, I'm so glad you were so pushy."

Moments later the staff for the meeting arrived. Outside it was business as usual. Ten minutes after we had started, there was a knock on the door and a head popped round the corner.

"Excuse me, Nats, but there's a delivery for Charlotte. The delivery boy is most insistent that he must deliver it personally."

"Send him in then," Nats said, a little irritated.

I was surprised to see it was the waiter from the Covent Garden bar that Anthony and Lloyd had taken me into the day before Nats offered me the job. He came over to the table and said, "This is for Charlotte."

Putting his hand into a bag, he pulled out an object that I had only ever heard about and never before seen, it was see-through and inside you could see the mechanics of the object, about eight inches long, with a little rabbit sitting further down the shaft, I looked closely in amazement open mouthed my chin almost touching the floor, not quite knowing what to think at first. It was an Ann Summers fucking rampant rabbit! He placed it down in the middle of the table, watching me as he did so. I could feel the flush rushing up from my toes to my face. What the fuck! I looked around the table quickly to see if anyone had noticed. Of course they had, it was a fucking rabbit sitting on the table! They were all looking at me to see what my response was going to be. Quick, think! What was I to say to this? Oh, for fuck's sake! Then out of nowhere I said, "OK which one of you bastards has set me up?" and laughed as I reached to pick it up. Then everyone began to laugh too, looking at each other, not knowing but suspecting everyone else for sending the rabbit. I knew who had sent it, and when I got home later I was going to let them both have it.

"Reply?" grinned the delivery boy/waiter.

"No reply. Thank you for brightening up our day," I said deadpan, and he went away, no doubt to report back to those two boys.

Nats tried to carry on with the meeting, but kept bursting out in uncontrollable laughter whenever she caught sight of the rabbit on the table. The hour went quite quickly and everyone left the office and went back to work.

I sat back in my chair and let out a sigh of relief. "Thank God that's over."

"That must have been one of the funniest things I have ever seen in my life." We burst out laughing again. "Your face when he put it on the table was just so funny, I didn't know what you were going to do. Well done, now that lot will speculate for weeks on which one of them sent it to you, but we both know, don't we?"

"Did you know they were going to do that?"

"No, I didn't, not at all!"

"What are they thinking, sending me a bloody rabbit, and when they knew today was the day of me staying here forever! A bloody rabbit, indeed!"

"Such a big rabbit too, it's a platinum rabbit, not just any old one. You should be flattered. If it was a bunch of flowers, it would be a fistful of orchids." We laughed again until tears were rolling down our faces.

Nats made us both a cup of coffee, and we sat down on

her sofa. I took out my phone and saw that I had two texts on it. Oh, here we go! I looked to see whom they were from. One from Anthony and the other from Lloyd. I showed Nats, then opened Anthony's message:

> Hi
> Congratulations on staying gainfully employed.
> Hope your day goes well and nothing pops up out of the blue.
> Ants xxx

"The bastard! Look at what he's said." Nats read it and laughed again. I opened the next text:

> Hi
> Hope you are well. Watch out for the unexpected, for it's the unexpected that might be expected.
> Lloyd xxx

"What the fuck does that mean?" I showed Nats the phone, just as it beeped with another message. No name this time, just a number.

> I am so sorry.
> They made me.
> Jake (the waiter)

"Oh the poor guy! It's the waiter saying sorry." I showed Nats the text. Then the phone beeped again. Another message from Lloyd:

> I am so proud of you.
> I'll meet you tonight for a drink and chat.
> Lloyd xxx

I showed Nats. "What is he on? What's wrong with him?"

"God knows. The pair of them are crazy men. Right, come on, we must do some work now." After work I got home to find Anthony and Lloyd in the lounge looking rather sheepish.

"I should be so mad with you two! A bloody fucking rabbit!" They sank down further into the sofa, clutching their glasses of wine.

"You should be ashamed of yourselves! Truly, you should!" I glared at them both, then burst out laughing. "You bastards, where's my glass of wine then?"

Anthony waved at the coffee table where there was a third glass of red wine. I sat on the chair and sipped my wine, watching them all the time.

"Which one of you is going to talk first?" my eyes danced between the pair of them.

"We thought it would help your confidence," Anthony said. "By all accounts you handled it so well." He sunk his head down into his shoulders.

"I didn't have any choice," I said, laughing. "You're lucky that Nats took it well too."

"Oh, we knew she would be OK with it," Lloyd said. They started to snigger. "Charlotte, the thing is, we like you, and we just like the way we can have fun with you, you always take things so well. Please promise us that we can always have a good joke with you." they looked just like schoolboys, who had been caught for the frog in the teacher's drawer stunt.

"Why, what else have you got planned for me?"

"Nothing yet." Anthony said.

"That's a relief, but the word 'yet' should that worry me?" I tilted my head to one side, looking at them I wished I could read what these two were up to.

"I have to go out. Are you and Lloyd OK for a while on your own?" asked Anthony, getting up from the sofa. "Maybe you can pick up from where you left off last time you were both left alone! Oh yes, been meaning to ask you – do fingernails have hangovers?" was his parting shot as he went out.

Lloyd laughed at Anthony's remark.

"I don't think you're funny, Anthony. You're already treading on thin ice!" I called, as the door closed behind him.

"That was a bit hasty of Anthony. It's unlike him not to finish his wine!" I raised an eyebrow and took a long lingering sip of wine to give Lloyd time to answer. After all, he had said he wanted to have a drink and chat with me this evening.

"Yeah, he's forgotten something and has to go and get it."

"Oh, OK."

"Anyway, you'll be pleased to know I've won another bet with Anthony. I told him you wouldn't fall apart." He looked very pleased with himself.

"What? That was a bet?" I wasn't pleased.

"Not at first, but this morning after we sent it to you we became a little remorseful, just a little, you understand. We wondered what you would think and the way you would react... Then we just thought again that it would be so funny, and then we thought maybe you'd crumble but we knew you'd really be OK as Nats would have sorted it. Nats phoned me not long after. She couldn't stop laughing – she thought it was one of the funniest things she had ever seen. She said at first she didn't know what to think, then you just turned it around and made out someone else from the meeting had sent it. So clever of you to do that!"

I laughed. "After the initial shock I did think it was funny. I've never seen one of those rabbits up close before, so it took a minute or two for it to sink in."

"See? I have mended you. I think you could now handle anything that was thrown at you."

"I wouldn't go that far," I said. "I've decided that I don't want any relationships ever again. I like being free and single, not answering to anyone. I think if someone asked me out I would go into meltdown and run a mile, to be honest. So no, I couldn't handle anything that was thrown at me."

"OK, so define relationships." Lloyd crossed his legs; here we go, the psychiatrist mode.

"I'm sure you know what I mean by a relationship. When two people get involved sexually."

"OK, but my definition is any involvement between two consenting adults. After all, what you have with me is a relationship, and although we have never spoken about them we have lines that we do not cross. So in other words, you could have a sexual or any other relationship without having to have all the shit you've had."

"Oh, here you go again, trying to make me think." I tilted my head to one side and leaned it in my left hand.

"Yes, but that's a good thing isn't it?"

"Why whenever you are here with me do you end up analysing me?"

"I'm not analysing you! Just trying to open your eyes, trying to get you to look at the bigger picture."

"What if I don't want to look at the bigger picture?"

"I think you do, you just don't know it, yet your curiosity will always get the better of you," he grinned. "Charlotte, a relationship is a two-way thing, and up till now you have only had a one-sided relationship, where someone has controlled you. You haven't had any say in it, and I think it would be a shame for you to give up on relationships just because you've had a bad experience."

"I've had two bad experiences. I seem to attract them."

I leaned my head to the back of the chair, looking up at the ceiling, trying desperately to give the impression that I really didn't want to have this conversation.

"Yes, you're right, you do attract the wrong guys for you but that's your nature, the very fact that you're caring and kind, and you have a vulnerable side to you as well. Control freaks see the green light. It doesn't take them long to work out that if they push all the right buttons they can control you." I put my head up abruptly and looked at Lloyd.

"I'm fed up with being treated like that, so I'll not have any more relationships. That's what I said when we started this conversation."

"Yes, I know that's what you said, and I've said relationships come in all forms, and you just have to find the one that is right for you."

I looked at him, eyes wide, and said, "A relationship is a relationship. You meet, you fuck and then in my case you get fucked! So why should I consider going through that again?" I tried to sip my wine and look graceful to hide the fact that I was getting very irritable.

"Right," he said, "OK, we're going round in circles. Let's try another tack on this." I looked at him then at the bottle of wine, as if to say OK, well, if we have to, then give me some more to drink, I placed my glass on the table then slouched back in the chair.

He picked up the bottle and filled my glass up.

"Yes, Charlotte, a glass of wine or two might help you understand better," I leaned forward to pick up my glass and our eyes met. He did have lovely blue come-to-bed eyes. I lingered while I looked. He slowly leaned back in the sofa, as if he really hadn't noticed me looking into his eyes.

"Right. Do you trust me?"

"Yes, you know I do." trying ever so hard to sip my wine

and act casual, but still thinking about his big blue eyes.

"No, would you really trust me to do anything to you?"

"I don't know what you mean. We've had so many talks about trust, so why again?"

"I trust you, and I know Anthony trusts you implicitly, so I'm going to tell you something about me and Anthony because I think you are a little too naïve to get the picture on this by yourself."

"Is this Anthony's secret? I think he should be the one to tell me if it is." I sat up with a slight urgency of interest, *don't you dare not tell me now you have started*, thinking this would be the best conversation of the evening.

"Yes, it is, but he has said I can tell you. In fact he insisted that I should tell you tonight."

"Oh, so that's why he ran off so quickly, then." I nodded my head and bit the bottom of my lip as the penny dropped.

"Yes and no. He does have something he has to do tonight, but we had already decided that you should know what we are about. What we don't want is for you to find out what we do through a third party."

"Oh my God. You're both gay. I knew it!"

"No, you really do have that wrong." He took a big gulp of wine, for some courage, I think. Then he said, "Anthony and I are in alternative relationships."

"Isn't being gay an alternative relationship?" I said as a matter of fact.

"Charlotte! There's more to life than just being gay or straight," he said sharply.

"Sorry," I muttered.

Lloyd continued "Alternative, OK? Or not so much alternative as non-vanilla."

"What the fuck...what? Why are you talking about vanilla?"

"Right, OK, you've only heard of gay and straight relationships, then."

"Er, yes – what other sorts are there?" My brain felt muddled as I tried to work out what he was saying. I fell back in my chair I felt quite exhausted again; these chats I have with Lloyd do that to me.

"This is going to be harder than I thought, if you have no idea of other types of relationships. Let me think." He finished his wine and topped up our glasses. "I think this is going to be a long night. Am I right in thinking that you have a day off tomorrow?"

"Yes, unusually. I don't know why, but the salons have some sort of party they are sorting out. They're closed to the public and they don't need me."

"Yes, the salons." He looked like he was in pain and I didn't know why. He screwed his face up "Oh God, I hope you're ready for this. Now, Charlotte, I don't want you to lose the plot. I want you to just listen."

"OK."

"Here we go. Anthony and I…" He paused and I thought to myself that he was talking about himself and Anthony as if they were a couple.

"Anthony and I are in…no, not in…we are Dom." He paused, looking at my face to see my reaction. What the fuck is Dom, I thought.

"You don't know what a Dom is, do you?"

I shook my head.

"OK. We are all consenting adults. That's the first thing you must understand."

"We all are consenting adults," I repeated. "What – you're into orgies?"

He laughed, tilting his head back. "No, Charlotte that's not it either. Have you ever heard of BDSM?"

"Of course I have. I don't quite understand it, though, all that bondage and stuff."

"That's a start. Anthony and I are into BDSM."

"OK, so you tie each other up. Maybe you should have been sailors, you'd have learnt a lot of knots." I teased.

"No, you're still going down the wrong track. We don't tie each other up, we have subs for that," he laughed.

"See, you should have been sailors. Where do you get submarines from, then?"

"No, not submarines, *subs*" He emphasized the word. "Submissive...subs are people that put their whole trust in another person, especially when playing."

"What? I don't understand." I took a sip of wine, was my brain going to explode?

"Charlotte, I need to explain this to you so that you understand everything. The Dom/sub relationship is a lifestyle. We have chosen a lifestyle that isn't the norm. I am a Dom. I dominate. I like to dominate my partner. She is a sub, she likes to be submissive, so I dominate her and she submits."

"What the fuck? You like beating the crap out of poor defenceless females?" I leapt out of my chair, placing my wine on the table as I did so. Waving my hands around and ranting I shrieked, "You're no better than the bastard! You think this is OK? Ow!" I fell over my heels and landed on my arse.

"Charlotte, are you OK?" He rushed over and crouched beside me. "Long nails, tall heels and red wine just don't mix with you, do they?" He pushed the hair back from my face.

"What the fuck! Don't touch me! You're the same!" I shouted.

He moved away from me. "I knew this was going to be hard but you're making it so much harder for me. It's not all that you think." He put out his hand to help me up and I took it.

"You said you trust me now. You either do or you don't, and this is a very big ask, but I want you to keep quiet while I explain some of this to you. I want you to keep trusting me and Anthony as we would never do anything to hurt you or anyone else."

"OK." The shock from the fall had quieted me a little. Lloyd helped me back to the chair.

"Dom/sub, relationships have many levels. When you find a partner you talk and you work out what you want from each other. Everything is controlled. We don't beat the crap out of each other like you think… You must have heard about slap and tickle, a little light bedroom fun, as most husbands and wives put it. Well, what we do is no different but it's controlled. The Dom usually does the control, they make sure that the environment and the game is safe for the sub. You usually have a contract and in that contract you set your limits on what you will and won't do. Do you understand so far?"

"Yes, I think so, but I still don't understand why you get off on controlling people."

"I do and I don't. The contract is a two-way thing and the sub says what they want or don't want. In fact a Dom won't do anything that the sub doesn't want. So we both have control but at different times, and this is what is called a non-vanilla relationship. You have different levels. Different people have different needs. The thing is, you have people that use the lifestyle. They are just nasty. On the whole, it's just good fun by two consenting adults. If at any time my sub didn't enjoy what she was doing, then I wouldn't enjoy it either. That goes for most Doms. Right, that's about it. Any questions?"

I sat with a blank look on my face. Any questions, he was asking me. Any questions? Well, of course I had questions but I didn't know what should come first. I didn't know how to ask questions about that sort of behaviour and when you have just found out that your best friend for all your life is some sort of fucking perv, where do you start? Oh my God, how the fuck did he get caught up in this? What happened to him for him to be so twisted? And Lloyd – he was supposed to be a psychiatrist so how could he be so weird? I looked at him and he said, "You're having trouble with this, aren't you?"

"Oh, that's an understatement, I think. How the hell do you think it's sexy to give someone a black eye? Let me tell you, there is most certainly nothing sexy in having one…" I started ranting again.

"No! No! No! Neither Anthony nor I have ever bruised anyone on purpose. We aren't into black and blue, thank you. Put it this way, OK? If you had sat down with the bastard and drawn up a contract, and in that contract it said that you would trust him to do anything to you as long as he never hit you or hurt you, that in the bedroom you would do things once a month to spice up your sex life, and that you would trust everything he did and said while that session was taking place, do you think he would have thumped you? Do you think if you were able to sit down with a potential partner and say, 'Look, I want a relationship, but I like this, this and this, and I need to know that we can talk about our relationship', that even you would be able to enjoy a relationship again? After all, it makes sense. Why shouldn't we all have wants and needs in the bedroom and the ability to make those happen with someone who feels the same way?"

"Yes, I suppose so, when you put it like that, but you still beat the shit out of other people, and I find it hard to understand how you, but most of all Anthony, can even think about hurting others in that way."

"Phew! I thought I'd lost you then," he said, relieved. "Charlotte, what you're talking about are hard limits, but that's not what Anthony and I are about. And anyway even when hard limits are involved, the playing is done in a controlled manner by the Doms, so please don't think it's about hurting people because it's not. Many girls like dressing up and role-playing. We all dress up and role-play to an extent. You do when you go to work, insofar as you wear a uniform and play a part of sorts. These girls just like to extend the idea to the bedroom and be more daring. Some girls like to be spanked, some like to be tied up. Some are voyeurs who enjoy watching others having sex. Some like sex in the country, in lifts or fast cars. Some like the Mile High club. You name it – it's all there for the taking, as part of the lifestyle. It's all about trust and control between two consenting adults."

"So it's all about dressing up and having sex in a fucking cramped loo in an airplane a mile up?! That's your lifestyle?" I looked at him and then at my glass, which was empty, just like the bottle, and I got up to go and fetch another one from the kitchen. When I returned he was leaning forward with his head in his hands.

"Another?" I asked, as I poured the wine into his glass.

"Charlotte, I have something else to tell you as well and I really do hope this won't blow your mind too much…"

"Oh God, Lloyd! I can't digest everything you've already told me, let alone hearing anymore! Why are you doing this to me? Do you know how hard this is for me to find out you're a perv?" I slouched with one arm over the arm of the chair and the other holding on firmly to my glass of wine, feeling quite bemused with all of this now.

"Yes, I do, but you need to understand something else, about Anthony's and Nats' other business. And I am not a perv." He sipped his wine.

"Oh my God, he's her pimp! I knew the salon was a front for something else!" I slouched deeper into the chair with my wine, how I wished it were just me and this glass of wine this evening.

"No, that's not it. They own a club. In fact they own The Room between them. It's a club for people who are into the lifestyle, who can go and practise whatever they are into whenever they want, and before you say it, no, it's not somewhere they go to beat the shit out of each other! They go to Joe's boxing gym for that!" he laughed.

"Oh, don't! Why did you tell me that? How can I look Nats in the eye again, now I know this?"

"Oh, trust me, you will. Charlotte, although I'm the one telling you this, the other two know what I'm telling you. We all want you to know. You're so close to the three of us now, it's only fair that you should know, and we didn't want you finding out from anyone else. We don't want to hurt you in any way or for you to feel pressured into doing anything you don't want to do. We have too much respect for you to let that happen. You're almost right on one thing, though, in that the salons do double up sometimes as venues for people who subscribe to the lifestyle. For instance, tomorrow night there's a big party at the club, and lots of people will no doubt want to be pampered in readiness, so they use the salons for that. Some of the Doms will bring their subs along for saunas and spas and to get their nails, make-up and hair done. For some, this is a big part of the play element. It's as important to them as the party itself."

"What, pampering together? Most men wouldn't be seen dead doing girlie things!" My interest seemed to perk up with this last comment of Lloyd's.

"That's one of the big differences with this lifestyle. It's about trust and respect and knowing and adhering to the limits. It's the choice of the Dom and the sub. I'm sorry if I've shocked you, but you needed to know."

"OK, so you've told me all of this, but I don't know what you're expecting from me."

"We're not expecting anything from you, other than trusting you to keep all of this where it belongs – within these four walls. And we all do trust you."

"If your lifestyle is so good, why all the secrecy? Why doesn't everyone know about it and practise it?"

"Good question, but the truth of the matter is that most people don't want to know about it or practise it because they can only cope with the idea of vanilla sex with their partners, and probably not even that very often either. The problem is that people who practise this lifestyle are immediately and very unfairly judged by others, as society tends to be hostile toward that which it doesn't or doesn't want to understand. But why shouldn't people have the privacy to do what they want to do, if it allows them to forget about their day-to-day life, even if only temporarily, and to become someone else for a few hours a month? It's escapism. But I'll tell you this, the ones who are married and practise the lifestyle have very strong marriages, with mutual respect and trust and love. In fact I don't know anyone who has ever divorced as a result of the lifestyle, so it can't be all bad, can it?"

"You make it sound so normal, but how can it be?"

"It is normal to those who practise it. It's people such as you who don't quite understand it who don't think it's normal." Lloyd smiled briefly.

"I think I might be vaguely starting to understand, sort of. I am trying to, although I'm still not sure about how and where I fit in."

"You fit in because you're our friend and for no other reason."

"OK. I thought for one scary moment you were going to say that you and Anthony had plans to tie me up on the rack in the kitchen to beat my fucking arse or something."

"No Charlotte, not unless you want us to?" Lloyd asked seriously.

"Er, no. I don't think so!"

"So you still love us all then?"

"Lloyd, I need to get my head around all of this, but let me just say, I might not approve of what you do...do I actually know what you do?" I shook my head in an attempt to reassemble my thoughts. "Anyway, OK, I might not approve, but what you guys do behind closed doors is your business, nothing to do with me. I still love you all, and I hope what you do will never come between us, but until I get my head around things I can't say much more than that."

"You're right. You don't know what we do. What you've said is fair enough and I'm sure that once you've spoken with Anthony and Nats things will become clearer, and I'm equally sure that you'll feel more comfortable with it..." He murmured something else that I couldn't quite catch.

"What was that, Lloyd?"

"Nothing, just...tomorrow, lunch? You and me, yes? We're going to go out, if that's OK with you?"

I got the impression he was trying to distract me. "Yeah, OK, but don't you have to work, doing some pervy thing like making someone call a sex line or something?"

Lloyd laughed. "Charlotte, you're so funny! One minute you're ranting uncontrollably and the next you're making jokes."

"Oh hold on! Is this one of your jokes now? If so, I'll bloody kill you, if you're setting me up on this! What the fuck? Not funny!"

"No, it isn't a joke. This is real. See, I rest my case: one minute talking, the next ranting! Oh Charlotte, I love you, truly I do!" He laughed, his whole face lighting up. "OK, back to tomorrow. We're going out. You'll see when we get there, so don't ask any questions about where we're going, as I won't tell you. I'm staying here tonight in the spare room and Anthony isn't coming home. What do you want to eat? My treat."

So now he was changing the subject on me? Why didn't he want to tell me where we were going?

"Oh yes, we haven't eaten yet, have we? I'd forgotten all about food, with all this pervy talk about whatever it is you do, or don't do…not sure which, but Chinese, if you're paying, would be great, thanks. You order. I must go and get out of these clothes and killer heels."

I sat down on the bed trying to work through some of the things he'd told me. I found it all a little hard to believe, though a lot of things were starting to fall into place, like when Nats first saw me she'd asked Anthony, "Someone you know?" meaning my bruising. He'd replied that not in his social life did he know of anyone who would do such a thing, so Anthony couldn't be in the Dom/sub thing. Or had Lloyd said something about there being different levels or limits or something? Oh what the fuck, I couldn't work it out! I slipped my feet out of my shoes and took off my stockings. I unzipped my dress and stood up to slip it off, still thinking, wondering what exactly was going on in their lives. Lloyd was right, dammit. I was now really curious to know more. What if you could have a relationship the way Lloyd had described, with rules and limits? Could that really work, and if so, would it work better than a normal relationship? Crap, if I kept thinking like this where would it all lead? I put on some joggers and a T-shirt and rejoined Lloyd in the lounge.

"You look worried, Lloyd!"

"Yes, well, I am worried. This hasn't quite gone the way I thought it would."

"There's the intercom. I'll get it." I let in the delivery boy with the Chinese. I carried the bag of cartons through to the kitchen, and unloaded them onto the bar before getting some plates. Lloyd came into the kitchen and we sat down and began to eat.

"If it's a big Dom party tomorrow why are you not pampering your sub, or whatever it is you do? Why are you babysitting me?" I asked, between mouthfuls of noodles.

"Because I don't have a sub. Well, not a regular one. The person I usually go with is a free spirit. Her name's Liz, she's a friend and she likes to surprise, or should that be shock." He shook his head as if to wake himself from a dream. "She likes to get herself ready elsewhere, on her own, and then make an entrance."

"Oh, so not all the subs get the five star treatment then?"

"Oh yes they do, but not always with the Doms. We just pick up the tab. They still go to the salon and have a pamper day. Some Doms can't get to the salons, so the subs go on their own. Some are allowed to make their own choices, but others won't know what they're having done till they get there: their Doms will have left specific instructions for them."

"Why do they use Nats' places?" I ask.

"For several reasons, but mainly because number one, she runs a tight ship and is the soul of discretion, and two, she's a Dom, a Dominatrix."

I looked up, a forkful of noodles half in and half out of my mouth. "*What*? But she's a woman. How the hell does that work?" I asked naïvely.

Lloyd laughs and said, "Women can be Doms too, you know. Some men like to be submissive."

With the noodles still hanging, I tried to bite through them neatly, and failed. "So, um, er..." I sucked in a few strays. "I wouldn't have thought she was like that. Everything she does at the salon is done with such diplomacy she doesn't strike me as being dominant at all. She's so kind and caring."

"She is very kind and caring, yes, and also very assertive. I keep telling you it's not about being a bully or a control freak."

"So what about the staff at the salons? What does she tell them when all the subs turn up to be pampered?"

"The staff, as you know, have all signed a contract. Not all of them know, only a few, and they live the lifestyle as well. The rest think it's some sort of photo shoot thing they're doing, and they all get paid very well, so they're happy. The people who make the outfits for some of the subs think it's for some sort of publicity stunt, so no one is any the wiser, although now there are people who specialise in BDSM clothing."

"What, you have people who make clothes for you all?"

"Yes. It does makes life a little easier," he smiled.

We finished eating in silence and then after clearing our plates went back to the lounge.

"Listen," I said, "I'm curious about this lifestyle thing, although I'm not entirely sure why. You've said one or two things that I just can't fathom. I'd like to know more, but to be honest I don't know where to start."

"You're curious! I thought you thought it was pervy?" He grinned at me with a devilish little glint in his blue eyes.

"Yes, I am curious, only because I want to see what the big attraction is, and maybe understand why Anthony's decided he's better off in a relationship with someone he can boss around."

Actually, thinking back to when we were kids, he was

always bossy after a fashion, wanting to be in control, so maybe it made sense. He'd always had a certain presence about him that made others do what he wanted them to, and if they didn't he could be very persuasive, but in a manner that was kind rather than menacing.

"Oh, and there was I thinking you were curious because you wanted to have an alternative relationship." Lloyd screwed up his nose in a cheeky way.

"No, never! I've had enough violence in relationships to last me a lifetime, and I'm not pervy, I'm normal."

"Define normal. What is normal? Who is normal? Who's to say that you're normal or that I'm normal and who or what isn't normal? Who sets the boundaries? Society? Or narrow-minded people who only see what they want to see?"

"Is that a rhetorical question," I asked, "or do you want me to answer it?"

"Do you have an answer?" He sat forward with an air of interest.

"It's tricky. I've learnt from my training as a nurse that you're right to question what normal is. It's usually measured by what the majority does or says or thinks, so society dictates and defines it. But then we're all individuals, so normality should accommodate individuality, I suppose. Well, that's what I think, rightly or wrongly."

"Indeed. Now you're starting to think for yourself and to look at things differently."

"I've always tried to look at things from other perspectives," I said. "It's just been over the last year or so that I've lost my way a bit. But you do make me think, and things are falling into place more about the way I was abused. And intelligent conversation…" I made air quotes with my fingers, "Has also helped to lift the fog."

"Anthony said you always used to be able to see all sides

of an argument and others' points of view. I am so glad that tonight hasn't freaked you out."

"I'll keep an open mind until I learn what it's all about. I think my initial reaction was because of my last relationship, but now that I've thought a bit more, and we've chatted, I think I have it more in perspective."

"Good. Right then, time for bed. You've got a long day tomorrow." He finished his wine and stood up.

"We're just doing lunch, you said?"

"Yes, but we'll be out from about ten, so be ready, Miss, and remember you need a clear and open mind."

"OK, I will. Night, then."

"Night," he said, and we went to our rooms.

Chapter Eight

The next morning we were in the kitchen drinking coffee. I asked where we were going and he said again he wouldn't tell me until we got there, when all would become clear. We left the house dead on ten and to my surprise we were walking, not driving. We came to a building that looked just like all the others.

"Here we are," Lloyd said, and walked up the steps to a grand Regency-style door, painted black with a brass knocker. He knocked, and a butler opened the door.

"Mr Hughes. Ma'am," the butler said, inclining his head.

As we walked in, I whispered, "Oh my God, how posh is that! Did you hear him? Where are we?" I was overawed, trying hard to keep up with Lloyd as I followed him down a big hallway, hardly having time to look around. How could anyone walk so fast?

We entered a room through double doors at the other end of the hallway. Lloyd stopped just as we went inside.

"Please, Charlotte, sit down." He gestured toward a sofa. I went over and sat down, looking at him. His manner had suddenly changed, his voice full of command. I didn't know what to make of it.

"Please wait here. I just need to check on a few things, I'll be back in a minute." He went out, shutting the door behind him. I'd never been in such a big room. There were five sofas in all: very luxurious green leather chesterfields, with little occasional tables at each end, and lamps on the tables. They looked like Tiffany lamps. There were two footstools to each sofa, also in green leather. The windows were tall with full-length curtains striped green, white and gold, and with folding wooden shutters behind.

Hanging from the ceiling was the most beautiful chandelier. The daylight caught it, dancing through the crystals. An emerald-green carpet covered the floor, and a rug in golds and reds lay in front of the open fireplace. Pictures hung on all but one of the walls, mostly landscapes. On the remaining wall were hundreds of photographs. I got up to have a closer look, and – oh my God, I was in The Room! Lloyd had brought me to Anthony and Nats' club! What the hell was he doing? Why did he think I needed to be here? I looked around in panic, trying to think how to get out, but there was no obvious exit other than the way we came in, through the front door, and I didn't want to bump into the butler. My eyes were drawn back to the photos. Some of them were of normal looking people…a little over the top in the way they were dressed, maybe, and some of the girls' make-up, but they were all very beautiful, like models. The men looked like average men…but then there were a few photographs which were a little more obscure. The people were dressed all in leather and some had dog collars and chains. Some of the girls were more scantily dressed.

The door opened. "Mad?" a voice said, as I swung round. Lloyd.

I raised an eyebrow. "Why should I be?"

"I knew you wouldn't want to come, and the only way to get you here was to keep where we were going a secret, but I thought bringing you for a look around would maybe help to answer some more of your questions regarding what this is all about."

The butler entered and put down a tray with two cups of coffee on one of the tables and left the room without uttering a single word. Strange, I thought, but who am I to question the behaviour of a butler!

Lloyd walked over to where I was standing, "I thought I told you to sit?"

"I'm my own person, and I don't always do as I'm told."

He was looking at the wall. "I see you've found some pictures."

"Yes, they aren't what I expected at all."

"Why, what were you expecting?"

"I haven't a clue, actually. None of this is what I expected. It looks just like a gentlemen's club, nothing out of the ordinary."

"That's exactly what it is, from the outside, but you're now behind closed doors. No one gets in here without an invitation or nomination by another member, so certainly it's a private club, yes."

"We got in without question."

"Yes, we did, because I'm a founding member of the club. Come, sit and have your coffee, and then we'll go on a tour, and I'll try to explain it all to you as best I can."

We sat on the sofa and he passed me a coffee.

"What about the staff here?"

"The staff are all people who follow the lifestyle, and they're paid exceptionally well. They are all utterly loyal and trustworthy, and would protect anyone and anything connected with this club. Its reputation for complete discretion is what makes it work, and they all respect that."

"Wow, you all take this so seriously!" I giggled.

"It is serious, very serious. OK, some rules before I show

you round. You are here as my guest." He rolled his eyes. "God help me with this one," he muttered. "Rule One: you don't talk to anyone unless they talk to you first…" Before he could say any more I was rising up to that one.

"What the fu…" But before I could finish he clapped his hand over my mouth.

"Shush, will you!" He took his hand away slowly. I looked at him, shocked.

"Charlotte, please listen to me. I am trying to keep you safe. There are people here who would expect me to spank you for talking to me like that."

"*What*?" I was taken aback. "You said you'd never do anything to hurt me."

"And that is why I need to explain the rules to you. This is serious," he repeated. "Rules: one, don't talk to anyone unless they talk to you. Two, don't question anything that is said. Three don't swear: it's not becoming to a young lady. And four, if there's anything, anything at all that makes you feel uncomfortable or unhappy, you must tell me at once, OK?"

"OK. I am not happy with the way you just grabbed my mouth. I am not happy with the way you've told me what I can and can't do. So stick that in your Dom's pipe and smoke it!" I finished, feeling pleased with myself for having stood up to him already when we hadn't even left this first room. Who did he think he was, telling me what I could and couldn't do!

"Charlotte, you're being very brave, but joking aside, this is my domain now, and Anthony's and Nats', and these are the rules. Why did I draw the short straw with babysitting a vanilla!" he muttered.

"If you don't want to babysit me you needn't have brought me here, and stop referring to me as an ice cream," I snapped.

He frowned, shaking his head. "That's not quite what I meant. You are being naughty now, and who mentioned anything about ice cream? These people deserve respect, and you must show them some."

"You have vanilla!"

"Charlotte, what are you talking about?" he said impatiently.

"You keep talking about vanilla, and that's a flavour of ice cream in my world."

"Oh Charlotte, you don't mean...? You do!" Lloyd burst out laughing. "You haven't a clue what I mean by vanilla, have you?"

"Why don't you try to explain it to me then, instead of laughing at me?"

"It means plain, regular, ordinary, in a sexual relationship sense. 'Same old', if you like." When I didn't respond he continued "Drink up, and let me show you around. All the rooms on this floor are the same so we'll start on the next floor. They're all playrooms of one kind or another, and none of them are being used till later."

We finished our coffee and went upstairs. The first room we entered was much smaller than the room we'd previously been in, but otherwise identical: two sofas, footstools, and occasional tables...

I looked around. "This is the same!"

"It might seem the same, but it's not." He moved over to a wall and pushed it. It opened.

"In here is the bit which you might feel is a little... no, you'll feel is very...it's probably easier if you just take a look." He held the door open. Inside, neatly hanging on hooks, were whips of all kinds. It was all for inflicting pain. I could feel my mouth moving but nothing came out. I stared at him, horrified.

"Now wait a minute, Charlotte, where is your open mind?"

"What the fuck do you do with these?" I felt numb.

"They're used. I thought I'd get this room out of the way first. Come and sit down, and I'll try to explain." He led me to a sofa. "Always remember that everything that's done here is done in a controlled way. No one gets really hurt. We've never had to take anyone to a hospital. We've never had anyone leave here looking like you did when I saw you that day at Anthony's. As I've said, everyone has different levels, and no one does anything they don't want to do. The club's rules would forbid it otherwise. Pain and pleasure are very close to each other: closer than you might think. Similar you might say to love and hate. Slap and tickle in a vanilla relationship is fine for most people, but for others they need a little more: this…" he gestured around him toward the whips "is the next stage on from slap and tickle. It's also the punishment room."

"So you do have punishment? It *is* about controlling someone by violence! I knew it! That's the bit you're not telling me about."

He laughed softly. "No, Charlotte, it's not like that. Have you ever seen a western movie: John Wayne, for example, when he grabs a woman and throws her over his knee and spanks her arse?"

"Yes, I have."

"Did you think there was anything wrong with that? Did you think it was violent? And what did he do afterwards? Did you think he was pervy?"

"No. As I recall, she was a spoilt brat and needed to be put in her place, and he did that."

"Exactly. He put her in her place, and that is what goes on in here. Remember no one does anything they don't want to do and no one does anything to anyone without their permission. None of the staff would ever allow it. Anthony and Nats would have them out of here, don't doubt that for a second. Right then, next room. We don't have long."

The next room looked like a French boudoir: very grand, with a tall four-poster bed. Candles stood on every surface, and there was a...well, I'm not sure what it was... in the corner. As I went over to it Lloyd said, "This is the fire and ice room. I like this room – it's one of my favourites. That's an ice machine. This room is very tactile: it's all about touching and feeling, and sensations."

I walked around the bed, holding onto one of the posts and swinging round it flirtatiously.

"I like this room. It feels so enticing, with the lighting, and all the lovely soft furnishings. It appeals to the senses. It's very seductive."

He looked at me. Was there a fleeting look of desire on his face? Then he turned the door handle saying "Come, there's one more room. The bondage room. All the rooms are soundproofed so no one can hear what's going on, but each room has a microphone installed and there's always someone monitoring the rooms to check if anyone sounds stressed or unhappy, at which point someone would go to that room to ensure nothing's got out of hand. There's also a panic button on the side of the fireplace in each room. It makes no noise in the rooms themselves but it lets security know that someone needs help."

"So why the microphones, or is that a pervy thing too?"

"No not pervy, just sometimes you might not be able to get to a panic button. It's just for added protection, mainly so the subs feel secure."

There was so much in the bondage room: ropes, tapes, chains and so on. I shuddered.

"I think you've had enough," he said, taking my hand. "Time for lunch and a chat, I think."

We went back down the imposing staircase and then into yet another room, a private dining room. It wasn't large, just big enough to accommodate a moderately sized table and two chairs by a window on the far side, and a real fire in the fireplace. We went over to the table as Lloyd pulled a cord hanging by the fireplace.

"Very *Upstairs, Downstairs*," I said.

"Yes, very much so, and Hudson will arrive in a minute," Lloyd smiled.

We sat down, and as if by magic the butler appeared with our food.

"I ordered the salmon salad for you. I hope that's OK." The butler placed the plates on the table and left us.

"So, do you have any questions?" Lloyd asked, with a 'please, God, don't let this be painful' look on his face.

"How the hell can you call it fun when you truss people up in chains like slaves?" I leaned over the table with my face close to his.

"Look, bondage is an art form. Here, I'll show you." He got up from the table and picked up an envelope. When he sat down again he opened the envelope and sorted through what looked like photos. He passed one to me.

"Look."

The photo was of a young girl with a subdued expression. She had ropes tied around her body in such a way as to make her look like an Egyptian mummy. Lloyd passed me another, this time of a guy wearing what looked like a pair of pants made out of rope. Ropes had been tied and plaited behind him in such a way as to make it look as if he had a tail.

"These are not what I expected."

"No. Expect the unexpected and the unexpected becomes the expected."

"Your text from yesterday. I did wonder what that meant."

"Things are not always what they seem. All you know about things like these is what you might have read in newspapers. Negative stuff."

"Do people have sex here too?"

"I assume so, as there are bedrooms."

"How many bedrooms are there?"

"Thirty."

"What! You're all running a knocking shop? Oh for fuck's sake! You sell sex too!" I hung my head in shame, but the shame was not mine, it was what they should be feeling and I didn't understand why they weren't. They were running a fucking brothel!

"No, it's not a knocking shop. All the rooms are rented out to people who live outside London but who work in the city and want a base here. What they want the room for is up to them, provided it falls within the club's rules. They can rent on a daily or weekly basis, first come first served, but there is no sex in the play/specialist rooms upstairs. There are, however, the dungeons. Now how the hell do I explain those to you…let's just say they're for stuff that's of a more sexual nature, and involve hard limits." Lloyd rubbed his forehead. "I can't show you them, or at least not yet. I don't want to scare the pants off you altogether."

My head was spinning with all this information. I still couldn't work out if I thought this was right or not. I couldn't help thinking it still sounded like taking advantage of weak, vulnerable people.

"How do I know that this is all what you say it is, and nothing bad or wrong? I only have your word for it."

"Like I've already said, it's all about trust. Trust on every level. It hinges and relies on trust. And you said you trust me. Look, that party is this evening. It's more of a social than a play thing, and I would like you to come with me so that I can introduce to you some friends from the lifestyle. Some are in it as husband and wife and some just as occasional friends."

"What, you want me to come here with pervy people...?"

"No, Charlotte!" I looked up, startled. Lloyd sounded angry. "You'll be coming here as my guest to meet Anthony's, Nats' and my friends. What they do behind closed doors is their business, remember, but if you talk to some of them it'll maybe help you to understand. I'd really like you to join me." His face returned to its former warmth and the look in his blue eyes melted through me.

"I'll try it, but only because I'm curious. I want to see what sort of people are into this."

"Good. Excellent, in fact! I am really looking forward to it already." He seemed genuinely pleased at the prospect.

"Anything else you want me to see here, then?"

"I don't think so, but I have to take you shopping, and afterwards Nats is expecting you at the salon."

"No, she isn't. It's my day off, remember?" I looked at him, puzzled.

"Yes, she is. You are going to be pampered for the rest of the afternoon, along with Anthony's sub."

"What! Do I not get any say in this?"

"No, not really. Well, you do, but we all decided that even if you didn't wish to join us this evening, you would need some pampering to relax, so we booked you in for a little R 'n' R. Nats wants to talk with you too, so let's get going." He got up from the table.

"Oh, what the hell..." I followed him.

First, Lloyd took me to a shop to get a package, and then we went to the salon.

"I thought you were taking me shopping?"

"I did." He handed me the bag.

"What's this?"

"Clothes for you to wear tonight."

"I have clothes of my own."

"Yes, but tonight you need to fit in a little and not look like you work in a salon, so I've bought you something to wear. I only hope you like it! Now get going! I can see Nats hovering, waiting for you."

I looked through the door. She was standing by the reception desk. I could just make out her outline through the frosted glass. OK, act normal, I said to myself, as if I didn't know anything about what she was or what she did in private...oh fuck, it was never going to work. I walked into the salon.

"Hi, Nats," I said calmly, though my impulse was to say, "You perv! What the fuck do you think you're doing!"

She came over and hugged me tight, whispering in my ear "Oh Charlotte, please don't think badly of me. I've known you for such a short time, and yet already you've become one of my closest friends. We just thought we should tell you... I bet your brain feels like it's going to explode, but trust me, things are not always what they seem."

She released me and led the way into the office. Closing the door, she turned and said, "I'll totally understand if you don't want to work here any more or if you don't want to be my friend, but what I will say is that if that is the way you're feeling, please take a bit of time, maybe have a few weeks off to take time out to think before making any decisions. I don't want to lose you as a friend or as my right-hand woman."

"You really mean that, don't you?"

"Yes, I do."

"It hadn't even crossed my mind, either leaving here or losing you, Anthony and Lloyd as friends. I do think you're all pervy, but that's your choice. As long as you don't hurt anyone, what's it to me?"

"Oh, thank God!" She visibly relaxed. "Are you coming to the party tonight? I see you have a bag with you. Have you looked in it yet?"

"No, I haven't."

"OK, let's see what he's got for you."

We opened the bag. Inside was a dress.

"It looks like a serving wench's dress from days gone by," I said. "He must be kidding if he thinks I'm going to wear this."

"You'll look stunning. The theme is Dick Turpin, so you'll not be the only one dressed like it."

"What, it's fancy dress?"

"Yes, didn't he say?"

"No, he didn't, although I'm not surprised. I think he's found me rather difficult to deal with over this. My reaction was a little all over the place, and I still don't really know what to make of it all. Do you hurt anyone?" I looked her squarely in the eye, hoping to see her reaction, only realising as I did so that she had her contacts in, which were distracting, as all I could concentrate on was today's colour, which was violet. Not helpful.

Nats answered firmly, "No, I don't. I never do anything my sub doesn't want me to do, never have and never will. I don't know anyone who has ever done anything to hurt anyone else, in fact. You had more bruising on you when I first met you than my sub does after I've whipped him."

"How can that be?"

106

"I whip him with care. The pressure and the amount of time I whip him for are all relevant: he says how hard and he says when to stop. He has a safe word and when he says it I stop."

"Do you like whipping him?"

"Not really, no, but he likes it so it's me giving him what he wants."

"What? It's his own choice, really?"

"Yes, hasn't Lloyd explained all of this to you?"

"Yes, but I'm finding it hard to take in, and I think the fact you've said you don't really like whipping him – that it's what he wants – has just put another slant on the whole aspect of this thing."

"Look Charlotte, you never, in any way, shape or form, asked for the beatings you got." She stroked my cheek. "No real Dom would ever do that to his or her sub, and in my eyes anyone who could do that sort of thing to another person is sick. Some people do hide behind the Dom mask to try and justify what they're doing, but trust me, it's not and never should be violent or against another's will." She went to the door. "Right, time's getting on and you need pampering. Come and enjoy your afternoon of leisure…"

We left the office and went down to the spa.

"Here's your first treatment." Nats opened the door to a changing room and we went in.

"Charlotte, this is Kat. Kat, this is Charlotte. Kat is Anthony's friend, and sub for tonight. Kat knows who you are, I've explained to her."

Kat was stunning: reed-slim with vibrant curly copper hair piled on top of her head, big green eyes and a perfect porcelain complexion.

"Hi, Charlotte." She gave me a friendly smile. "Here's a bikini to pop on for the spa. I'll see you in there." She went out through a door on the other side of the changing room.

"I'll leave you to it," said Nats. "I've booked the spa for just the two of you for about an hour, so you won't be disturbed. Enjoy, and ask her questions. Anything you like. She'll be honest with you."

"OK, thanks, Nats."

I slipped on the little red bikini and joined Kat in the spa. I got in and immersed myself, looking everywhere except at Kat, who giggled and said, "Come on, don't be shy. Anthony's told me all about you, so I have the upper hand, I think."

"I don't know what to say to you. You're the woman who my best friend gets off on when he hits you and hurts you."

"Whoa, now hold on just one second! He doesn't hit me, and he never hurts me." She stood up. "Look! Look at my arse. He spanked me last night. Look! What do you see?"

As she bent down and planted her arse in my face, I had no option but to look. To my astonishment there wasn't one bruise or a scratch or anything.

"Answer me then, what do you see?"

"N-nothing," I stammered. Was that the way subs were supposed to behave? I thought by their very definition they were timid people who wouldn't say boo to a goose.

She turned around to face me. Thank God she hadn't farted while her arse was plonked in front of me, I thought.

"OK, so no bruising. Get it straight, lady! No one bruises me, and I mean no one!"

"Hey, but hang on, aren't you a sub? Aren't you supposed to be quiet and timid?"

"Only when I want to be, and only when Anthony and

I are playing. You don't think I'd really let anyone walk all over me, do you?"

"No, I can see you are quite able to look after yourself."

"Too right I am. Just because I'm a sub doesn't mean I don't have a voice."

God, she scared me! And she was the sub. If she was so feisty, what were the Doms like? I sank down below the bubbles of the spa, hoping she wouldn't have her voice for much longer.

Maybe Kat guessed what I was thinking because she said in a softer voice, "Charlotte, I'm sorry, but I get fed up with people assuming that Anthony hurts me. Some of my vanilla friends know what I do and they really don't understand and I get very defensive when they start on at me. They should mind their own business and leave me to mine. After all, I don't tell them how to lie in the missionary position, do I? No I don't."

I thought about what she'd just said. That was the only sex I'd ever had, and come to think of it I hated it, lying there while he rolled on, then rolled off. I'd never thought about it before, but yes it was plain, boring vanilla. How could I judge when all I'd had was my own definition of plain, boring vanilla, and I hated it when I had it? I also hated it when I was unable to compare things properly.

"Thank you, Kat. You're the first person who has helped me to see clearly on this. You're right – how can people judge when all most of them have had is the one vanilla experience? They can't compare, and shouldn't judge."

Kat was clearly taken aback.

"What do you...?" Then changing tack, she said, "Tonight is going to be such fun. Lloyd texted me saying you were coming, and I'm to take you to the suite. I love it when it's fancy dress and a themed night, and I'm sure you will too, Charlotte. I must say you're not what I expected. I thought you might be trouble: a typical vanilla friend who would judge without even wanting to know what it's all about. I love the lifestyle: it's given me confidence in who I am and I've changed so much since I started."

"In what way, and how did you get into it?" I hit her with both questions at once, as she seemed to talk without taking a breath and I thought maybe she would give me the answers in one go.

"I was fed up with him indoors: every time we had sex it was the same – he was always drunk, and would literally fall asleep on top of me half-way through, but not before either farting or burping in my face. I just guessed there must be something else out there to try. The last time he tried to fuck me he belched and threw up all over both of us. It was disgusting, to say the least. I pushed him off, and went and showered. Then, after sticking a Post-It on his head with the words 'Bye, arsehole' on it, I left, in the middle of the night. I went to a hotel for a few days until I sorted out a flat, and when I moved in I decided to do some research on relationships and found a site for Dom/sub chat rooms on the internet. I started chatting to some very nice people who explained what the lifestyle was like. Then, one of the Doms invited me to The Room, but he made a mistake. He told me where it was...and I went and knocked on the door and asked if I could see someone about the lifestyle. I explained to the butler I was very worried about meeting someone off the internet as I didn't know who or what he was and I wanted to check if it was all right. He told me he would fetch someone to talk with me, and that's when I met Nats. I talked to her a few times over several weeks until she was sure I was OK with the idea, and the rest is history. And I've never looked back. I love it!"

"What about the person who told you about The Room?"

"I don't know who he is, and he doesn't know who I am. I used a false name and I'm sure he did too."

"And your relationship with Anthony?"

"We play and have fun together. He looks after me and I him, but no ties."

"So you don't want to live with him?"

"God, no! We're friends and consenting adults, that's all."

"Don't you want more?"

"Why should I? I have everything I need. If and when things change and I want to have a full relationship, I'll talk with Anthony. If he wants one too we'll draw up a new contract and sort things out, but if he doesn't then we'll go our separate ways, no hard feelings."

"Sounds very cold."

"No, it's very grown-up. No hang-ups, just trust and truth."

"I can't believe it's that easy."

"It's not that easy, you have to work at it, trust me. Some of them get themselves in a right state, but that's often because they overstep lines or don't keep to their contracts. You do have to be quite level-headed to do this, and you'll find the ones who mess it up are the ones who are off with the fairies, in that they think the lifestyle's what they want but deep down it's not. Some people are right for the lifestyle and some people are vanilla and never the twain should meet. And of course you also have the occasional nutter who should be for neither, as they give both vanilla and the lifestyle a bad name. Guys like your ex, for instance. Anthony told me, I hope you don't mind?"

"No, it's OK."

"So do you think you might feel able to join the lifestyle?"

"What, me? No way! It scares me."

"Oh? So why are you going tonight then?"

"Curiosity, that's all, and because it's all happened so fast today, and I'm trying to get my head clear as to what I do think."

"I think you would love it, just like me, but if you're not ready certainly don't be pushed."

"I'll remember that. Thank you."

After we finished our spa we went to have our nails done. Mine were a bright pink with silver lines, and in the nail of one of my little fingers I had a hole punched and a little pair of handcuffs attached. They looked quite cute, although signifying something more than I cared to know about.

Then it was time for hair and make-up, none of which I had a choice over, which I found a little intrusive as I was used to making my own requests as to what hairdressers did to my hair, but I went along with it.

When Nats had finished she looked at me in the mirror and asked what I thought. I looked at my reflection. My hair was piled in curls on top of my head, with a few loose tendrils softly framing my face. A few fresh daisies had been secured amongst the curls, adding a suggestion of innocence to a look that was both elegant and sophisticated. It looked lovely, although I felt it said bridesmaid at a wedding rather than guest at a Dom/sub fancy dress party. My make-up looked very modest compared to some that I'd seen during that afternoon, with liner highlighting my eyes, and false lashes that curled so high they touched my eyebrows. A soft pink lipstick with a gloss over the top completed the look. I had to admit I looked stunning.

"It's how I'd always imagined I'd look on my wedding day."

"Good. You'll do, then." Nats laughed. "Now go into the office. You need to try your dress on."

I went to her office and put on my dress. I looked like I was the rose-seller from *Oliver Twist*. My boobs were fighting either to escape from or stay in my dress, I wasn't sure which. I came out of the office and stood in the salon, and everyone turned and looked at me.

Nats said, "You're going to blow everyone's mind tonight. You know that, don't you?"

I felt the flush work its way up my chest and neck and reach my face. I still wasn't used to being complimented. I didn't think I'd ever get used to it.

"Right, you two, it's time for you to go! Charlotte, change back out of your dress. Kat is taking you back to the suite at The Room. Anthony and I will be staying there tonight too. Kat, when you arrive ask one of the butlers to bring you both something to eat and drink. Charlotte, I've briefed the butlers to keep an eye out for you tonight. If for any reason you want to return to the suite just ask one of them and they'll escort you back."

We left as soon as I'd changed.

Chapter Nine

At The Room, Kat took me to a lift. As we went in she pulled at a chain she was wearing beneath her top. Dangling at the end was a key, which she inserted into a small lock to the left of the panel of buttons, and turned it. The lift started to go up.

"We're going to the fourth floor – the top floor. No one can get up here without a key."

The doors opened and we stepped out into an oak-panelled hallway where a butler was waiting for us.

"Evening, ladies, I trust you are both well?"

"Yes, thank you. We would like some refreshments, if you wouldn't mind. Red wine and something to eat, please?"

"Certainly. I'll organise that for you."

Kat opened a door and we walked into a lounge much the same as the one Lloyd and I had been in earlier that day. (Was it really the same day? It felt like so much longer ago than that.)

"OK, that door over there leads to a hallway. The first door you come to is a toilet, the second door is your bedroom and you have an en suite. That door is the kitchen, and the other is the office, where Nats and Anthony spend most of their time working when they're here. They also have a secretary, when they need one."

How the hell could Anthony afford all this? I didn't know what I was most shocked at – the fact he was pervy and I never knew, or the fact he had all of this and I never knew.

"Right, I must get ready for Anthony, as this is his evening, and he'll expect me to do as he wishes tonight."

"What do you mean 'do as he wishes'?"

"Tonight is Anthony's night, so I must do everything he has asked and will ask of me. After all, I'm his sub, and he works hard so he needs to be looked after. We've talked about what we both want tonight so I must be ready for when he walks in."

"He won't mind if you're not quite ready, surely?" I protested.

"Oh yes he will, mark my words! I must change. I'll be back in a minute..." and she rushed off, bags in hand.

By the time Kat returned the waiter had come and set down some sandwiches and poured two glasses of wine.

"Wow, you look stunning!" I said. She was dressed in a period dress but with a modern twist – a ball gown with a bustle, but short, falling to just above the knee, and her boobs also looked to be fighting to defy gravity.

"Thank you," Kat said. "Anthony always chooses so well for me when we have parties here."

"What, he doesn't choose for you all the time?"

"No, just for occasions such as tonight. The rest of the time he trusts me to be dressed in a manner that befits the evening. He does pay for my clothes, though, and salon work too."

"That seems cheap."

"No, not at all. My friends all go out and get their hair done, buy make-up and clothes, all paid for from the pockets of their partners, so why should this be any different, just because we have a different arrangement?"

Good point, I thought, why should it? She's right again.

"We choose to live apart and to have a double life – this one and an everyday life – but we're still partners. We share, and he buys me things and I buy him things. I treat him to the theatre and he treats me to weekends away. What's so different? I trust him and he trusts me."

"Do you love him?" I asked – intrigued to hear what she would say.

"Yes, I do love him."

OK, not what I was expecting to hear. "If you love him, why don't you want to be with him all the time?"

"Because neither of us is ready for that. We both know what we want as we talk all the time. We talk as Dom and sub and we talk as friends, so we both know exactly where we're at and what our needs are. He knows what I like in the bedroom, both when we're playing and as a friend, and vice versa. How many vanillas do you know who know exactly what each other want, and when and where?"

"Well, I don't, most of my friends always moan that he or she doesn't know them or know what they want."

"Exactly, and what happens? They go from one relationship to another looking for what they're missing instead of talking and telling each other. Oh, the lift is here! I must go, excuse me," and she got up to stand by the door, head down and her hands out in front of her. I had to fight not to laugh.

Anthony walked in and gently placed his jacket over her hands, then lifted her chin with his finger, and softly kissed her lips.

"Evening, Kat. You look lovely, but I think that as we have an important guest and friend here you can be yourself until the party."

"OK," Kat said, smiling.

Anthony turned to me. "Hi Charlotte, you look great too." He leaned down to kiss my cheek, then whispered, "We're still bestest friends in the world, I hope?"

I whispered back, "You're a perv, and even that isn't going to get rid of me. We're friends for life!" I kissed him back on the cheek.

He smiled down at me and winked. "I knew you'd be OK eventually. Lloyd says you've been hard work. I'm glad you gave him a hard time! He says he's mentally exhausted, and you've been worse than having a full day of his most difficult patients."

"Oh dear, I am sorry."

"Did you enjoy your pampering?"

"Yes, I did, thank you."

"Don't thank me, thank Lloyd. He's the one who organised and paid for it"

"I hope that doesn't mean he thinks I'm his sub for the night and can boss me around like he has on some occasions."

"No, silly, he's going to escort you tonight but he didn't think you should come along unless you'd had all the trimmings too. He thought that was only fair. He'll look after you when you're downstairs."

"Why? Do I need looking after?"

"Not really, but we don't want you to get yourself into any situations, that's all. You have to remember this is a different world that you're about to enter, with different rules, and you might just find it a little daunting at first."

"Yes, well, I confess it does worry me a bit, and if I'm honest I'm not completely sure I want to go." I fidgeted uncomfortably in anticipation.

"Don't worry, you'll be fine. All you need to remember is that the only reason we've told you about this is because you're so close to us, and it was getting more and more difficult for us to keep it a secret. I could have hung Nats when she offered you the job, as it made you so close to where it all happens, and we couldn't just keep shutting you out. We didn't think that was right. Tonight is a party. It's mild, but you need to know, to understand, why people are like they are. This is how we live our lives, but we don't expect you to live it like this just because we do. It's a personal choice. Kat made her choice after about six months of talking with Nats while she was trying to find what she was looking for. She's been living her lifestyle now for five years, and that's her personal choice. Lloyd and I would never think any differently or worse of her if she had chosen a different lifestyle. She's still our friend, and if after tonight you choose never to set foot in here again that's fine, and if you choose never to be at the salon when these guys are there getting ready, again your choice, but this I will say – we choose to keep you as our friend, as a salon employee, and as a flatmate...our choice. Now you had the choice to come tonight, to ask questions, and to see what it's all about, and then to make an informed decision. It might take an hour or a year, who knows, but that's for you to choose."

"Wow, Anthony, that's deep!"

"I want, no, *we* want you to know that you have choices, and what you choose will in no way make us think any less of you. Today has been a bit of an overload of information for you, and Nats has decided to give you the rest of the week off – call it thinking time – as she wants you to be sure about what you choose to do. We don't want you to feel pressured in any way. I hope you understand why we decided to tell you."

"Yes, I understand all, or mostly all, of what I've seen

and heard so far. I'll go this evening as you suggest so that I can see for myself."

"Good."

"How can you run this place and be a lawyer?"

Anthony sighed. "With great difficulty, I can tell you. It's a long story, how all this happened, and I will tell you one day, I promise, but right now we have a party to go to. Kat, will you go and help Charlotte get ready, please? Lloyd will be here in about half an hour."

"OK, come on. Charlotte, let's go to your room and get you sorted." She gave Anthony a little kiss as she walked past him. We went to the bedroom. It was decorated in exactly the same way as the bedroom I had been into downstairs and my eyes lit up. "Never thought I'd be sleeping in such a luxurious room! Why are all the rooms the same? Is it cheaper that way?"

"No, not quite. It has something to do with the guy who used to own it. Nats decided to keep everything as it was when he died."

"Who used to own it?" I asked.

"I'm afraid I can't tell you, but I'm sure Anthony will explain all the details to you when he has that chat with you. I don't want to say anything out of turn, if you catch my drift."

I didn't press her further. She helped me into my dress and sat me down at the dressing table.

"Your hair only needs tweaking, which will literally take a minute." She started fussing with it even though my hair still looked great to me.

"I could get used to someone fussing over me like this! Thank you, Kat, you're very kind."

"That's OK, I like doing it. I always wanted a little sister but the stork never found my mum again after she had me," she laughed. "Right, you'll do, we'll go back to the lounge and wait for Anthony to finish getting ready, and we can have some more wine. You would probably benefit from some Dutch courage. Now, have a look at yourself."

I stood and turned. There was a full-length free-standing mirror just the other side of the bed, and as I caught sight of my reflection I felt for a brief minute confused, as if my brain was telling me I didn't belong here, either in this lifestyle or this room, styled from an age long gone...

"Come, I hear the lift. It'll be Lloyd." Kat said.

We rushed to the lounge. Why the hell was I rushing for a man? As we arrived the door from the hallway opened to reveal Lloyd standing there.

"My, my, ladies, we do look grand! Hello, little Miss," he pecked Kat's cheek, "and who is this? A new serving girl by the looks of it?"

"Quit, Lloyd, I am no one's servant girl, and you'd do well to remember that."

Lloyd stepped back in amazement. "Do you hear that, Kat? She dares speak to me in such a manner!" He winked at Kat and they both started laughing.

"What's so funny?" I demanded, hands on my hips.

"You..." Lloyd grinned. "Wine for you two lovelies, before we get into a fight, Charlotte? I need one even if you don't!" He poured some wine into clean glasses on a tray. Someone must have cleared away and set out new ones while we'd been gone.

"Honestly, you turn your back for five minutes in this place and everything you've been using has gone and been replaced with fresh, eh?"

"Indeed," Lloyd smiled, "It's the butlers. They keep the place perfect at all times."

"Don't the butlers have names?" I asked. "And how many of them are there?"

"Yes, they do have names, all twenty of them, but they are just known as the butlers. I don't know why, they just always have been."

"Don't they mind?" as we all sat down.

"No, not at all. They see it as part of their job."

"Why do you need twenty?"

"Because it's always been that way. We have twenty maids as well."

"That's a huge number of staff!"

"This is a big operation, and it's what everyone expects."

"It all seems very indulgent to me."

"Good, that's what it's supposed to be, so goal achieved!"

"How do you pay for it all?"

"Members' fees, and they pay substantial amounts of money for this place to stay the way it is. Take tonight for instance – this is ticket-only entry and the tickets cost around a thousand pounds per person, so that in itself brings in a lot. Then you have sales of rooms and extras as well, and that's before what they'll have paid for their sub's pamper day, and for their own as well if they've had one."

I sat back in amazement, not believing what he'd told me.

"That's shocked you, hasn't it? This is an exclusive club, and exclusivity is expensive. It costs a lot to keep it going, so those who want to use it have to pay for the privilege. If they want it badly enough they'll pay, and they do."

"But why the cloak-and-dagger secrecy? When you're making so much money, why have your day job as well?"

"Although it's hard work and sometimes means juggling two lives, this place pretty much runs itself. We'd get very bored if we didn't do something else as well."

"But isn't this Nats' and Anthony's place?"

"Yes, it is...well, Nats owns the building and the business is owned by both of them, and I, well, I manage the staff, for a twenty percent share of the business. Anthony and Nats are the brains and I'm the worker, not that the staff here need any telling what to do. They're incredibly experienced, capable and efficient, and just get on and do their job. We're very lucky they're all so good."

Anthony came in.

"Hi, Lloyd, you not getting changed then?"

"Hi you. Bloody hell, you look like Puss in Boots!"

Kat and I turned round and laughed to see Anthony standing in the doorway transformed into a swashbuckling handsome highwayman.

"Anthony!" My mouth dropped open.

"God, Charlotte, you've been here all of five minutes and you've already made my sub laugh at the way I'm dressed."

"I didn't say it, Lloyd did!" I protested.

Lloyd got up. "My turn, I must change. Back in five minutes." He disappeared down the hallway.

"Charlotte, I must say Lloyd has chosen wisely for you tonight, you look fantastic! And notice I am not laughing at *you*." Anthony sat down and took a glass of wine from the tray as he looked me up and down, checking every detail of my dress.

"Charlotte, some rules, OK?" he said seriously. "You mustn't wander off, and please do exactly what Lloyd says. If you get separated from him, go stand with a butler, and they'll find him again. Don't talk unless someone talks to you first, and please don't go upsetting anyone, and don't enter any rooms unless Lloyd is with you."

"Why don't you just shackle me to him and be done with it?"

"That can be arranged, but I wouldn't go suggesting things like that downstairs or you might just find yourself in a situation you don't want to be in."

"What's that, Charlotte already got herself into a situation?" Lloyd said as he came back into the room dressed as a musketeer. Lace, three-cornered hat, even a sword. My God, he looked so damned hot! Bloody hell, I thought, where did that come from? I shouldn't be thinking that! Nevertheless though, I thought, remembering a film about the Three Musketeers, I would happily roll around in a haystack with him if it was on offer. I shook my head to bring me back to reality.

"Lastly, Charlotte," Anthony was still talking, "before we go down, remember that should you wish at any stage to come back up here, just tell Lloyd and he'll bring you back. Remember we're your hosts as well." He got up and led the way. As we walked to the lift, Lloyd leaned toward me and whispered, "Are you OK? You look like a Christian about to get thrown to the lions! Don't be scared, you'll be fine. Here, take my arm." He held it out for me.

Downstairs it was very busy. So many people had already arrived. The butlers were serving glasses of champagne and the maids offered platters with caviar canapés. I could feel my heart pumping. Lloyd got me a glass of champagne and said, "Here you go. Try to relax a little and don't forget to smile! This is all normal."

Normal? This was not normal! There were girls wearing next to nothing, although still adhering to the highwayman theme. There were people with their hands tied and someone holding the rope so they couldn't run away. Some women in a corner were holding dog leads, and when I looked down I saw people behaving like dogs. For fuck's sake, this was not normal! Why were they behaving like this!

"Charlotte, you're staring. Let's go in here for a minute." Lloyd dragged me into the private dining room we were in earlier in the day. I was really not believing what I was seeing, and I couldn't take my eyes off them.

"Charlotte, are you OK?" Lloyd asked.

"Why are they behav..." I pointed to the door, "them... what the fuck... I have never seen such a thing!" I was still staring and waving my finger at the door. "Why are some people tied up like that...in public?"

"Charlotte, look at me please. Look at me and calm down. It's people's limits and this isn't public. It's all part of what they like...remember, like-minded people? I thought you would have a problem with this bit, so I've asked my friends to come in here and talk to you, so you can see for yourself. They can explain better than I can. You up for that?"

"Oh, er... I...er..." I paced around the room. I felt as if he was asking me to jump off the edge of a cliff or something. It was a cliff, mentally, to me, and one like I had never faced before.

"Charlotte, calm down! They're only people, just like you and me." He sat me down and looked me in the eye. "You look so beautiful tonight, Charlotte, and I'm so proud of the way you are handling all this, when I know it's still all a huge shock to you—" But before he could say another word I lunged at him with a kiss. Bloody hell! My heart was pounding and I hadn't a clue what I was doing. My brain felt overloaded. What the hell was I doing, kissing my friend? He *is* my friend, my brain kept telling me, but I couldn't stop kissing him, a kiss that showed no sign of stopping, and he was kissing me back! Oh my! What the...where the hell... why did I... I pulled back. Oh shit! Looking at his face, it hadn't even fucking shocked him. He was just sitting there looking at me, as if women kissed him like that all the time.

"Feel better? Was that fight or flight?" he asked, completely unfazed.

"What? Oh shit, what...oh, for fuck's sake! What do you mean, fight or flight?"

"That was a little extreme, that kiss, don't you think? Usually when people panic as much as you our fight or flight reflex takes hold and..."

"I know what fight or flight is, don't give me that bloody caveman crap, but why bring it up now?"

"As I was saying before that rude and certainly not as nice an interruption as the previous one..." He pondered for a second or two. "What I was saying, or rather asking, was whether you were fighting against what you saw or wanting to run away from it?"

"Neither, in fact. I don't know what came over me. I just... I just...well, I think it's this bloody stupid costume. I've got caught up in all this character stuff." I kicked myself for not being able to think of anything clever or witty to say.

"Exactly, and that's what all the people out there have done too. They've put on a costume and become whatever they want to be. They just want an opportunity to escape briefly to another world, and for some it's such an important part of their life that without it they feel as if they'd go mad, so they find like-minded people to help them do what they want to do."

Oh crap, how the hell did that happen? How did I walk straight into that one? I didn't even see it coming, but what he was saying made sense, because I'd never in my life kissed like that before, and I'd never have made a move on him if I hadn't been here dressed like this with these people around...

"Oh for fuck's sake, I've turned into a perv!" I hung my head in shame. Did I say that out loud? Fuck!

"Charlotte, no one here is a perv. In here tonight they are doing what is normal to them, and they're enjoying being able to do that rather than being dictated to as they usually are by the confines of society."

"I...but... I..." I stuttered, trying to say 'I kissed you'.

"Charlotte, that kiss was panic...nice, but panic. I don't want you like that. I want you as my friend. And if one day we do kiss as more than friends, well, I want it to be about more than panic, is that OK?"

I shook my head as I really didn't want to say anything right now as anything I did say would more than likely come out wrong.

I spoke to some of his friends. I even spoke to one of the dogs. His name was Dulux, but he wasn't shaggy at all: not a single hair anywhere that I could see. They explained to me what they did and why: that a lot of it was just role-play, dressing up and pretending. One couple explained how it started for them with a little dressing up. They said it was fine in the house but then they wanted more, so they came to The Room and practised Dom/sub, but they were switchers so they would take it in turns to play each role. They told me about the contract they had between them even though they were husband and wife. They even said that if they hadn't talked to each other and realised they wanted to do this they would probably have been divorced by now. It saved their marriage and fulfilled them both, in so many ways.

Dulux fitted his name perfectly: big and plodding like a sheepdog. We sat talking about how he'd started in the lifestyle. He'd met his partner in a puppy pound where he worked as a dogcatcher. She went to rescue a dog and ended up going home with him. They found, after weeks of talking, that they both liked experimenting with the alternative lifestyle, and she had said jokingly that she'd gone to get a dog, so he must be her substitute dog, and that was how he became Dulux. Again, role-play in the house left them wanting more, and they too had a contract with all their limits clearly defined. She took control all the time. Although his being a dog was a little bizarre, they were clearly very happy with their lives. They didn't get involved with vanilla people at all.

The stories were all the same: none of them ever got hurt and they loved what they did and for similar reasons – to try and have a better life with a little spice and without having hang-ups about it. The ones who were having affairs were also happy for the most part, but felt their wives or partners would never go for the alternative lifestyle, and some wanted to protect their other halves from the lifestyle and what it involved as they knew they'd never understand and they didn't want to hurt them. So they had companions whom they saw just to meet their needs. Maybe that was right, maybe wrong, I didn't know. I did know that people who find out the person they love is having an affair end up very hurt indeed, so in that respect it was wrong and I felt for anyone who did find that out. But, at the same time I met a couple and the wife did find out, but she was just mad that he hadn't told her about the lifestyle. She felt he'd left her behind and couldn't understand why he hadn't asked her if she wanted to share the lifestyle with him. They worked things out and were now happy with their new lives as Dom and sub. The more I chatted the more I came to understand how cruel society was to not let people be who or what they wanted and needed to be so they didn't have to hide away. Everything I heard was about people having harmless fun behind closed doors, with a few little differences or fetishes, which we all have from time to time: we dream about our knight in shining armour coming to sweep us off our feet to a happy ever after, and this seemed to be the same. They'd all dreamed and then gone and found what they wanted.

After I'd finished talking with people Lloyd took me out to rejoin the party. I felt a lot calmer now I was a little more in the know. I felt happier now being amongst them, and not so out of place. Lloyd handed me more champagne, and I was starting to feel like I was glowing by the time I'd finished the glass. As I looked around the room I noticed everyone looked beautiful in their costumes. It was like a scene from a period drama, with a few handcuffs and dog leads thrown in. Suddenly I was aware of someone grabbing my arse. I was just about to turn round when Lloyd took my arm firmly, pulling me close to him, and said, "You have no right to touch her."

"It feels ripe for a spanking to me, and I'll be glad to do so if you don't want to."

Lloyd pulled me even closer. "If you touch anyone here without prior permission, I can promise you you'll never be allowed in here again." Lloyd steered me toward a butler and said in the man's ear, "Watch him. If he touches anyone like that again he's out. Tell the others, George, please."

"Yes, Lloyd, no problem. As I recall, he was a little handy last time he was here. I think I'll have to have a word with him next week."

"OK, George, I'll leave it to you. I'll be upstairs in the usual room if you need me."

"All right, Lloyd, but I doubt I'll need you."

Lloyd was still holding my elbow as he marched me upstairs. I tried to pull away from him but he didn't let go. We went into the fire and ice room and he closed the door.

"What the fuck was all that about, Lloyd? You hurt my arm!"

"Sorry Charlotte, I just had to get you away from that man before you said something to him or vice versa."

"I could have told him hands off."

"No, you don't understand. If you had answered him back or he'd thought you were being disrespectful to him, he could have challenged me to a public spanking of you, some people like all that being spanked in public, they'll deliberately be disrespectful just so they get the attention they crave. The members and the club have rules which are there to protect the limits of everyone, but they can also be broken and if you break a rule well then be prepared for the consequences and I really didn't want that to happen to you. We'll just stay up here for a while, out of the way. George will get rid of him as soon as he manhandles someone else, which I don't imagine will be long."

Feeling rather light and giddy in my head, I walked seductively over to the table with the ice machine on it, and some glasses filled with champagne. Opening the icebox I took out a lump of ice and held it to a flickering candle.

"What happens in here, with all this ice and fire around?" I bent down to look at the flame through the ice. Lloyd came over to me. Taking the ice from my fingers he dropped it into a glass of champagne. Handing me the champagne he asked, "What do you think we do in here?"

"Oh now Lloyd, if you're going to insist that I use my brain maybe we should go back upstairs for a consultation." I turned away from him and went over to the log fire, "Why? Do you need a consultation?"

"I should ask my doctor. He should know if I'm due a consultation."

He picked up the other glass of champagne and came toward me. "If you're trying to seduce me, I would say you definitely need a consultation."

"Why would that be, Lloyd?" I looked straight into his eyes. They held an expression I couldn't read.

"Because we are friends," he smiled. Damn, that burst my bubble. He turned away and dropped onto a chair, putting his glass down on the table. He had a grin on his face. I hate you, I thought, as I sipped the champagne and went to sit on the sofa, watching him as I went past him. He grabbed my waist and pulled me onto his lap. My heart leapt and I closed my eyes as he whispered into my ear "Charlotte, I have always fancied you like hell. I have always wanted you, and maybe the truth is because I never thought I'd get you. But tonight is not the night, not for what you think. There is too much about me that you need to know before I even think about making love to you, and trust me it doesn't matter how beautiful you look or how seductive you are, I won't have sex with you until I'm sure you know everything about me."

I looked at him in astonishment. "What?" was the only word I could find. Most men would have taken it while it was on offer, no questions asked.

"It's called control, Charlotte. I practise control. But mainly it's because I want you and only you, forever. Anthony has always known what I feel for you, but I have to make sure you want it too. I don't do one-night fucks, I never have done."

"I don't understand."

"It's easy. I fell in love with the person you are the first time I met you, all those years ago. I don't want to mess up anything we may have just for a little mindless sex. I want to play with you, have fun with you, court you, show you who I am, what I am. I want to find out what you like, and I want that forever – not just a fuck because you've had too much champagne and got carried away with the moment."

"I had no idea you felt like that. Anthony has never said…"

"I asked him not to, because I want this to be about us, and not with a go-between."

I suddenly felt very sober.

"So, confession over. Now you know how I feel, what about you? I know it's probably the wrong time to have confessed, but I couldn't let you carry on thinking something might happen tonight."

"Lloyd, until tonight – well, maybe a few times before as well – I've thought that if things were different I would fuck you willingly, but I've never thought past that point. After all a fuck is a fuck, isn't it?"

"Not in my world, it isn't. When I have sex, I seduce the mind, body and soul, long, hard and seductive. Sometimes it can take weeks of playing physically and mentally before the act itself happens."

"Isn't that mental cruelty?"

"No, it's not, its foreplay, and the longer it goes on the better the sex is, believe me."

"Really?" My eyes lit up.

"Now you're just thinking about the end product, the fuck."

"You're already being cruel to me," I pouted.

"Aww, don't pout your lip at me like that, young lady, or I'll spank you, and God knows you have already tried my patience today."

I jumped up from his lap. "You wouldn't dare!" I snarled at him. Before I knew it he had flung me over his knee, my skirts and petticoats falling over my head. Pinning my body to his legs with his other arm, he grabbed my pants and pulled them down below my buttocks and above my stocking tops, and began to spank me.

"Five, I think."

I started yelling with the first blow.

"Please Lloyd, no!" I tried to catch his hands as he spanked me. My head was in a whirl with confusion at this point a memory of the bastard hitting me flashed through my mind. After two he stopped and rubbed his hand softly but firmly where he had spanked my arse, and leaned down to my ear. "I wouldn't dare, would I? Had enough, or do you want to play some more?"

"Lloyd, please don't, I give in, OK?" He released his grip on me and I clambered off his knees trembling and then from nowhere out of my mouth it flew.

"That was only two anyway," and before I knew it he had pinned me back down saying, "Only two? You saying I can't count now?" He hit my arse again.

"Lloyd!"

"I think nice and long and slow for you this time... One."

Slap! He rubbed my skin.

"No, Lloyd, you got to two before so that's three surely!" my brain was saying this isn't right, it can't be right, this is no better than the bastard, but my mouth was just being contradictory not only to my brain but to everything that Lloyd was saying and doing to me.

"No, my dear, I let you off three spanks because I was feeling generous... Two," and another long lingering rub. This wasn't too bad. I liked the rubbing. It was very sensual indeed, and it seemed to calm everything else that was running through my brain, *after all I know that Lloyd isn't really going to hurt me*. It was just a bit of a shock at first.

When he got to five he rubbed my arse and said, "Now, how's your smart-arse mouth?"

"Fine, it still fucking works."

"Wrong answer." He raised his hand and brought it down. My buttocks clenched. He stopped just before contact.

"Anticipation, Charlotte."

"Yes, it's natural, isn't..." I relaxed a little.

Slap!

"For fuck's sake, that was hard!" He rubbed to soothe my skin.

"How's your smart-arse mouth now, my dearest?"

Crap, what should I say? "Please Lloyd, let me up?"

He lifted me up from his knees and looked into my eyes. Some of my hair was falling down along with my skirts.

"That looks better. You look more like a serving wench with your hair a little messy. Are you okay?"

"To be honest maybe a little insulted, shocked even, but yes I am ok, it all seems a little hard to digest."

He kissed my cheek, then stood up, put his arm around me and took me over to the bed. This small action from Lloyd made me feel a little more secure, in the fact that this was playing and not for real, that nothing was going to get out of hand, that there was no way that he was going to hurt me.

"Do you trust me to do anything to you? I want to show you something."

"Like what?"

"Just answer. Do you trust me?"

"OK, yes."

"Right, let's play a game."

What did he want to do? I tried to think what sort of game he'd want to play. I tried to see a clue in his eyes. He didn't blink. He just kept eye contact with me.

"What sort of game?" I asked as I watched his eyes.

"It's a game of trust, to see how far you will or can trust

me, if at all." He was still looking straight into my eyes.

"What does it involve?"

"If I tell you that, there wouldn't be much point in the game because you'd be expecting it." His eyes gave nothing away. "At any time you can use a safe word, a word that will make me stop, and you must use it if you feel unsure or uneasy, or if you feel you've had enough. You must never push your limits."

"Safe word? What about 'fucking stop'! Will that do?" My patience was wearing thin.

"That will do if you wish, yes. Fucking stop it is. Might make things interesting," he grinned.

I felt myself tensing with frustration, but also curiosity about what he might be thinking about playing. I'd never played adult games before, if you could call them adult games.

"OK then, as long as you promise me you'll tell me everything you're doing?"

"I will, but I'll only play if you promise to trust me and tell me when you've had enough."

"I asked you to stop when you were spanking me and I didn't see you stopping then."

"That was different, you were enjoying it. Your pathetic pleas were more like 'Please stop, Lloyd. Aww please! I'll give you five minutes to stop doing that!'"

Of course he was right, I did enjoy it a little, and it wasn't half as bad as I thought it would be, and if the bastard hadn't popped into my head giving me such mixed signals, maybe I would have enjoyed it more.

"One thing to be sure about is that I was only playing when I spanked you. I can spank much harder than that when I want to, believe me." He grinned at me, and I could almost imagine little devil horns briefly appearing on his head. "So, do you promise me?"

"Yes, go on then, let's play." I said, thinking what the hell.

He leaned over to the pillow and picked up a sleeping mask. "Right, this is for you. I'm going to put it on you, then I'll lay you down on the bed, and I want you to lie perfectly still. I'll lie on the bed next to you and talk to you. I'll tell you what to do and when to do it, do you understand?" Suddenly he was very serious.

"Yes," I said.

"Let's begin." He did everything he'd explained to me and after each step he asked if I was OK. I felt strangely vulnerable: aware of a tingling in my fingers and my heart pumping. My senses heightened and I started breathing heavily. I was suddenly aware of his hand on my shoulder.

"Charlotte, are you OK? What's wrong? Answer me now."

"I'm finding it hard to breathe and I don't know why."

"Charlotte, do you want the blindfold off?" His tone was urgent.

"I don't know if I want to do this, but…"

"Sit up and take off the blindfold." I did as he said, and when I took it off I saw I was OK and there was nothing different about the room. Lloyd was still at my side. He had his hand on my leg and was rubbing it soothingly.

"Are you OK?"

"Yes, I'm still here and everything's the same."

"What did you expect?"

"I don't know, but both my mind and body went into overdrive and I couldn't control my breathing. It's better now that I can see again."

"Was it that you didn't trust me?"

"No, I don't think so. I don't really know, to be honest."

"Were you frightened of being hurt?"

"I don't know. My senses heightened and my heart started racing, and I couldn't breathe."

"OK, so you panicked when you felt your senses heighten?"

"I guess so, yes. Why did that happen to me?"

"I took away your sight and your mind made your other senses step up a gear to protect you. That's what's supposed to happen: as a nurse you must know that a blind person will have very good hearing and a deaf person very good eyesight? Well, the same applies here. That's all that happened. Do you want a drink?"

"Yes, may I have a glass of water please?"

He went to the table and poured me some water, adding ice to the glass He came over and sat on the bed, leaning over to give me the water. "Better?" He lay down casually beside me.

I nodded my head and sipped the water. It was nice and cold.

"What do you want to do now?" he asked.

"Oh, have I spoilt the game we were playing?"

His eyes were warm as he said, "Charlotte, by being truthful you'll never spoil a game, that's all part of it. I asked you to trust me and I also asked you to tell me if you felt there was anything wrong. I trust you to do that, otherwise I'll not know what your limits are or when you've reached them and that's when people get hurt. I really don't like inflicting discomfort or pain on anyone, so what you've done is shown me that I can trust you, so no, you haven't spoilt the game."

"Oh God, there's a lot to this, isn't there?"

"Yes, but if you want this you'll get the hang of it. Just remember, you are the one calling the shots on your limits."

"So what you're saying is that this is all about me if I become a sub?"

"Most definitely yes, within reason. Just don't ask me to stick pins in you, because that's one of my limits, and I won't go there."

"OK, round two." I put the glass down and picked up the blindfold, but he grabbed my hand.

"What are you doing?"

"Having another go, now you've explained to me."

"Are you sure?"

"Yes, I am."

"OK, but same rules."

I covered my eyes and lay back down. For a minute or two he didn't move. I could hear him breathing, and strangely I could feel him looking at me, his eyes burning through me with passion, or so I imagined.

"How do you feel?" he whispered.

"Fine."

"Do you want to play?"

"Yes," I said, and my breathing quickened.

"OK, let's play." I was aware of him getting off the bed and moving around the room. I turned my head, following the sound of his footsteps. Then silence. I couldn't hear him. Where was he? I moved my head from side to side, straining to hear him.

"Still want to play?" he whispered in my ear, making me turn my head with a start.

How did he do that? How could he be there and not over where I last heard him?

"Yes."

"Good. I am going to give you instructions and I want you to do exactly as I say. I want you to keep your arms firmly on the bed at your side, and I don't want you to move. I want you to trust me."

I put my arms down by my sides and lay as still as

I could. As I did so I realised that once again I couldn't hear him breathing. Where had he gone now? I moved my head from side to side again, trying to hear him.

"I said keep still," he whispered again.

Something touched the skin of my chest, and my body went rigid. I felt him get onto the bed again beside me.

"What's wrong, Charlotte, are you OK?"

"Yes, I'm fine."

"Are you sure? Anything you want to say or ask?"

"No."

Something touched my chest again. It felt thin and flat, like a knife...what the fuck! He had a knife! I panicked and started moving.

"Charlotte, I told you to keep very still. Use your safe word if you want to stop."

"Fuck you!" I ripped the blindfold off and saw a feather in his hand. A feather! I looked at it and then at him.

"It's a bloody feather you bastard! I thought it was a knife you had to my chest!"

"Nope, just this feather." He ran it down my arm, and it felt soft now that I could see what it was.

"You broke a rule, didn't you?" he said.

"That's hardly fair, is it? You knew it would freak me out, you bastard!"

"Now, now, Charlotte! I asked you not to move, I asked you to trust me, and I asked you if you were OK when you first started to move. Despite that, you have twice now shouted profanities at me, and I don't like that."

"Oh? And what are you going to do about it then?"

"I could spank you again, and normally that is what I would do to a sub if she spoke to me like that, but this is a game we're playing and the point of this game is to see what some of your limits are, so lie down and relax, will you?" I lay down. He started twisting and stroking the feather across my chest.

"You see, something as innocent as a feather can feel so different, given the right circumstances." He raised his hand and positioned the feather on my temple. I closed my eyes as he ran the feather gently and slowly down my nose. A shiver travelled the full length of my spine. My mouth opened slightly as a moan escaped from it.

"See, when you know what it is, the sensation is what you expect, but you get different sensations from not knowing."

I opened my eyes. He was looking at me very tenderly.

"Seduction is just as much about the mind as it is the body. It's the art of getting to know what gives each other pleasure." He held up my hand with the pierced fingernail. "This trinket is a memento for you from me of your first experience of the Dom/sub world. That's all tonight is and has been about. Where you go and what you do with it from here is up to you. There is absolutely no pressure, and all I'll say is that there's a world out there for you whichever path you decide to take, Dom/sub or continuing as you are, but no matter what you decide, I'll always be there for you to help guide you if you want me to." With that he leaned over and planted a brisk kiss on my forehead. "Come on, up, we have to go and rejoin the party."

"What... Is that it?"

"Yes, that's it, come on."

"What..."

"Come," he said, going to the door.

I felt frustrated and confused. Had I done something wrong? My body wasn't feeling satisfied the way it was expecting to be. Lloyd looked me over. "Just the way you should look." He opened the door, and holding my hand he led me out of the room and back downstairs. I saw Anthony coming toward us, "Wow, you two look as if you've been enjoying yourselves!"

I blushed, but Lloyd smiled. "The party is good." He grabbed some drinks from a passing waiter and handed one to me.

"Where's Nats?" I asked.

"She's here somewhere," Anthony said, looking around. "I hope this has enlightened you, Charlotte, and not scared you too much?"

"Yes, I think so, and no, I wasn't really scared, although it all still feels a little strange."

Anthony leaned toward my ear and whispered, "I see Lloyd has enlightened you a little as well..."

I blushed again.

"Did you enjoy your little spank?" Anthony asked. How the fuck did he know...? "Your hair and face is a giveaway. See you later." He grinned, and left us.

What the...how... "How does he know?" I whispered to Lloyd, my head hung low.

"Your face is glowing, and has a look of wanting more."

"I don't want more," I snapped. Certainly, if everyone could tell that easily, then I didn't want more.

"We'll see, but maybe not tonight." He looked around the crowded room.

The party went on well into the small hours of the morning and at about two o'clock Lloyd took me back to the suite. I was very tipsy but not drunk. He helped me into my bedroom and the last thing I remembered was him saying, "Come on. Bed for you."

Chapter Ten

I woke to a tap on the door. I opened my eyes – bad idea! – and shut them again. My head pounded. Shit, how much had I drunk? The door opened and Lloyd came in.

"Good morning, and how are we this morning?" He was carrying a tray with some breakfast which he brought over to the bed and set down next to me.

"Are you going to open your eyes today?"

"I've already tried to."

"Oh, that bad, is it?"

"No. Worse."

"Good job you have the day off, then, isn't it."

"What, another one? I should go in and see Nats." I tried to push myself up onto my elbows but my body felt like a lead weight.

"Jesus, what the fuck is happening?"

"Probably champagne poisoning," he laughed. "Here, let me help you." He propped me up to a sitting position with some pillows. "That's better, now drink this." I half-opened my eyes and he gave me a glass of orange juice which I drank straight down. It felt wonderfully cold and refreshing against my sandpaper mouth.

I looked at Lloyd. He looked so bright and refreshed and not in the least hung-over. And...oh no! What the fuck did I do last night? Memories came flooding back…

"Oh crap, I have made a complete bloody fool of myself, haven't I?"

"I don't know what you mean."

"Me, you, in that bloody room!"

"No, you didn't make a fool of yourself. I didn't let you."

"You…you spanked me if I remember rightly. You bloody spanked my arse. How bloody dare you!" A burst of indignation momentarily overcame the shame.

"Careful, that's how it started last night, remember, with you daring me?" He got off the bed and went over to the door on the other side of the room. "I think you should drink your coffee and eat your bagel before you get into any more trouble. I'll run you a bath," and he disappeared into the bathroom.

I drank my coffee slowly but I just couldn't manage anything to eat.

"Your bath is ready. You have a choice," Lloyd called out. "Do you want me to bathe you or can you manage yourself?" He came back into the bedroom.

"I am quite capable of having a bath and washing myself, thank you."

"The only reason I asked is because it's normal in my world for me to pamper you today, and as…well, as you're so hung-over, I feel responsible."

"So you should feel responsible. You were the one who kept giving me champagne, and you were the one who… who…" I was going to say 'took advantage of me', but then I remembered it was me who kissed him first and me who tried to seduce him.

He came over to the bed, leaned down and said, "I see that smart-arse mouth of yours might just get you into more trouble if I don't leave now," and he planted a swift kiss on my forehead. Going to the door he said, "As you're so capable I'll leave you to your bath, but if you need anything just pull the cord over by the fireplace and I'll come straight in." He opened the door, then turned and said politely, "Thank you for a most enjoyable evening," and went out.

Oh my God, I'd made myself look stupid yet again. What the fuck was happening to me? I was confused, and the past few days had been a lot to take in, but I'd still thought I had life sort of worked out until two days ago, and now I just didn't know. After my bath I went to the lounge where Lloyd was sitting reading the papers.

"Where's everyone else?" I asked, looking around.

"They left hours ago for work."

"Why haven't you gone to work then?"

"I have a few weeks' holiday."

"Oh, you never said."

"You never asked. Coffee is on the table if you want it." He didn't even raise his head from the paper. He seemed so cold this morning.

"Do you want one?" I asked as I poured mine.

"No, ta."

OK, two could play that game. I picked up a paper, but every so often I couldn't help but peek over the top at him. He was reading as if I wasn't even there. I started to feel my blood boil. How could he just ignore me like that, after everything he said last night, and after everything he did? I turned the pages faster and louder as my frustration grew. He still ignored me. I peeped again. He looked exactly the same. Crap, this wasn't working. As I flipped the next page I caught a glimpse of my nail with the trinket hanging from it and remembered something Lloyd said to me last night: one of the most important things was to talk and to be honest about how I was feeling. Right now, though, he was being so bloody rude I didn't want to talk to him. I scowled over the top of the paper. No, if he wanted to talk he could go first. Maybe he didn't want to talk, but why should I give in first? He turned the page and I looked up, hoping he'd put it down, but no. I crossed my legs, trying to act casually, but as I lifted my leg my foot hit the coffee table and everything clattered. Shit, why did I have to be so clumsy! Still he didn't look up at me. I wondered if it was killing him as much as it was me, or was it that he just didn't give a fuck. I looked back at the trinket for some inspiration, but nothing – or nothing other than to talk, which I wasn't going to do.

He flipped another page. Was he really reading that? Most men I'd known sat farting when they read a paper, and he hadn't farted once. Maybe I should say that. Yes, that would surely get his attention.

"Most men I've known fart when they sit reading the newspaper, so I don't think you're really reading it, are you?" Oh my God, I said it! I actually said it out loud and I didn't even look in his direction as I was saying it! I felt so proud of myself, until I realised that yet again he hadn't answered me. Enough of this, I thought angrily. I folded the paper and dropped it on the sofa next to me.

"Your rudeness has just proved you're no better than or different to most of the men I've known. You're all the same in how you act and react." That would annoy him for sure. He'd have to say something now. I looked at him as he flicked another page. What the hell! Had he got his iPod headphones in his ears or something? I got up and went over to the window. The sun was shining. A lovely day out there. I went back to the sofa and sat down again.

"The sun is shining. It looks so nice out there," I said.

"Is it?" He spoke! Hah, got you! So he could hear me

then? So why hadn't he responded to anything else I'd said? Well, just you wait, Mister, I too can play that game and only talk when I want to. I picked up the coffee pot and poured myself some coffee.

"Yes please," he said but didn't look at me. How could he do that? I picked up the pot and poured him a cup. I didn't say anything to him, just glared. Did I have to wait until he'd finished reading that paper before I got his attention?

"Thank you."

"Oh I get a thank you do I?" I snapped at him.

"Smart-arse mouths and bad-tempered bitches get spanked, hangover or not," he said.

"At least I got a reaction from you."

"Be very careful what you wish for, Charlotte, or the reaction might not be the one you are expecting."

"I am not a bad-tempered bitch, thank you very much."

"You're welcome."

What did he mean? I was welcome? What the fuck did that mean? I thought he said he was going to pamper me today, but this was hardly pampering. His phone rang and he answered it.

"Hi…yes she's fine. She's here in the lounge." He looked at me. At last he was looking at me.

"Yes she has. Yes, she has what I think. You can say that again. An understatement to say the least." He laughed. "Yes, OK. No, I haven't told her yet, I'll wait a while…"

Hadn't told me what? What hadn't he told me? I couldn't take any more surprises. I'd had enough.

"OK, see you then. Bye."

I tried to pretend I hadn't heard any of that. He put his phone and the newspaper down beside him and sat back on the sofa folding his arms and just looking at me, as if waiting for me to do something.

"Out of all your protests this morning, Charlotte, I have noticed the only thing you didn't protest about was when I said smart-arse mouths and bad-tempered bitches get spanked. Can I assume that you're warming to the Dom/sub lifestyle?"

What, what...how has he come up with that? Where did he get that one? I looked away.

"Come now, Charlotte, no need to be shy."

"You've finished reading your paper then, and actually want to talk to me now?"

He immediately reached for the paper, saying, "I can always start reading again if you prefer?"

My mouth dropped open.

"No, I didn't think you did." He let the paper go. "I assume your behaviour since you came into the lounge is because you want to talk?" I looked away again, and Lloyd laughed. "Charlotte, you're so funny, I can read you like a book. You're curious about last night, you're curious about what I get up to, and you're as frustrated as hell."

He paused. I wasn't going to answer him. Why should I?

"You should answer me, Charlotte. Well, not answer me so much as talk to me, otherwise how do I know what the problem is? Not talking and stamping your foot just isn't going to work."

"I haven't stamped my foot. I don't stamp."

"A figure of speech, as you know full well. Will you please stop with the attitude?"

"Why should I? You're the one who's been ignoring me all morning."

He got up and came over to me, grabbing my arm. "Up, come with me." He tugged my arm and pulled me up, frog-marching me to the bedroom. I tried to protest but he was having none of it. He twisted me around and looked me straight in the eye, saying, "Right, you frustrated obnoxious little madam, I can either fuck your brains out, to use your phrase, or spank you. What do you want me to do?"

I stepped back and tumbled onto the edge of the bed. "Neither," I said in a low voice.

"No, you have a choice, just like you did last night, and your choice today is either sex or spanking."

"That's not fair of you. You said you wouldn't push me into anything that I don't want to do."

"I also told you that you had to talk to me and tell me your feelings, and that no matter what you decided I would be there for you. No promises, just trust, and as you have chosen not to talk but instead to be a brat I can only assume you want me to take the lead. So choose: your mindless fuck or a spank. Which is it to be?"

"You don't do mindless fucking, you said so last night."

"Right, so you're choosing a spank, then?"

I shook my head. "That's not what I meant."

"So what did you mean?"

"I don't know what I mean. You're confusing me."

"Why am I confusing you? I have just given you two options: sex or spank. How can that confuse you?"

All I wanted right now was a cuddle. Looking up at him from the bed I knew he didn't want to just fuck me. I knew by the way he was looking at me and from what he said last night that he cared for me, and I liked what we did last night, even the spanking, because it was all part of the fun, but right now I just wanted a cuddle. I wanted a cuddle when we were on the bed in the fire and ice room, I wanted a cuddle when he came in this morning and I wanted a cuddle when I was in the lounge with him.

"Charlotte, what is it to be? You have until the count of three and then I'll choose for you. One...two...thr..."

"I just want a cuddle."

147

"What?"

"A cuddle. Please, I need a cuddle."

"Why didn't you say so before, instead of all the sulking?"

I shrugged my shoulders. He sat on the bed and put his arm round me.

"Why do you need a cuddle?"

"I want to feel you cuddle me, that's all."

He snuggled me into his body, and I suddenly felt warm and secure like I'd never felt before. None of my farting paper-reading partners cuddled me like this. I liked being cuddled. I really liked it.

"This is lovely," I said softly. "See, you don't have to spank me to get me to behave."

"What, you think this is instead of a spanking? Let me tell you now it's as well as, unless you can come up with some good reason why not?"

"Because I don't want one."

He laughed. "Is that the best you can do?"

"It's the truth."

"My dear Charlotte, we need to talk."

We lay with his arms wrapped tightly around me and me snuggled so close it would have been hard to slide a sheet of paper between us.

"Charlotte, do you want to give us a go? I know I said I wouldn't pressure you, but I'm getting so many signals from you that say yes, without you actually telling me yes, that if I don't ask the question now I think it might take us the rest of our lives to get there?"

"I know and yes, I would like to. I'm just so scared."

"I know you're scared, but try not to be. You've no reason to be, and I've said I'll be there to help you all the way." He pulled me closer to him. "We have to agree on some rules and a mini contract while we get to know each other more. I know you're not sure, and I know that you want to know more, so I'll be kind on the contract bit. How about six months, at which point we can review where you're at and what you want to do?"

"OK, sounds good."

"So a six-month induction, then?"

"Yes."

"This is very irregular, and I don't want you telling anyone, not even Anthony or Nats, that we're starting with a mini contract, OK? I don't want to look soft."

"OK," I agreed.

"OK, subject to contract, you now belong to me in your entirety for six months."

"What? I don't belong to anyone. What the fuck…"

"What have I said about the way you talk to me?"

"Oh come on, what the fuck…you make me sound like a car or a house you're buying, for Christ's sake!"

"You, madam, have been asking for this all morning, and now you are going to get it…"

In one movement he released me, flipped me onto my front, lifted my skirt, and pulled down my pants.

"Noooo, cuddle please," I begged him.

"Not this time. I gave you a chance to stop and you still continued."

Slap followed by a rub.

"Ouch!"

"Oh come on, Charlotte, that wasn't an ouch. *This* is an ouch."

SLAP! Lingering rub.

"For…" I bit my tongue.

"Was that what I thought it was?" as he rubbed my arse.

"No," I said hastily.

"Oh Charlotte, I am going to enjoy these six months!"

Slap, rub. My body clenched, trying to absorb the slap.

"You must tell me the truth at all times, that has to be number one on the list, I think. Number two, I think, should be that I can spank you any time I wish. Wouldn't you agree they should be the first two? You choose the next two."

Slap, rub.

"I want a say on when you spank me, under number three."

He laughed. "Then number two will say 'non-negotiable' after it."

Slap, rub.

"OK, number three will say you must ask me before you do anything to me."

"OK, good one, and may I suggest that number four will be that you talk to me?"

Slap, rub.

"How many are you giving me?"

"Rules? As many as you need," he says.

Slap, rub.

"Awww, I meant spanks. How many?"

"It's not really for you to ask that."

Slap, rub.

"Last one." He flopped back onto the mattress, put his hand back on my arse and started rubbing it in circles.

"Sore?"

"No."

"Do you want another, then?"

"Another what?" I asked.

"Another spanking, as I think you're not being truthful."

"Maybe a little sore, yes."

My arse was smarting, but soothed by the way he rubbed it. It felt nice and sensual, and I started to move my arse in time with his hand-rubbing. He stopped.

"Why have you stopped? That was so nice!"

"Yes, I know, and you're getting turned on."

"You can't just stop like that! What about my needs?"

"Yes, I can just stop like that, and what needs are those? The mindless fuck needs?" he snapped.

"What's wrong with you fucking me?"

"Nothing, but not yet."

I buried my head in the pillows, wanting to scream loudly with frustration. I felt his hand reach to the nape of my neck as he took hold of my hair. Pulling my head up, he said in my ear, "Charlotte, you really are going to have to learn to trust me. I am not just going to screw you and that's all there is to it." He turned my head and moved to kiss me but stopped and hovered just before my lips. I tried to reach my head toward his and he said, "You really want this don't you? You really want me to kiss you?" I tried to tease him by licking my lips, still trying to get my head closer to him as I did so, but his grip tightened. I opened my mouth, unashamedly begging. He moved his head closer until his lips were just a fraction away from mine and I could almost feel them. Then he pulled away and looked into my eyes. "No, Charlotte, I am not going to. Seduction is a state of mind as well as body, remember."

Drawing his head away from me he rolled me onto my back so I was lying down flat. Then he pulled my hair so it fanned out above my head. Sitting astride me he grabbed my hands, and holding them above my head, he wove my hair around them. "Yes, just about right, I think. Another rule: you can't have anything done with your hair without my permission." Holding my hair by its ends he lay down on top of me. "Now you can't move. Nice isn't it?"

He started to gyrate his hips on top of mine. Oh my

God! Oh my, what the…wow! This was fucking lovely. It was so sexy and full on… I closed my eyes…and he leapt up off me, saying, "Right, come on, we're going out."

What? What the fuck? I wanted more! I sat up and looked at him as he straightened his clothes.

"What do you mean? Are we not going to finish this?"

"Charlotte, you look just like a good sub should, flushed and all sexed up with a wanton look in your eyes. Now come on, we're going out."

I threw myself back onto the bed in protest.

"Charlotte, I hope that isn't a little foot-stamp you're doing there? I'd hate to be late for lunch because I have to spank you yet again."

I looked at him, desperately trying to think of a way to get him back onto the bed so that maybe he would get carried away and we could go on.

"Charlotte, please can I have you up and sorted so we can go, and don't think about any tricks for when we return, or so help me God you'll be over my knee again." He winked. Oh, that wink sent shivers down my spine! How did he do that? He grabbed my hand and gave me a gentle pull up off the bed, and I went to sort myself out and brush my hair.

"Where are we going?"

"I'm taking you to lunch."

The restaurant he chose had dim lighting and simple décor. It smelt expensive. We were shown to a table set with four places. Lloyd asked the waiter to bring some wine.

"How are you feeling?" he asked me.

How was I feeling? How the hell did he think I was feeling! Twice now he'd started something and stopped without even getting close to finishing.

"Frustrated," I said curtly.

He smiled, and leaning toward me said, "Foreplay is such a wonderful thing, don't you think, my sweet?"

I clenched my teeth as my body tingled at the thought of what he called foreplay.

"I bet that even though you're frustrated you're already anticipating when your next chance will be to see if you can make me go all the way? I bet you've even thought about what it would be like to fuck me."

Oh God, he was still playing, here in this restaurant, in front of all these people! I fidgeted on my chair, trying to contain myself. Oh God, I wanted an orgasm! I needed an orgasm!

"Sit still, Charlotte," and he ran his hand slowly down my back. I closed my eyes. He was so right, dammit!

"Charlotte, you OK?"

I opened my eyes and looked up to see Anthony.

"Hi, um, yeah, just a bit hung-over still." A little embarrassed in seeing Anthony standing at the table beside me, just at that moment of intense tingling up and down my spine, I felt a flush of redness across my face.

"OK, as long as that's all it is." He sat down. "Where's Nats? Late as usual, I bet." He pretended to be cross.

"Here she comes," Lloyd said.

The waiter came with the wine and filled our glasses as Nats sat down.

"Hi all. Hi, Charlotte, how's you then?"

Oh goodness I think everyone can see right through me the way they are asking me if I'm ok singling me out, I felt the flush return as I replied.

"Oh, I'm fine, thank you."

"So you and Lloyd then – are you two finally getting somewhere? I can't believe you've never noticed how he swoons every time you walk into the room," she said.

"We're going to see how things go for a while. Take things slowly." I didn't look at him.

"Yes, we're just friends," Lloyd said. He wasn't looking at me either. "No promises – we'll just see what happens. Neither of us is sure what we want yet, and to be fair, Charlotte has had a lot to deal with, so far better not to rush into anything, right?"

"Yes, Charlotte, you've had a lot to take in, and I must say you're taking it all incredibly well, considering your background." Anthony put in.

"I have corrected her about a few things," said Lloyd, and winked.

Nats looked at me. "Come, Charlotte, I need to powder my nose. Keep me company?" She got up from the table. I got up too and followed her. Once inside the ladies she looked me in the eye.

"Right, girly talk, are you really OK?"

"Yes, strangely enough, I am."

"Don't you think this is all a bit quick? I mean I know Lloyd has had a thing for you for ages. Anthony told me that he fell head over heels for you the first time he met you. But it's all right for him, he's never had a relationship that's been violent or gone so wrong. I'm worried about you getting hurt. This lifestyle we're all in works for us as it's something we'd been looking for one way or another for a long time – we knew what we wanted. But I'm not sure you even really know yet what you want from your vanilla life, let alone from one like this."

"What are you saying, that I shouldn't get involved?"

"No, I want to make sure that you're really OK with it. I don't want you to be a crumpled mess on my office floor in a few weeks' time because you've made a mistake. I don't want to see either of you two hurt."

"I know, and yes, things have happened very fast, and I'm not yet completely sure about this lifestyle, but I do feel comfortable with Lloyd, and for the first time in my life I feel alive, as if I'm finally waking up. When Lloyd was first trying to explain to me what the lifestyle involved I'll admit I was horrified and wanted to run for the hills, but once I'd calmed down and begun to see things more clearly it all started to make more sense. Talking to everyone last night really helped as well. They're all so happy, or seem to be. I never knew relationships like this could ever exist, let alone work."

"So is this thing you've got with Lloyd Dom/sub or is he standing down from it to accommodate you?"

"I think it's sort of fifty-fifty right now. He wants to take things slowly and to know that I'm comfortable with everything we do."

"You know that this is about control of the body and mind? And not just control, but ultimate control. Used correctly it can be fantastic and you can have the time of your life, but I worry that if you haven't yet got over your last relationship... I guess what I'm trying to say, or ask, is are you sure you're mentally stable enough to take this on, after all you've been through? After all, you haven't gone looking for it, it's found you."

"I think I am. I like Lloyd and I've grown quite close to him over the weeks."

"Is that as an emotional crutch, though?"

"No, I don't think so, although I admit that's a factor I hadn't thought about, but up until yesterday Lloyd has kept his distance and been very careful not to be a psychiatrist, so to speak, and not to crowd me. He's tried to keep everything as friendly advice rather than professional."

Nats still looked doubtful. "OK, but just promise me,

Charlotte, that if you ever feel alarmed or unhappy you'll come and talk to me? Anything you say to me will stay in my office between the two of us. And talk with others if you get the chance, as well. Everyone will be happy to guide you."

"You sound as if you're trying to put me off Lloyd."

"Oh God no, I'm not doing that. He's fantastic, and has always treated all who've subbed for him with the utmost respect. No one has ever had a bad word to say about him. But he is hardened to this life, and I can't see him stepping down to a vanilla lifestyle. He wouldn't be happy and the two of you wouldn't survive together. You have to step up to the mark, and it's you who'll have to change, and don't think for one minute it's going to be easy, because it's not."

"You're right. Everything you say is right. Had you asked me even a few days ago if I wanted another relationship I'd have said no, but I think that what's on offer now is so much better than I've ever had before that I want to try it. I want to find out what it's about."

"As long as you understand then I'm really happy for you both. Let's get back or they'll think we've abandoned them."

As we came to the table Lloyd smiled at me. A man smiling at me when I returned from anywhere was a first. It feels so reassuring, warm, and cosy, like sitting in front of a big log fire, hot chocolate in hand, on a cold winter's day. I gave Lloyd a little smile back.

"You both took so long we figured we'd better order for you or we'd never eat today," Anthony said. "So what are you two doing for the rest of the week?" He grinned at Lloyd. God, they were worse than girls with their coded little smiles and body language. Lloyd screwed up his face as if Anthony had said too much. I assumed then that Anthony knew exactly what would be happening.

"Charlotte, I've arranged an excursion for us, if you'd like it?"

"What have you arranged?" My eyes lit up.

"Oh don't be too excited, it's nothing too great."

"What is it?"

"We're going shopping for the afternoon and then back to The Room. Nothing very exciting."

"Oh shopping! I love shopping!"

Anthony pulled a face as if it was an effort for him not to say something. Lloyd continued, "I've planned for us to have a few nights there. I want us to be able to do as we wish when we wish."

"In other words, Charlotte, he wants to put you through your paces," Anthony laughed.

Lloyd scowled. "No, it's not like that, Anthony."

"Stop it, Anthony!" Nats said. "I'm quite sure Charlotte doesn't need you to put your two pennies' worth in. Charlotte, take no notice, I'm sure you'll be absolutely fine."

Chapter Eleven

Later that afternoon we returned to The Room after shopping. I felt relieved that the afternoon had gone well, and Anthony and Nats seemed to like the fact that Lloyd and I were together, although Nats obviously had her reservations about the relationship.

I took my things to my bedroom then returned to the lounge. Lloyd had disappeared. I sat down and was pouring wine for us both when my phone beeped.

> I'll be with you when I can.
> In the mean time I want you to think about this: me undressing you slowly and laying you blindfolded on a bed and...
> Talk soon xxx

What the...! Again he was leaving his intentions unfinished, but the thought of being naked and blindfolded on a bed made my imagination run wild. I fidgeted on the sofa, took a sip of wine. My body felt all tingly just from a text... I liked this game. I was sitting with my eyes closed, lost in thought, when suddenly I felt someone touch my hair. I jumped, and spun round. "Lloyd! You startled me."

"Did I, and why was that? Who were you expecting to touch you?"

"No one else, I just didn't expect you right then."

He leaned on the back of the sofa and smiled. "That's OK then. What were you so deep in thought about?"

"I wasn't, I was just..."

He raised his eyebrows. "Charlotte, I thought the rule was that you must tell me the truth." He moved around the sofa and sat down next to me, picking up his wine. "I want to talk to you."

I turned toward him and sat back. He reached his hand down and lifted my skirt so he could see the tops of my stockings. He ran his finger gently over my skin, just above the tops. I closed my eyes and sighed, a deep breath full of anticipation that he might even go further. I felt him tuck his finger under the stocking. Oh shit, it was bloody fantastic. His touch was so light. I began to float away on the moment, willing his fingers to move up my leg. I opened my legs as an invitation. Please don't stop...keep going...

"For fuck's sake!"

"Charlotte, what have I told you about the language you use in front of me?"

I opened my eyes. Lloyd was looking straight at me. What? Did I say that out loud? I cringed as I saw his eyes full of displeasure.

"So you should cringe, madam, but I'll deal with that later," he said, sitting back. "Right now I want to talk to you."

What, no spanking? I was disappointed. How the hell could I talk now when I felt so, so... I wiggled my hips. I could feel myself getting moist.

"Charlotte, please control yourself or I'll have to do something to control you," he said sharply. I found all this strange; in the past if a man spoke to me sharply I would have taken it as a sign of aggression, but for some reason nothing that Lloyd said or did to me felt aggressive or controlling.

I knew for the most part that it was a game, and when he spanked me it was done in such a way that it was fun and sensual, gentle but controlled. He never lost control of himself or me, and although he spoke sharply, and sometimes I was taken back by it, I know he was only trying to make me take control of my action. The fact he didn't lose control was probably why I didn't feel threatened by anything he did.

"Look, all day long you've been turning me on and off like a tap, so unless you're going to fuck me I don't see how you're going to stop me, do you?" I gave him back look for look, as if to say bring it on, I'm ready for you.

"Sex isn't on the agenda, and you'd be surprised what I can do to make you stop. But I am not going there just yet with you."

Oh man, would nothing move him to respond to my sex needs?

"Now, if you've finished…" He looked down at my lap. Don't just look, touch! I wanted to cry out. The physical ache inside me was now so strong it was painful.

"Oh Lloyd, do we have to analyse every little detail like this? Why can't we just do it? I have everyone asking me if I'm all right and happy and sure about this, and I am, so can we please get on with it?"

"I need you…"

"Oh here we go again. You need me what? For crying out loud, if this was a regular relationship we'd have fucked weeks ago, for fuck's sake!"

He didn't reply, just grabbed my arm, pulled me to the lift and thrust me inside.

"Where are we going?"

He still didn't say anything. When the doors opened on the ground floor he pulled me out by my arm and walked me down the hall. There were other people there.

"Let me go, I can walk on my own!"

He took no notice. He went up the stairs and past more people who stopped and watched as he hustled me along. I tried to pull back but he would have none of it. He entered the fire and ice room and threw me on the bed.

"Stay there!" He closed the door, leaving me on my own. Oh my, why hadn't I kept my big mouth shut? He was really pissed with me. I got up off the bed and walked around the room. Although maybe it wasn't going to be so bad, I thought, remembering last night. I sat on a sofa by the fire wondering why he'd left me here on my own. He seemed to have been gone for ages. I realised I hadn't got my shoes on. Crap, I would ladder my stockings if I wasn't careful.

The door opened and Lloyd came in.

"Hello," I said, subdued.

"I told you to stay on the bed. Would you please get back onto it?"

OK, he was still pissed. I got up and swaggered my arse over to the bed. He grabbed my shoulders and threw me onto it.

"Lie down!" he ordered. I knew that would get him. He retrieved the blindfold from the other pillow and put it on me. I could do this, yes, I could, and it would be quite different now. I knew what he was going to do with feathers. My hips twisted in anticipation.

He moved me over to the middle of the bed and he fastened my legs by the ankle, one to each of the posts, and then my arms to the top posts. I was spread-eagled on the bed unable to move.

"What are you doing?" This wasn't right. He didn't do this last night.

"What you wanted me to. Didn't you tell me to get on with it?"

"This isn't what I meant—" Before I could say any more, he cut me off.

"You are in an alternative relationship now and things are done differently. Now you have to deal with the consequences of your actions, or should I say of your smart-arse mouth."

And with that I heard him move away from the bed. I listened for him moving but all I could hear was the crackle of the fire. Someone knocked on the door and I heard him move to open it.

"The things you ordered, sir."

"Thank you." I heard the door close.

"What have you ordered? Some food and drinks for us?"

"The only reason I haven't gagged you is because you're new to all of this."

"You haven't answered my question."

"Take the hint, Charlotte."

OK, he wanted me to shut up. I heard him walk to the table and then back to the bed.

"This is better: you with your mouth shut and unable to move." He stroked my leg gently, and, so quickly I might almost have imagined it, at the same time something touched my face. I flinched away. Then it touched my arm. I flinched again.

"Oh Lloyd, I don't like this. What are you doing?"

"What's wrong, Charlotte? I thought you wanted to get straight into it?" Something touched my leg. I struggled to get out of the restraints, but I couldn't.

"Please, Lloyd, this is too far. Please let me out!"

I felt him undo one of my hands.

"Here you go. You're completely safe." He took off the eye mask and cuddled me tight. "Look at me. You're safe, see?"

"Lloyd, I don't like that."

"I don't like the way you talked to me." He undid the other restraints and lay next to me. "The reason you don't like it is because you aren't ready for it. I've told you I don't want to have sex with you until I'm sure of what you want from this. Otherwise, if I do I would only be taking advantage and I don't want to do that. I want this, us, to work. Now we do this my way or no way at all, or we'll both end up being hurt."

"OK, your way, I'm sorry. I know nothing about this. I thought I did but I realise now I don't."

"No you don't, and that is what everyone's been saying to you when they ask you if you're OK and if you're sure about all of this. They want to make sure you understand."

He held me tight as we lay on the bed, but I still felt uneasy. I really hadn't liked it at all, what Lloyd had done to me. I felt so vulnerable and insecure. What if I couldn't do this? I felt his hand run down my back and slip inside my skirt.

"I've been mean to you the last few days and you've coped very well." His hand cupped my buttock and he started to rub. "Your arse is so very soft, just how I like it." He pulled my hips toward him. Careful, girl, don't get carried away. "I like exploring subs' bodies. Every time I make love I like it to feel like the first time." He nibbled on my ear, and I was putty once again, forgetting all about what had just happened. He wound his hand into my hair and pulled my head back. He kissed my neck softly then made his way down toward my breast creating a trail of tiny kisses as he did so.

"Your hair is the right length for me to grab and wrap it around my arm," he said, and I was back in that place I was in just before we came downstairs, but for some reason my lust now was more intense, my need greater. I wanted him so much. I tried to move my arms but one arm was under him and the other under his top arm. I tried to reposition my legs but he quickly put his leg on top of both of mine so I couldn't move them.

"Now Charlotte, why would you want to move from here? I'm very comfortable." He kissed my neck slowly and tenderly. My eyes closed as I longed for him to continue down as he kissed me. I wanted him to kiss my breasts. I tried to raise them to his lips, but he tightened his grip on my hair. "Please stay still."

"Is it really the reason you've said that you don't want to fuck me?" I whisper to him.

"It's not that I don't want to have sex with you. It's that I'm not going to, and yes, for the reason that I've said."

He pushed himself into me, and I felt him big and hard, pushing at just the right place. My body shivered in response and I groaned. He released his grip on me, sat up and released my legs, then got up off the bed, saying, "Besides, I am enjoying this too much to stop right now." He held his hand out, I put my hand in his and he pulled me to my feet. He took me to the sofa and on the table was a tray with sandwiches and wine.

"Let's eat."

What did he mean, *eat*? He was doing it again. Why couldn't we ever finish? I was a big girl though; I wasn't going to run home to Mum if it didn't work between us. I could take it.

He poured me some wine and passed it to me. "What I was trying to ask you upstairs was whether you wanted to play tonight, but as you so rudely interrupted me and we're down here anyway, I think the answer is yes, whether you want it or not!" he grinned.

"Why are you teasing me so?"

"I'm not teasing you. I told you – this is all foreplay."

"It's nothing like foreplay I've ever done before. Usually it's a grope, a fumble and Bob's your uncle."

"Did you enjoy it?"

I suppose I didn't, usually. I didn't really remember much about it – just another fuck.

"Not every time, no. I didn't."

"Are you enjoying this?"

Bloody hell! Well, of course I was, did he think I was frigid or something?

"Yes, it's nice." I leaned toward him. God, how I wanted a kiss! But just as I got there he put his glass up to his mouth. Pants. I moved away.

"There you go, then. You already have more than you did in your vanilla life."

"I'm worried that some of the aspects of my vanilla life will come back and haunt me." I shuddered at the thought of being beaten again. Lloyd put his hand out and held mine.

"That's one thing I can promise you, Charlotte, and that is I'll never ever beat you in temper. I'll never mark you like you were, and anything you're uncomfortable with I will stop straight away. I don't do scared shitless like some do."

"You scared me just now," I said.

"Nothing I do is to scare you, you just don't take the hint, but you will get it. I did stop when you asked me to, and I cuddled you until you felt safe again. I don't enjoy you scared, I enjoy you the way you are now – frustrated!" He grinned, pouring some more wine into our glasses.

"Can I ask you about Kat, please?"

"You can. I don't promise that I'll be able to answer, but if I can I will."

"Yesterday, when she heard Anthony coming she bounced

up to the door and stood there waiting for him with her head down. What was that all about? She seems such a strong woman and for her to behave like that just seems out of character."

"Well, Kat is totally submissive when she's with Anthony. She trusts him one hundred percent and he can do anything with her."

"Like what?"

"That I can't answer. All I know is they have a good time and enjoy whatever it is they do."

"Why can't you tell me? Is it that bad, what they do?"

"Would you tell someone everything about your ex-boyfriend's love-making?"

"Oh God, no!"

"We don't tell each other what we do...not unless that's what we're into!"

"How do you know what to do – how to do it safely?"

"We have demonstrations. Some people like to be on show when they're playing, it's all part of their thing. They'll show you and explain all the dos and don'ts, what's safe and what is not. We learn from each other as well."

"Didn't you tell Anthony what we are doing tonight? I had the impression, by the way he looked at you, he knew exactly what was going to happen. You two seemed to be talking in riddles at the restaurant."

"Not at all. All he knows is I wanted to play this evening with you. He doesn't know what I wanted to play. Just like girly talk, Anthony and I chat about things, but not in detail."

I raised an eyebrow, thinking he had never been on a ladies' Saturday night then.

"What do you want to play?" I asked hastily before he started to quiz me about what I was thinking.

"I don't know if you're in the right frame of mind now

or not? I need you very relaxed, but now I don't think you will be." He looked at me long and hard, flicking his eyes all over me.

"Can't we try?"

"No, not tonight. It's not the right time."

Oh God, nothing was ever the right time! He wouldn't fuck me because it wasn't the right time, he couldn't play with me because it wasn't the right time. When was anything going to be the right time? And then it was out of my mouth before I could stop it.

"For fuck's sake!"

He gave me a hard look. "Was that what I think I heard?"

"It depends what you thought you heard."

"My, my, Charlotte! We can do this one of two ways."

"Do what?" I asked innocently.

"Punishment."

"Punishment for what?"

"For having such a smart-arse mouth and for having such a smart-arse answer, what did you think it was going to be for? I think you should get on your knees while we discuss what we should do with you."

My mouth dropped open. "You have got to be kidding, right? Or maybe this too isn't the right time!" I burst out laughing.

"Do I look like I'm kidding? Maybe it would be a perfect time for you to do as I say."

Oh shit, he was deadly serious. He wanted me on my knees. "Oh come on! Why can't I just stay here like a big girl?" I said teasingly.

"Because you're behaving nothing like a big girl. You have till the count of three."

Well, how much worse could I behave? He was going to spank me, no matter what.

"Look Lloyd, you're gonna spank me, so get on with it!"

"One…"

I sipped my wine.

"Defiance isn't where you want to be right now. Two…"

I looked at him. He pointed to the floor. OK, I thought, I give in. I put my glass on the table, and knelt down. I looked him squarely in the eye and he took hold of my hair. I drew in a sharp breath as he tilted my head back.

"Charlotte!"

He kissed me with passion and lust, not like he kissed me last night. This was different. My body tingled. He pulled my hair upward. I clasped his hand with both of mine and rose to my feet with him still kissing me. Bloody hell! I'd never been kissed like this! I could feel my juices oozing from me, and my nipples were so erect that the movement of my T-shirt rubbed on them. He sat back down and I thought, this is it he has got to want me now. He kept my head with his while kissing me. Then suddenly I was on my stomach across his knees. What the fuck happened? This wasn't right – not after a kiss like that. Oh shit, I could feel him pull my panties down.

"Charlotte, your panties are very damp. Would you like to explain why?"

What? Didn't he know he'd being turning me on and off all day, and he couldn't work out why my panties were wet?

Slap! Shit, that hurt!

"Hey, I thought we were going to talk about my punishment first!" I protested, trying to get my hands up to protect my arse.

Slap!

"I asked you a question! You didn't answer!" Aww, he didn't rub me. That's not right either.

Slap!

"Ouch! Can't you rub it in between, like you did last night?"

Slap! "No, I can't. This is punishment, and last night was playing."

Slap!

"What was this morning, then?"

Slap! "This morning was fun."

Slap! "Or was it not fun for you?"

Slap!

"*Ow*! That one hurt!"

Slap! "It's not supposed to turn you on, but then again by the feel of it you can't get much more turned on, can you?"

Slap!

I squirmed. "How many more?"

Slap! "I am waiting for my answers."

Slap! "Mind you, I am enjoying this." He stroked his hand over my arse and then down between my legs. "Yes, you're even wetter than you were. This is turning you on isn't it?"

I didn't answer. I was lost in the moment. He slipped a finger—oh that's sensational.

"Oh that feels so wet I should think you're moments away from letting go completely. You feel so nice, so ready, but this is a distraction." He removed his finger.

Slap!

Shit, that hurt! His finger returned and I moaned as he pushed it deeper into me.

"Charlotte, you surprise me. Tonight when you got on your knees I didn't think you would. I thought I would be waiting for a very long time before I would get you to do that."

I didn't answer. My body tingled all over and my hips began to move, trying to punch harder into his fingers.

"Charlotte what are you trying to do?"

I wanted to burst. I needed to burst. It was too much for me. I wanted my juices all over his fingers; my body was aching for it.

"Charlotte, will you please answer me?"

"Please, please," I moaned.

"Are you begging for something here?" Without another word his finger was out and...

Slap!

"Ow!" A sharp blow to my arse brought me back out of my dream. He pulled my head up and whispered, "Had enough, or shall I carry on?"

In my orgasmic state I whispered back, "Yes, please," not realising what he meant. He lowered my head.

Slap!

"*Ow*! What the hell was that for?"

"You said yes please." He laughed as he rubbed my arse.

"I said yes please to...to..." I stopped. What had I said yes to? Oh crap, I should have clarified what he was saying but I was so much in the moment I didn't.

"Why are you hesitating? What did you say yes to? Charlotte, answer me!"

I couldn't tell him I'd said yes please to an orgasmic moment.

"I said yes please to one final spank."

"OK. Your wish is my command. One final..."

"Nooooo!"

Slap!

"Fuck!"

"What was that, Charlotte? Did you say something?"

"Er, no."

"I didn't think so."

He took hold of my hair and lifted my head.

"I didn't think I would say this to you so early in our relationship but I think you'll make a very good sub." Lifting me off his knee he stood up and took me to the bed. He laid me down then he lay next to me. Cuddling up, he said, "You OK?"

"Yes, I am, I think."

"Really?"

"Yes."

He held me tight. My body tingled. He rubbed his hand to and fro over my arse.

"Stinging?" he asked.

"Yes, a little, but it's strange – it feels quite warm and more sexy when you touch it."

"Shall we go upstairs?"

"OK, if you like."

Returning to the suite he led me into the bedroom.

"I'll run you a bath, please let me bathe you this time." He went into the bathroom and turned on the taps. Taking hold of me, he pulled me toward him. Undoing my zip, he let my skirt fall to the ground and took off my panties. Then he rolled down my stockings, planting tender kisses on my legs. As he did so, my body started to melt. He pulled my T-shirt over my head, planting little kisses on my face when it appeared from under the T-shirt. Cuddling me, he undid my bra, stroking my back. God, he even made undressing for a bath seem sensual.

He felt the water. "Just right." Turning off the taps he held out his hand and helped me into the bath. I eased myself down as the water reached my arse.

"Ouch!"

"A little sore on the derrière are we?" He picked up a sponge and soaped it to start washing me.

"I could get used to this." I lay back in the bath. God,

this had never happened in my adult life: a man content to bathe me softly, gently. It was heaven, it was what things should be like, peace with each other, understanding each other, getting to know each other, and it was so perfect. Nothing so far seemed so unnatural that I wouldn't be able to live with it...that I couldn't get used to it.

From my feet he moved up my legs, Oh God, he looked so good down there washing me. I closed my eyes as I was swept away with the moment. Why couldn't every relationship have this in it? He was above my knees now and my hips twisted with anticipation. He rubbed the sponge up my inner thigh. Oh yes, here we go, I thought. My body just wants more. He didn't really have to do anything much, I was putty in his hands. He just brushed my lady button with the sponge and I could feel my nipples hardening as he moved higher to the sexiest place on my body. Then he bypassed it, straight to my tummy, oh, oh nooo! My body cried out for more, but he worked his way to my breasts and soaped them up with the sponge, making me twist with orgasmic pleasure. I had the desire to touch my lady button and slipped my hand slowly down my body.

"Oh Charlotte, you look so sexy!"

I rubbed my button and he leaned down and gently kissed my breast. Oh, this was one of the best moments in my adult life. Water streamed around my body as I moved, responding to the touch on my button. His hands slid down to meet mine, but he held them firmly and said, "No don't, not yet." What? It isn't your party, buster, I thought, it's mine, or haven't you noticed?

"What?" I snapped.

"Not yet, wait, please wait!" He held my hand so tightly that I couldn't move it. "Let me finish washing you, please."

"What?"

"I'm saying no. Do you want to argue and spoil the moment?"

He was a fine one to talk about spoiling the moment. He'd been doing that all day and now it looked like he was going to be doing it all night too. I thought that when he went to his room, if nothing had happened by then I would find my own orgasmic experience, get rid of some of my frustration.

He went on washing me all over, teasing me with the sponge. Then he lifted me out of the bath, took me back to the bedroom and laid me on the bed. He then began to dry me, starting at my feet. He worked his way up – when he got to my inner thigh I was gone. He kissed my thigh, gently working his way up. Oh here I am, I thought. Please don't stop!

"Charlotte," He climbed on top of me, looking me in the eyes. "Have you enjoyed yourself so far?"

"Yes," I gasped, and he kissed me long, hard and full of passion. He took my hands and held them above my head. "I have to tape your hands together. I can't do this, they'll get in my way."

He leaned over to the bedside table and took out some tape. He taped my hands to the bedpost.

"That's better," he said, "you've been very amenable to everything I have wanted from you today. You never even argued when I said I was going to tape your hands, you just let me do it. Your trust in me has started to build already. I really didn't think it would, for a while, but here you are only a few days after freaking out about what I do and I like, willing to please me. I like that so much. Are you happy? Truly happy? Do you really think this life can be for you?"

Oh come on, I thought, I've been turned on all day, close so many times to orgasmic satisfaction and you have to ask?

But he is right – I have surprised myself in all of this. It is the first time in my adult life that I have a say in everything I do. All I have to do now is find a way to say what I want, and explain my likes and dislikes to Lloyd.

"Yes, I am happy."

"You looked so beautiful in the bath, rubbing and moving your body. I didn't want your first time to be in the bath, I want your first time of complete pleasure to be shared by us both, although you playing was one of the sexiest things I have ever seen." He kissed my neck and then down to my breasts. "Oh God, I want to tease these babies!" He felt gently around my breasts then kissed my nipples. "Oh what I can do to these! I have some fantastic toys for them." He cupped my boobs. "I love 36Ds, just right – a handful."

He was like a kid at Christmas unwrapping his presents and not quite knowing what he wanted to play with first. He placed his thumb and forefinger on my nipples and pulled as he twisted. I moaned and felt a gush as my hips moved beneath him.

"Oh my God, you are so ready. I think I could make your passion burst just by playing with your nipples." He kissed all the way back up my neck to my ear.

"Shall we try?" Before I could answer his mouth was over mine, kissing me so hard I couldn't breathe. His finger and thumb manipulating my nipple harder and faster, his tongue in my mouth. I suddenly felt I wanted to come up for air but he pinned down my hair so I couldn't move my head. His feet locked on the insides of my knees as he pulled my legs slightly apart and pinned them to the bed, stopping me from wriggling. Then in my panic to breathe my body trembled and I was bursting in a way that had never happened before. I could feel every muscle in my groin tighten with excitement as my pleasure grew. I wanted him, I wanted him inside me and I wanted him now. His kiss became softer as he started to pull his head away. He kissed my lips and bit them softly.

"You OK?"

"Yes."

"Good. Ready for Round two, or do you need a break?" What, more? Where was the burp before he passed out on me?

"OK, I'll take that as yes then." He worked down my neck and chest, kissing as he went. My body tingled and twitched as he started nibbling my nipples. He moved so that he was lying beside me, and slid his hands slowly down my body. Slowly he rubbed my button. I could feel it swell, and pleasure overcame me. Bloody hell, two in one night! I was going to pass out I just knew it. He kissed back up to my ear and nibbled it.

"I want you to keep your hips still. I want to talk with you while I play down there so I don't want to have to hold you as well. Please keep still or I might have to take you back downstairs to a room you haven't seen and I don't want to do that yet." I gasped in anticipation of what he could mean.

"See? See what the power of suggestion can do." He slowly pushed a finger inside me. "This is wetter than it was downstairs. Maybe I should spank you more often. Maybe I might be able to make you burst like you just did just from spanking you."

I felt a clench deep within me, the muscle inside me tight around his finger.

"Aww, you are so tight! This is so nice." He ran his thumb over my button. I moaned, my hips arching. "Keep still, I said, or I'll take you, naked as the day you were born,

downstairs to the other room, I don't care who sees you."
Oh God, his voice, demanding, controlling, adding fuel to
the fire that was burning deep within me.

He kissed my lips gently, took hold of my hair then
kissed me deeply. Then he pulled away.

"No, I want to watch you this time. I want to see your
face, want to hear you loud as I make you come." He put
another finger inside me. I could feel them deep within,
moving and wriggling.

"After you have come I want to taste you, taste your
fresh juice."

I twisted with the thought of him tasting me. Why, oh
why, hadn't this ever been done to me before? Why was
he so good at it when others couldn't even manage to find
a boob? I was in heaven. Then his fingers stopped. Oh,
don't stop. Keep going! I tried to move my head to kiss him.
Please don't stop! Not now!

"No, baby, this is all yours if you want it. You do it!"

I moved my hips, raising them up and down trying to
reach his fingers. He had them just out of reach. I could
feel his fingertips but I couldn't get them in me, "Come on,
baby, you can do better than that! If you want it, get it, or
maybe you don't want it badly enough?"

Every time I moved he took his fingers away, watching
me with a smile on his face. "I love watching your frustration
when you can't have what you are so desperate for!"

His tantalizing fingers were just out of reach, teasing,
tempting me on. My body was aching from frustration.
I could feel the tape around my wrists tighten as I tried to
get closer.

"You can have whatever you want if you work for it,
baby."

"Please. Please...that was so nice. Feeling part of you

deep inside me was so nice, it made me feel part of you, please let me, please."

"Let you what? I'm not stopping you." He said gently

"Kiss me – kiss me like you did before, so that I'll burst. Please,"

He smiled. "What, do you want me to kiss you or to carry on? What do you want?"

"None of them."

"What, none?"

"No."

"We'll stop then."

"No, please let's not stop!" I twisted my hips

"You just said you don't want to play any more."

"No I didn't. I said none of them. Please don't stop."

"What do you want to do, then, Charlotte?"

"I want to feel whole, I want to feel part of you, one with you." I lifted my head to see if I could tempt him for a kiss, but no such luck.

"Is this lust talking?"

"No, it's me, what I feel. I don't want to fuck, I want to feel part of you."

He kissed me hard and plunged his fingers deep within me and in no time at all I was arching my body in pure passion and I came all over his fingers. He stopped kissing me.

"That was intense. Are you OK?"

"Yes," I panted.

"Do you want to play some more or do you want to rest?" What, again? Oh fuck, I couldn't take any more. He ran his finger lightly down my body and I twisted and moaned.

"Sensitive, are we?" He grinned wickedly. "What can we play now?" as he did it again.

"Please, please," I gasped as I tried to move away from his teasing fingers.

"Come now, Charlotte, are you going to deny me my pleasure when I have just given you so much? It's my turn now. Your body is so nice and sensitive I want to play with it, but first a blindfold, I think." He got off the bed and opened a drawer. Returning with a blindfold he placed it over my eyes. I heard him move across the bedroom.

"Where have you gone?" I felt disoriented.

"I'm here, Charlotte, here beside you."

His fingers journeyed down my body, startling me.

"We are going to play a game. Trust me, I won't hurt you." Something touched me; fell on me, not heavy. It feels cold, I thought, and then there came a slightly different feeling. It was strange but I liked it.

"Mmm," he said, "you react in just the way I thought you would. Do you like it?" The touches on my body became more frequent.

"What are you doing?"

He let his hand linger on me. "Just playing." Then something else touched me on the arm. Oh God, it was sensational! My body was still tingling and alive, and the slightest touch just sent me into orgasmic meltdown. The whole of my body was so sensitive that the littlest touch was enough to send me to heaven. I tried to work out what it was that was dripping on me but I couldn't and quite honestly who cared at this moment in time. What was he doing?

"Do you need a rest?" Something dripped on my leg. Oh God, I wanted to burst again.

"No, but I would like to know what you're doing."

"Not yet. I've loved tonight. It's been quite intense for you and you have handled it well." He lay back down on the bed and lifted the blindfold. "I think you should have a rest now. I'll take this tape off you." He un-taped my hands and rubbed my wrists gently. "Are they OK?"

"Yes."

"Good. Come, cuddle up with me." I cuddled into him and we wrapped our arms around each other.

"Do you want to talk? You know, pillow talk or anything?"

Oh my God, I have won the lottery! Pillow talk as well as orgasmic experience!

"This is so nice, cuddling up. What were you doing when I was blindfolded?"

"Did you like it?"

"Yes I did, but I couldn't make out if it was hot or cold or what it was. I felt a little disoriented."

"It was just ice water. I was holding an ice cube in my hands and letting it melt, dripping onto your skin. It was nice to see your body so sensitive. With each little drop it reacted differently."

"What, it was just water? But sometimes it felt different. It felt like there were different things dropping on me."

"No, it was all the same thing – ice-cold water. It was because your senses were heightened so much and your imagination was running wild."

"Having sex like this isn't everyday sex, is it?"

"Why isn't it, Charlotte?"

"Well, you know, the honeymoon period and all."

"If I just had sex with you, within in a week I'd be fed up with it, but it's not just sex, it's about us – what makes us whole as individuals and as a couple. And yes, we wouldn't be able to play like this every night of the week as we have to go to work, but when we do play it will be fantastic. I'll pamper you and spoil you, just as I've done this evening. All I want is for you to be totally sub. There will be evenings when I'll want you as you, and evenings when I want you to be...a whore in the bedroom." He let his fingers stray

down my back and I squirmed. "Still very sensitive, then."
He kissed my forehead. "But most of all I need you to be
totally happy. You can say anything you want to me."

"I don't think I can."

"Why not? What can't you say?"

"I can't say 'what the fuck'."

Lloyd laughed. "Oh, Charlotte, you can say 'what the
fuck' as you put it so ladylike! It makes things interesting.
But not when we are playing, nor in the company of any
Doms or subs. It's disrespectful."

"Oh, so all of today you've been playing."

"Yes, Charlotte, *we've* been playing!" He rolled me over,
sitting astride me, and pinned my arms behind my head.

"You're naked!" I hadn't seen him without clothes on
before.

"Yes, I am, and I have been, ever since I blindfolded
you."

I looked at his body. Well fit! He had a six-pack. Who
would have thought it? "Wow, what the fuck! Great view!"
I looked at his body, wanting to touch it.

"Excuse me?" He raised an eyebrow.

"Oh it's a compliment! Great view – I like what I see."

"I understood that bit, it was the other three words
I was referring to."

Oh crap, here we go, I thought. Give the Dom a compliment and he'll find a way to spank you.

"You said I could! Besides, I was amazed. I never realised
you had such a good body underneath those sloppy shirts
you wear."

"I said, when we aren't playing, and when there are no
others around."

I looked up, half-expecting someone to jump out and
say 'Surprise!'

Lloyd shook his head. "We are alone, Charlotte. I wouldn't do that to you...well, not yet anyway."

"Oh, are we still playing, then?" I gave him a cheeky grin. He would have to get a load of Post-It notes and stick them on his head, so I'd know what I was supposed to do and when. Otherwise I could see we wouldn't be doing anything other than spanking. I giggled.

"What's so funny? Care to share?"

"No," I said, trying to contain the giggles.

"I can wait here for the rest of the night if you wish."

"Oh, that would be cool! I could look at you for the rest of the night, I'm enjoying the view so much."

"Charlotte, that isn't what you were supposed to say at all!" Laughing, he rolled off me and lay down.

"What was I supposed to say?" I rolled over to look at him but he shook his head again.

"No, nothing, the moment has gone. You make me laugh. That's all. I've really enjoyed the last couple of days with you. I didn't think for one minute that I would have you here with me. I thought you would run a mile at the sheer thought of all of this, and Anthony thought he would have to find a new best friend."

"No," I said, "if anything, I think I'll be even closer to Anthony now. I think I was quite narrow-minded, afraid of people who are different to me. I was judgmental even as a nurse. I can see now that was wrong but it's the way we're conditioned within society. So I've learnt that I should give individuals their space, look at the person inside to understand them, rather then being totally dismissive about their differences. That said there are things in today's society that I'll never be able to get my head around, and probably in your lifestyle as well that I won't understand. I think that's to be expected."

"Like what?"

"I read an article once, on – you know – really nasty movies."

"No," he said, "don't go there. That has nothing to do with our lifestyle. It's completely different. It's sick, twisted people who have lost touch with reality. Nothing to do with the lifestyle."

"See, that's what I was going to say. Vanilla and non-vanilla will always have something that they agree on."

He cuddled me close. "There is one thing I do know. No one will ever do anything that is against your will ever again, be it vanilla or not. If it's the last thing I do."

"I don't think I could ever go back to being vanilla after tonight." I trailed my fingers down his chest. He breathed in sharply and closed his eyes.

"Charlotte, nothing would make me happier, but there is still so much you need to know and experience before making that decision."

"Like what?"

"All in good time and good time is when I think you are ready, not before."

"If it's when you are good and ready, I might just as well go to work tomorrow," I said.

"I don't think so!"

"Why not?"

"Because you have a lot to learn, choices to make. I have taken this time off to be with you, to explain things. Nats has given you this time off for you to get your head around things."

"I like work. I feel I'm letting Nats down, she has so much to do."

"Look, trust us. We don't want you getting empty-headed ideas about something, and then having a nervous breakdown because you haven't understood. It does happen. You may think we're wrapping you up in cotton wool, but given your past we have good reason, and remember this has found you, you weren't looking for it, like most. We've told you that, so do as we say."

"OK, so what are we doing tomorrow then?"

"We'll see what tomorrow brings, as it depends on your mood and mine."

"OK."

I let my hand slip down toward his groin. He shuddered slightly. I kissed his chest. Oh wow, he didn't push me off, saying 'not now'. No farting or burping, blimey, maybe he didn't come from Mars. I skirted my fingers around to the outside of his hip and down his leg, crossing over the top to the inner thigh, and started going up. Shock, horror, as I realised... Oh my God, he was bald down there as well!

"Fuck! You shave down here!"

"No, Charlotte, I don't!"

"What, you have premature baldness of the pubes?"

He laughed. "Charlotte, I wax! Talking of which, you shave your bikini line don't you?" I went red. That wasn't something your man was supposed to say to you in bed.

"I think I know what we're doing tomorrow now," he said.

"Oh no, oh no no no, you are not going to wax me!" My body tensed and I moved away from him.

"You're right, I'm not. Come here." He pulled me close to him. "Would you like to carry on where you left off before you thought I had premature baldness of my balls? It was very nice."

I started to trail my fingers down his chest and he instantly relaxed to my touch.

Suddenly an alarm sounded.

"Charlotte, stay here, don't go anywhere please. I have to go, I'll be back when I can."

"What's that? Is it a fire alarm?"

"No, it's a panic alarm." He hurried into his clothes.

"What would be wrong?"

"I'll be straight back." With that he was gone.

What was happening? Why would we hear the alarm in here? The rooms were all soundproofed. My mind worked overtime on what could have happened, what could be wrong, had someone been hurt? I lay on the bed, my body still tingling, feeling cosy and warm and I began to drift off to sleep.

Chapter Twelve

I woke to a smell of fresh coffee. I didn't want to open my eyes to find out that last night had been just a dream. I felt Lloyd's hand stroke my hair.

"Good morning, sleepyhead, or should I say afternoon?" He was still here. I felt I was floating on a cloud. Everything was perfect. "Are you OK?" he asked.

"Shush."

"Shush? Why are you shushing me?"

"I'm trying to enjoy waking up with you."

"Oh, I see." He kissed my lips. "It's time for you to get up. I've brought your breakfast."

I opened one eye and squinted at him. I didn't want coffee. I wanted more of what we had last night. My eyes widened when I saw he was showered and dressed. What about breakfast, and not the sort you eat.

"You're dressed!"

"Yes, I've been up for hours watching you sleep. Nice dreams, hope I was with you, with all that squirming you were doing." He looked at me quizzically.

I turned red. I now felt he'd been peeping. Or would they class it as voyeurism? It was a hot dream.

"Drink your coffee. I'll turn the shower on for you." He handed me a mug of coffee and went into the bathroom.

"I've put some clothes out for you on the chair. I'll leave you to it. I've got some work to do. I'll be in the office when you've finished." He left the room.

I thought he was having a holiday. I drank the coffee and showered, the water enhancing the tingling sensation. I felt fantastic. I went to the bedroom and dressed – skirt, bra, stockings. Oh, he'd forgotten my panties! I got some out that matched my bra. I did my hair, half up half down. That looked cool.

When I was ready I went to the office. Opening the door, I peeped in.

"Hi, come in," Lloyd said, "I've nearly finished."

"What are you doing?" I asked.

"Just a report of last night."

"What the…"

"Charlotte!"

Why was he writing a report about what we did last night?

"I'm writing a report on the reason why the panic button was pushed."

"Oh, I'd forgotten, sorry. What was the problem?"

"Basically someone out of their depth, didn't follow their rules, decided they knew best, ended up having a massive panic attack, and needed to be sedated. This is why we need you to take this slowly."

"What if you hadn't been here? What if you were at home? Who would have sorted it then?"

"Charlotte, this is my home. I live here. I thought you knew."

"No, I didn't realise. Does the alarm go off often?"

"No, but when it does, as the owners we like to be in control of everything that happens here. I am the doctor on call, twenty-four seven, so to speak."

"No one explained that to me."

"I just have."

"No, you know what I mean."

"Done...come here." He swung round on the chair. "You look absolutely lovely, you're glowing!" He took hold of my hips and felt through my skirt. "Er... I don't remember putting panties on the chair for you this morning?"

"No, you forgot them, so I got some out that match my bra."

"Oh good, I like these games. How many pairs of panties do we have, matching this bra?"

"Just the one," I answered.

"Good." He leaned across the table and picked up a pair of scissors from the pen holder. He lifted up my skirt and slipped a finger into the top of my panties. Looking in my eyes he pulled the panties away from my skin and snipped, that grin of his is just so evil sometimes.

"What the fuck have you done that for?"

"For the same reason I am now going to do this, for disobeying me." He flipped me over his knee.

"How the hell did I disobey you?"

"You got dressed in something other than what I gave you to dress in."

"I didn't know, did I? I thought you had forgotten them!" I was trying to cover my bottom with my hands. "You can't spank me for that because I didn't know."

"I am not spanking you for that. I am spanking you for your smart-arse mouth and lack of control yet again. I've already stopped you once from finishing the sentence, then you go and do it again, and will you get your hands out of my way, please. I don't want to have to tie you up so early in the day, we have things to do."

"That was the shock of you cutting my panties off."

"Would you rather have had me rip them off and risk hurting you?"

"No," I snapped. "I would have preferred you fucking asking me to take them off."

Slap. "Smart-arse mouth again, Charlotte."

"I liked those panties," I protested.

Slap.

"Like I like the bra…"

Slap.

"You didn't have to fucking cut them off!"

Slap.

"Fuck!"

"Smart-arse mouth."

Slap.

"What do you expect when you cut off a girl's panties?"

Slap.

"Oh, I am enjoying this. Me talking and spanking and then you smart-arse mouthing. We are going to be here for some time." Slap.

"Oh please, please don't!"

Slap.

"Charlotte, you are getting spanked for using words I don't like and for no other reason. I have asked you not to." Slap.

"Oh, but you don't know what…oh!"

Slap. "I don't know what, Charlotte?" Slap.

"Nothing."

Slap. "Charlotte the thing is, when you are with me you'll only wear sets of underwear that match, so if a bra is put out in the morning and it has no panties to go with it, it's what I want you to wear." Slap. "So if you have no matching panties you can't be tempted to put them on, can you?" Slap.

"Oh please, Lloyd! I understand now, please let me go!"

Slap. "Are you going to be a smart-arse mouth again today?" Slap.

"I will try."

Slap. "You will try to be a smart-arse mouth? Wrong answer." Slap.

"Lloyd, that's not what I meant and you know it. I mean… I'll try to not to be…and you are fucking twisting things!"

Slap. "Smart-arse-mouth again, Charlotte. You must like being here like this. Let me see how much you're liking it. Just as I thought, you're getting turned on. We must go now." He flipped me back up and clasped my wrist and we left.

"Where are we going" I asked when we were in the lift.

"Going to see Nats."

"Oh? OK, that will be nice."

"Yes, and I want you to behave. I'll be taking stock," he said severely.

"Hi, Nats!" I said as we entered the salon.

Nats turned from the customer she was advising. "Hi, Charlotte! Ready for your wax?"

"What the—" I began.

"I'm taking stock," Lloyd said in my ear.

"You said you weren't going to wax me!"

"I'm not," he grinned.

Nats led the way down the hall to one of the waxing rooms. "Here you are. Have a coffee, Dawn will be with you shortly,"

What the hell! I hadn't even been consulted!

"You can't let them wax me now!" I protested.

"Yes, I can."

"My arse!"

"Which arse would that be, Charlotte? This one here?"

He put his hand up inside my skirt and rubbed my arse, "or your smart-arse mouth?"

I glared at him and tried to sit down. "I'm not having you do that here!"

He pulled me closer still rubbing my arse. "It feels nice and warm, ready for another. Here, if you wish."

I scowled. "It's all red, and everyone will know I work here don't forget."

"Don't forget that they all have contracts, and Dawn is a sub so it's nothing she hasn't seen before."

Oh my God, he was really going to make me do this!

"Don't forget I'm taking stock, so no smart-arse mouthing from you while you're having it done."

"You won't know, because the room is soundproofed. You won't hear a thing," I snapped back.

"I'll be here with you."

"Oh no! Oh no, you can't watch! That's not right!"

"I can and I will." He said forcefully, such a turn on with that glint of naughtiness in his eyes.

The door opened and Dawn came in.

"Hi Lloyd, hi Charlotte! How are you both? Enjoying your holiday?"

"Yes thank you, Dawn," we said simultaneously.

"Good. Let's get started. On the table please, Charlotte."

I hesitated, looking at Lloyd, hoping he would take pity on me, but no such luck, of course. He just gave me a look as if to say he would put me there himself if I didn't get a move on.

I climbed onto the table. Dawn pulled up my skirt and covered my top half with a towel. This wasn't too bad, I thought, just like having a scan at the hospital. Then she put some wax on me. At least she had warmed the wax. NHS gel was usually cold. I felt her placing a strip on me.

"Ready?"

Rip.

"Fuck! Jesus, what the fuck!" My head reared up off the table. "That fucking hurt! What the fuck did you do?" I could feel Lloyd's eyes burning into me, but honestly I didn't care.

"Charlotte, is this the first time you have ever been waxed?"

What did she think? Of course it was the first time I had ever been waxed and it was going to be the last fucking time as well. Who in their right mind would have this done? "Lloyd, you must be off your fucking rocker!"

Dawn laughed. "Oops, sorry, Lloyd," she said politely, and put some more wax on. Oh no, not again!

"Ready?"

Rip.

"Mary, Jesus and wee black donkeys, what the fuck! Is that it now? It's finished, say it's finished!" Agony ripped through my groin. This wasn't pleasure; this was sheer bloody pain, a thousand needles sticking in me. I felt Dawn applying more wax.

Rip.

"Fuck! You didn't say 'ready'! Why the hell didn't you say 'ready'?"

"She's a bit sensitive today, Dawn," Lloyd apologized for me.

Rip. My eyes watered

"I can see she's sensitive, Lloyd, I'd know your handiwork anywhere."

What! They were having a conversation about my arse right over the top of me, as if I wasn't...

Rip.

Fucking here!

191

"I am fucking here, you know! I can hear you both!"

Rip.

"Fuck! Hello, are you both fucking deaf? Have you finished now?"

Rip.

"Fuck! Oh obviously not. My mistake, but there can't be any more left to fucking pull out!"

Rip.

Shouldn't she have told me what she was doing, like Brazilian or something? The differences between all the... Rip... Fuck!...different styles?

"Jesus! Call the fire brigade, I'm on fire down there!"

Rip. Rip...rip...

"How's Peter?" Lloyd asked.

"Oh he's all right. Overworked... Rip...rip...rip... "He's away in America at the moment."

How could they talk so casually at a time like this? My eyes were full of tears. "I want to go home," I said, clenching the edge of the table I could actually feel the knuckles on my hands turning white.

"There, Charlotte! Finished."

My body was shaking, every muscle tense. My head felt like it was going to explode. Christ, I was on fire.

"I'll leave you to it, Lloyd." Dawn left the room.

"How are you feeling? I'm sorry for this, but truly the first time is easier when you're not expecting it."

How was I feeling? Well, if the pain wasn't so bad I would be able to talk and tell him I was feeling fucking crap. *Not so bad if you don't expect it!* If I could talk I'd tell him it couldn't be any worse than it is right now, and that he doesn't look that sorry.

He leaned down and kissed me on my forehead. "I'll look and see what she has done."

I could tell him what she had done, all right. She had inflicted more pain on me than I ever though possible, and if he thought in his wildest dreams that I was ever going to have it done again, the answer would be fucking dream on.

Lloyd pulled up my skirt. "That looks better. I'll rub some moisturiser on for you. It's nice and cold. They keep it in the fridge."

What, not content with seeing me writhing around in fucking agony, now he was going to fucking freeze me.

Lloyd started to rub in the cream and my head jerked up. Bloody hell, that was fucking cold! Oh...oh, that felt better! Soothing. I laid my head back down while he rubbed gently.

"It will calm down soon and you'll be OK. That should do it. Ready?" he asked me, and pulled my hand to sit me up. Jesus that hurt! He swung my legs off the bed. I felt swollen between my legs. Oh shit, how the hell was I going to walk? I eased myself off the table and my legs turned to jelly. "Oh fuck, I can't stand!" I said.

"That's just shock. It did the same to me when I first had it done. You'll be fine. Here, sit on the chair. I'll get you some water." I sat down gingerly and he handed me some water.

"Where in the fuck was my choice in that?" I demanded.

"I'm still taking stock," he said. "Quite a few smart-arse mouths in that little display you put on."

"You said you wouldn't hurt me!"

"Correct. I think that was Dawn waxing you, not me."

I clenched my teeth hard. "Grrr, you're twisting again, you're fucking twisting words! I never thought in a million years you would let anyone hurt me."

"This is different, Charlotte, totally different. This is for pleasure, you'll see. Anyway, don't all you girlies say 'no pain no gain'?"

193

"What the fuck do I gain from that?"

"Smart-arse mouth! Do you really want a spank right now right here on top of your waxing, because I can put the lock on the door and my palms are getting itchy."

"Well, how do you know my palms aren't itchy?"

"Because you are sub, and you are my sub, and smart-arse-mouth-subs don't spank. They get spanked, that's why. Do you really want to go down this route and find out?" He raised his eyebrows at me. I glared back.

"Charlotte, I am waiting for your answer." He folded his arms. I looked away from him. I wasn't going to answer. Why should I when he had put me through that?

"OK, if that's the way you want it, fine. I would have thought you would have learnt from yesterday: when you stamp your foot I don't respond in the way you want." He went to the door and pushed the bolt across, then to the coffee machine. He made a coffee then sat down next to me.

"We can wait all day here until I get an answer – one that is fitting – and, trust me, the longer I wait the worse it will be for you when I decide what to do with you."

He crossed his legs. I thought, I'll just get up, unlock the door, and walk out. What could he do? I got out of my chair and tried to stand as straight as I could. He watched me with a small smile on his face. Jeez, my waxing was still smarting. I walked to the door.

"You don't... No, you really don't want to do that... you have already disobeyed me this morning. Do you want to do that again?"

"Oh, come on! This is a little different from this morning. You have subjected me to real pain and I'm in agony here, or haven't you fucking noticed!"

"Smart-arse mouth. Yes, I have noticed and I know

what it's like when you first have it done but next time it's not so bad."

"Next time? Next time? You'll plait fog before I have it done again. I'll never have this done again! What do you think I am, for God's sake?"

"Smart-arse mouth is pushing it. Smart-arse mouth will have it done again, and smart-arse mouth best come and sit down."

"I'll sit," I snarled, "but not for any other fucking reason than I am in pain and I don't think I can quite make it to the fucking door."

I sat down again and the smarting intensified.

"Smart-arse mouth is really pushing it."

"We're alone and I am not playing."

"No, we are out together, and I wish that smart-arse mouth not to be used. Is that clear?"

"Yes," I said sulkily.

"Right. Back to the answer. I want to get back home sooner rather than later. Do you really want to go down that route when we are here on why you get spanked and not do the spanking?"

"No."

"Good. Now we can go." He opened the door and helped me up. We walked down to the front desk in the salon and he paid Nats.

"Are you OK, Charlotte?" she asked, looking at me anxiously. "It wears off quite quickly. We didn't realise it was your first time. It won't be half as bad next time." with a hint of sarcasm, as if she didn't know it was my first time.

Lloyd shot me a look, as if to say 'don't start'.

"No, I'm sure it won't be," I said politely, knowing that was for sure because I wasn't having a fucking next time... Anyway.

Back at Lloyd's – I could call it Lloyd's now I knew he lived there – I rushed into the bedroom and stood in front of the big mirror to see what Dawn had done. I lifted my skirt. What the...what the fuck... My eyes were on stalks.

Where the fuck were my pubes? I looked like I had localised fucking scarlet fever! In the mirror I saw Lloyd leaning casually on the doorframe. "And before you start saying fucking smart-arse mouth, I am not fucking happy!"

Lloyd spread his hands. "I'm not saying a word because you're so good at saying it for me."

"God, I can't fucking win, can I."

"Not really, because you're not in control."

"No, would you be in fucking control if your crazy-arsed boyfriend took you to be waxed and waxed you bald?" That would shut him up.

"First of all I'm not crazy-arsed, and secondly I don't have and don't ever intend to have a boyfriend, so I wouldn't know, but I wouldn't lose control, that's for sure."

"You wonder why I've lost control? Look! This is why I've lost control!" I spun round on the spot with my skirt held under my chin. "See that? See, not a fucking pube where it should be, for fuck's sake."

"Yes, very nice view!" Oh shit, I was waving my new bald patch at him as if it was my best shirt and the colour had run. I flipped my skirt down and felt the redness burn into my cheeks. Shit, they felt like they had just been waxed too. I lowered my head so he couldn't see my blush.

"That's a better view," he said and came toward me. "My little sub with her head lowered in my presence looks so hot and sexy, blushes and all." He took hold of my hair and tilted my head back.

"How can you do this to me when I am so upset? I'm not in the mood for playing!"

"I know that and if you can't take control of yourself, then I'll have to."

"I am in perfect fucking control of myself!" I snapped.

"Can you still kiss?"

What? What is he asking me that for? "What the fuck has can I still kiss got to do with anything?"

"Charlotte, I'm waiting. Can you still kiss? Answer my question, please."

"Yes, I can still fucking kiss!"

"Kiss me then, before I have to spank you for your mouth." With that he pulled my head further back by my hair and kissed me long and hard just like last night, a drop-dead stop-breathing kiss.

When the kiss ended, he said, "Have you finished now, Charlotte? I do hope so, or you are going to find it difficult to know where the smarting stops and finishes down there. You won't be able to tell the difference between waxing and spanking, that's the choice you have today."

"Yes, I have finished," I said.

"Let's get some ice on you, calm down that redness you have. We'll go to the fire and ice room, I think, and have some dinner brought to us. What do you say?"

I had nothing to say, so we went to the fire and ice room and he laid me on the bed.

"Aww, it does look sore, but we'll sort it." He got some ice and a towel, and returned to the bed. He wrapped some crushed ice in the towel and put it on me. I gasped, and every muscle in my body tightened.

"Jesus, fuck! That's fucking freezing!"

"Smart-arse mouth, Charlotte. We really need a talk about control. It's very important for you to understand."

"What do you expect, Lloyd? You take me for a wax without telling me, and...oh yes, you then have a casual conversation over my body and ignore the very fact that I am there in pain! What the fuck was that about?"

"That was about not giving in to your little display of lack of control, just as you are doing again now." Jesus, anyone would lack control when someone was pulling their pubes out one by one, for fuck's sake.

"Do you want ice for your arse as well as for here?" He applied pressure on the towel, pushing it down firmly on the place where my pubes used to be.

"Fuck! That hurts! And no, it isn't too bad, thank you."

"Smart-arse mouth. I didn't ask if your arse was fine or not. I asked you if you wanted ice for it."

"Why the fuck would I want ice for my arse if it's fine?"

Instantly he flipped me on my front. "Charlotte, when will you learn?

Slap!

"That smart-arse mouths get spanked?"

Slap!

"Lloyd, no!" I put my hands over my backside to stop him. "Please no, I'm too sore...please!"

"Charlotte, move your hands and move them now!"

"No, Lloyd, please! I'm too sore!"

"Move them, or you'll find yourself not being able to move. I'll restrain you."

"Lloyd, please don't...please!"

He grabbed one of my hands. "Are you going to move them?"

"No." I said defensively.

He put my hand into a restraint and did the same to the other one. "Right, let's see if you can be quiet, shall we?"

"No, Lloyd, please! I choose for this not to happen!"

Very carefully he placed the towel with the crushed ice underneath me.

"No, Charlotte, you have chosen for this to happen. Let me explain and while I explain I want you to shut up please."

"Oh Lloyd, anything but this. Please don't! Not now!"

"'Anything but this' is a very interesting choice of words, Charlotte." He began to rub his hand over my backside. "Let me think about that 'anything else but this'. You really should be careful what you wish for, Charlotte."

Slap, rub. Fuck, the ice was so cold and now my arse was going to burn too. What was going through his mind?

Slap, rub. At least he was rubbing as well. It wasn't so bad when he rubbed.

"OK," he said. "I have thought. Spanking it is, and I shall explain why you chose spanking."

Slap.

What, no...

Slap.

Where was the fucking rub?

Slap. "I told you, smart-arse mouth, that you had a choice: stop and take control or I would take control for you."

Slap.

No, please rub!

Slap.

"Oh come on, this isn't fair!" I protested strongly.

Slap.

"So this is me taking control. I've given you chance after chance today as I thought we could cut a little slack..." Slap. "But you have taken advantage of my good nature."

Slap, rub.

He leaned to my ear. "Feel better, do we?"

I didn't answer.

"Or should I continue your choice?" Slap.

"No, no…"

Slap.

"You don't feel better?"

"No, you didn't give me a chance to finish!"

Slap.

"It's a one-word answer. Yes, or no?"

Slap.

"Yes, yes!"

He rubbed my arse. "Thank goodness for that. I thought I was going to have to get a paddle for you."

"A paddle?"

"Yes, my hand was starting to hurt and I don't like hurting my hands on a sub's arse."

"What are you talking about?"

"A paddle is what we use for spanking sometimes."

"You're not using one on me! I don't mind your hand, but nothing else."

"We'll see," he said.

"Can you undo me now, please?" I asked.

"No, I like the view. A nice red arse. I think we'll have a nice quiet afternoon with you there and me here just looking at your red arse, and if the redness goes I can always give it a little tap so it pleases my eye again."

"What? You can't leave me like this all afternoon!"

"I can, and I will if I so choose." He got onto the bed and lay down beside me, put his head on one of my arms and looked at me. "How are you doing?"

"I'm doing fine, thanks."

"Cool. Not too much for you?"

"The waxing was too much, yes. The spanking, OK."

He looked worried as he asked why that should be.

"Why do you look worried when you ask that?"

"Because I don't want to overdo it. Though you seem

to be coping with it very well, I don't want to go too far."

"I'm OK at the moment, thank you."

"Good. You haven't forgotten your safe word, have you?"

"No, it's 'fucking stop'."

"Yes, although it's a bit hard to know if that's what you mean or not. You use the word 'fucking' a lot, and that's why we need to talk about control, and you losing control."

"You're the one who's in control, aren't you?"

"Now *you* look worried," he said. "No, we're both in control and it needs it to be like that."

"Why do I need to be in control? You're the one who's doing everything and I'm the one that you're taking control away from by restraining me to the bed."

"Good point, but you need to be in control of the way you react to things. I'm learning how your body reacts in different circumstances. I'll know by your reaction and your body language if you like something or not, without you saying a word. I can only do that if you don't lose control. Tell me something – while you were being waxed, why didn't you use your safe word if it was so bad for you?"

"I don't know. Maybe because there was someone with you. Maybe because I was embarrassed."

"I don't know why you were embarrassed. You could have used your safe word, if you'd wanted to, and if you had I would have made her stop, but you didn't say the safe word, and yes, it is painful. You lost control and Dawn just carried on because you had lost control. I think we need to get you a new safe word – one you can use anywhere at any time, so if we are with mixed company you can use it and I'll know you want to stop. How about we use 'Time out'?"

"OK."

"That's good. Now you need to start controlling what

you're thinking and saying, because when you're ranting you're never going to be in control and may very well get hurt – not by me, but there are others out there that will use that against you. I'm only saying that in case you don't stay with me but desire a different Dom. In fact, by the time I have finished with you, you'll be able to control any Dom better then he can control you." He smiled at me. "How are you doing there?"

"Fine, thank you."

"Are you sure? How are your sore bits?"

"Not so bad."

He laid his hand on my arse and gave it a rub. "My favourite part of you at the moment. How's it doing?"

"It's fine as well, thank you."

"It feels as if it's cooled down a bit."

"Yes, it has." It felt nice with him rubbing. Feeling was coming back to my body.

"Do you want me to take the restraints off now?"

"No thanks." He'd probably put them back on again in five minutes anyway.

"Oh? Why not, Charlotte? Do you think you're going to have to be put back in them for something?"

Oh crap, how did he know what I was thinking?

"No, I like lying here like this." What? Why did my mouth say that? Although there was something dead kinky about it – my hands restrained and him lying on my arm talking to me, not bad.

"Oh, you like them? Well, that's good to know. We might use them a lot more often then. I must say it was very sexy last night when you were taped up, and I controlled what your body did, but you should learn how to control all of that too." He pushed his hand down between my legs and I moved my hips in response.

"Not hurting so much now? Has the ice helped cool it for you?"

"Yes, thank you."

"Charlotte, you've got very polite suddenly. I like this in you."

"Thank you." What did he mean? I was hardly going to tell him my real thoughts when he had me at a disadvantage, was I? Jeez, he was stupid sometimes. Maybe he did come from Mars after all. He removed his hand.

"I am not going there now, although it would be fun to see how much you could take."

"Go on then, do it." I looked into his eyes, daring him.

"You aren't challenging me, are you, Charlotte?"

"Might be, and why shouldn't I?"

"You can challenge me as much as you like, but our lunch will be here in about five minutes. Are you going to get up from there? Or I have time to spank you again if you like."

"No, I'll get up, thank you," and he undid the restraints.

Our lunch arrived – salmon salad and red wine – and we ate.

"How's your arse for sitting?"

Fucking sore, I thought to myself. "It's OK, thanks."

"Have you had enough for today? Shall we be just Charlotte and Lloyd for the rest of it? All this can be quite mind-blowing at the best of times."

"What, you mean I can say and do what I want?" I asked eagerly.

"Yes, Charlotte, you can," he laughed.

After lunch we went for a walk in the park. We sat and had coffee outside, and we talked about everything and anything, we held hands and cuddled as we walked. It was so nice to have quality time together, though in fact it had all been quality time ever since we started this, even the waxing. How many men did I know would come with me to get me waxed? Most wouldn't even go food shopping without a fight. I held his hand, thinking when will it end? Nothing this good would ever last.

We dined out, and walked back to Lloyd's in the dark. Lloyd poured us some wine and we sat on the sofa together, his arm around me.

"Enjoyed yourself today?"

"Yes, thank you. It's been fantastic."

"Even the waxing?"

Ah, the waxing. Well, still smarting a little, but not so bad.

"Yes, even the waxing, it's fine."

"OK, glad it's better in time for some play and I do like to play with something freshly waxed." He put his hand down on my knee and slowly worked his way up my thigh. I fidgeted and he got close. "I think I might give you a lesson in the art of control this evening, are you up for it?"

I could almost see his devil horns appear. "Can't we just do what we are doing? It's so nice sitting here."

"Yes, Charlotte, but afterwards when we play in the bedroom, I can't just go to sleep without a little teasing, can I, but you're right, it is nice sitting."

Oh, he was agreeing with me! How nice.

"Especially where I have my hand now – just where I want it to be."

Oh crap, no, he wasn't agreeing, he was twisting my words again and he thought he was going to sit fiddling with...with...ooh, that was nice, I could get used to this, he sure knew where a girl had her sweet spot...ooh...

"How have you learnt to do that?"

"By practice, asking and understanding."

God, it was amazing, just the right pressure, the right speed, everything, it was just...just *right*. I drank a little wine and let my head fall back, eyes closed, enjoying every movement. He kissed my neck and I began to tingle... oooh... I was in heaven...

"Charlotte, you realise I'm playing with you, don't you?"

Well, if it wasn't him down there, who the hell was it?

"This is a game I'm playing, a game about control, so snap out of it! I want you to control your body in every way. I don't want you to burst."

What? He was the one rubbing, for fuck's sake! How the hell would I do that? What sort of evil monster was he and what fucking planet was he from? Did he know nothing about girls? He controlled that button, especially when he was pressing.

"Wha..." I said like a teen talking to its parents, not quite grasping that he was even thinking such a thing. Me control him? You have the fucking button, moron! I shouted silently.

"Charlotte." He stopped rubbing. Noo...not good! Where had he gone? Come back! Oh shit, no!

"Charlotte, I want you to try and stay in control of everything this evening – your feelings and your frustrations and your satisfactions. Now it's quite possible for you to do this."

Too late, buster, I thought. My frustrations were well gone over the fucking wall along with my sanity. I couldn't believe he kept starting things then telling me I had to control it and when I didn't that was it – cut off without a penny, nothing for me until he was good and ready. Right, when he wanted to touch me again I was just going to turn away and ignore him, he would be but a figment of my imagination. Pure and simple.

"Charlotte, are you listening to me?"

No, not really but hey, if he wanted me to concentrate on my own satisfaction, so be it. That was what I would do. I slid my hand under my skirt and began rubbing.

"What are you doing?"

"Er, taking control of my satisfaction. You see, us girls, we were born with two hands as well and, unlike most men, women have always been able to use them both at once."

"I can't believe you just said that to me."

Yes! I had him on the ropes! That one had to be the quote of the century if you said it to a Dom. Hah. My eyes closed as I rubbed, enjoying the moment.

"Charlotte, are you sure you don't want to retract that last statement? I'll give you one chance to do so."

Retract such a perfectly formed sentence? Right time, right place, right moment? Yes, yes, it must be a Martini moment. Ooh... I was almost there... Retract? He was only saying that because he couldn't think of a reply. Probably jealous too.

"Charlotte," he whispered.

Yeah, he had nothing, but nothing, to say. Got you now, Mr Big Dom!

"Charlotte, do you want to come?"

"Oooh..." Yeah, he was just as much into me bursting as I wa... "What the fuck...?" I shrieked. Ice water hit me, and great lumps of ice. He had emptied the ice bucket over me.

"What the fuck was that for?"

"I told you. Every time you lose control I'll take it back from you."

"Is this in our rules?"

"We don't have any rules yet, but to be sure it will be in there when we get them."

"What, you're going to have 'I can throw a bucket of ice over Charlotte any time I want'?"

"Well, if it wasn't going to be there it sure will be now. Shall I phone Anthony and ask him to put it in especially for you? I can phone him straight away. Try me – see if you dare."

"You seem to be ranting a little. Are you losing control?"

"I haven't lost control and I am not ranting either," he said quietly. "I'm quite calm, unlike you."

How did he keep so calm all the time? Surely throwing a bucket of ice over me was losing control?

"I'm going to get changed." I began to stand up.

"Sit back down!" He grabbed the back of my skirt and tugged sharply. I fell back onto the sofa.

"Oh good, you decided to sit down again. Very wise."

I tried to tell him I thought he was being unfair. After all, I was soaked to the skin with ice-cold water. How the hell did he think I'd chosen that?

"Now, Charlotte, I love you to bits but you can sometimes be very—"

"Distracting?" I suggested.

"No, Charlotte."

"Enjoyable?"

"No."

"Cute?" Come on, it had got to be cute! I moved my nose to his and Eskimo-kissed.

No answer, no reaction.

"Look, how the hell did I ask for a bucket of icy water to be thrown over me? How the hell can that be my choice?"

"I asked you to take control and you didn't."

"Yes I did!" I protested. "I did take control! I started where you stopped! If that's not taking control, I don't know what is!"

"No you didn't. You took my control and carried on with it."

I knew he would find a way to twist it, I bloody fucking knew it!

"God, life must be so hard for you and Anthony. I bet you can twist the nuts off each other, it must be very painful."

"Charlotte..."

"It's the truth, isn't it?"

Lloyd began to laugh. "Charlotte, this is one of the things I really like about you. You make me laugh. Go and get dry. I'll be in the bedroom soon."

I went to the bedroom, sorted myself out and got into bed, a big, soft, comfy bed...

Chapter Thirteen

I woke in a half-daze, a little disoriented. Lloyd wasn't there and he hadn't been in bed either. It was light outside. Still feeling a little woozy from the wine last night, I got up, opened the bedroom door and stepped outside. Anthony was in the hall, going through to the lounge.

"Morning, Charlotte," he said, and I followed him into the lounge. Lloyd was there on the sofa pouring coffee. He raised his eyebrows at me.

"Er – morning, Charlotte. Coffee, maybe?"

"Um, yeah." I went toward the sofa.

Anthony said, "I like your new hair cut," and sniggered.

What new hair cut? Had Lloyd done something while I was asleep? I felt my head. My hair was still there.

"Still a little red, though," Lloyd said.

What the fuck! How dare he discuss my wax with Anthony!

"Don't tell Anthony about that! I don't think he really wants to know, do you, Lloyd?"

"We don't have to discuss anything, Charlotte, he's quite capable of seeing for himself." Lloyd nodded his head at me. I looked down. Oh shit, oh pants! I hadn't any clothes on! Oh fuck!

I turned and ran back to the bedroom. "I don't think

either of you are funny! I can hear you both fucking laughing at me, you bastards!" I slammed the door. Oh shit, how embarrassing, how bloody embarrassing! How the hell did that happen?

Moments later there was a knock on the door.

"Can I come in? It's me, Anthony."

"Hold on!" I called. I pulled on a T-shirt and skirt. "Come in," I said, still doing up the buttons.

Anthony entered and closed the door. "Charlotte, I am so sorry, sweet, but I couldn't resist. I wanted to tell you were naked but didn't quite know how, and before I knew it was out. I am sorry for embarrassing you like that."

"Oh that's OK. I'm just finding everything hard at the moment and Lloyd keeps playing games with me and my mind doesn't know if it's coming or going, just like you used to do with me."

"Oh yes, you used to get yourself into a right state back then."

"I feel quite emotional this morning and for some reason I don't know why."

"Have you told Lloyd?"

"No, I haven't seen him yet. Is it normal to feel emotional?"

"Yes, it can be, but you really must tell Lloyd."

"OK, I will, when I see him to talk to."

"It might be that he has been too hard on you or you're being too hard on yourself."

"No, he has this thing at the moment about me being in control of myself and he says it's so important that I control my feelings, thoughts and my body, but I don't see that, because he's the one in control. He's the Dom."

"No," Anthony said seriously, "he's right. You need to be in control as well. Look you trust me, don't you? Trust me on this – stick with it because it doesn't matter what you do next, vanilla or lifestyle, you'll be prepared for it. You'll be able to spot an arsehole a mile off, and if you don't and you end up with one then hopefully you'll be able to control him before he controls you and give yourself time to get out. I never want to see you like that again, neither do Lloyd or Nats." He took my hands and gave them a little shake. "Lloyd knows what he's doing. He also knows that you might choose vanilla and go on your way. That's the chance he's taking, but he's still taking it. Ask yourself why, Charlotte, why would he?" He stood up. "I have to go now. I'll see you this evening."

He left my bedroom, leaving me pondering his question. Why would Lloyd do that for me? I lay down on the bed, trying to find the answer, but I couldn't fathom it out. My brain seemed such a mess this morning. Suddenly I was aware of Lloyd sitting on the bed. He looked worried.

"Charlotte, are you OK?"

"No, I don't know what's wrong with me. I feel a bit emotional and I don't know why," My eyes filled.

"Hey, it's OK! Don't cry, we can sort this." He lay down and cuddled me. "Listen, this is normal. You're leaving a comfort zone and entering a zone you know nothing about. Your feelings and everything are all over the place. You don't know if you want this or if you want the safe option, and that's OK. Remember, it found you – you weren't looking for it." He held me tight and I felt safe again.

"Charlotte, a straight question. Will you give me a straight answer?"

"Yes."

He held me by the shoulders, looked me in the eye and said, "Do you still want to carry on with this or do you want to stop?"

I remembered the things that Anthony had said to me. My answer was clear: I was never going to be dog meat again.

"Yes, I do want this."

"OK." He held me tight again. "By the way, Anthony said you can have a clause saying I can throw a bucket of ice over you any time I want, if you really liked it that much."

"Lloyd!" I pushed him away, looked in his eyes and we both laughed.

"That's better! So what do you want to do today, then?" He got off the bed and put some clothes out for me to wear.

"Will you always get my clothes out for me every morning? I like it, not having to think what to wear."

"If you want me to, yes I will."

He went into the bathroom and ran a shower for me.

"Go get in the shower. I'll get you some fresh coffee."

After I'd taken a shower I felt much better. My mind felt a little clearer too. I joined Lloyd in the lounge.

"Better?" he asked.

"Yes, much, thank you."

He passed me a coffee. "So, we need to talk. You need to unscramble a few things, I think."

Oh, at last he'd noticed. "I just feel so emotional today. I felt strange when I woke up this morning and noticed you hadn't been to bed. It unnerved me, that's all. I didn't know what I'd done wrong. I felt very insecure, just like I used to with…"

"Is that it, Charlotte? I came to your bedroom, which by the way is usually my room, and you were sound asleep. I sat and watched you for hours. I even went and got some work and did some work in there. You looked so lovely, so beautiful, and to be honest it was the first time all day that you had shut up, and it was nice. About five o'clock

I went for a shower and to get ready for Anthony's breakfast meeting with Nats and myself. We always have one once a week. I was just about to bring your breakfast in to you as we'd finished when you arrived in the buff. You haven't done anything wrong and I haven't run off with some tart I found in the pub last night. I am not going to beat you because you came out here unclothed in front of Anthony, I find things like that very amusing indeed."

"So you've had no sleep."

"No, I've been watching you most of the night."

"Why didn't you get into bed with me?"

"Because I didn't want to disturb you."

"I wouldn't have minded."

"You've been on a roller-coaster ride ever since we told you everything. You needed the rest."

"What about your rest?"

"I'm fine, this is my life, remember? Look, I'm playing with your mind and you are playing with your mind. It's mentally exhausting. You'll find it'll play tricks on you and you'll lose reality."

I then remembered something the bastard would do when he didn't get his own way over something. He would keep me awake for days until I couldn't cope any more, and then he would make me believe it was all me. I had no control because he took it away from me and I let him.

"So I can't keep control if I'm exhausted?"

"No you can't. You have to make sure you have control all the time. The art is knowing when to switch the game, knowing how to switch the game, knowing your partner. I already know how to switch you on and off, how to piss you off, but quite honestly I can't do it as well as you can," he grinned.

"What do you mean, as well as I can?"

"You do such a good job of winding yourself up, Charlotte, and it's such good fun watching you do it, too," grinning again.

"So what winds you up? What gets you going?"

"Nothing. I have learnt how to stay in control. It's been hard but I've done it and you'll learn too."

"You throwing ice on me last night – that was loss of control, wasn't it?"

"No, I kept control all the time I was talking to you. I was calm."

"Didn't it piss you off because of what I said?"

"No, it didn't. If you had opened your eyes you would have seen me laughing. I thought it was so funny. No one would ever dare say that to me, other than you."

"Oh."

"What I did was change the game, as it wasn't one I wanted to play."

"That's not fair, just because you wanted it changed."

"Charlotte, we are learning about each other at the moment, finding out. If and when you decide to be my sub completely you'll know what I expect and what I don't and I'll know what you want and what you don't. You'll learn how to use your body and your mind to switch games if you don't like it. You'll learn how to play games with your mind and you'll also learn how to stay one step ahead and when to anticipate what's going to happen. I'll know within seconds if you aren't enjoying something we are doing. You'll very rarely have to use your safety word, because it will stop before you need it. This is a two-way thing."

"You, Lloyd, what is it you like?"

He looks at me. "You, I like, Charlotte."

"So why do you want to change me?"

"I don't. All I want to do is give you skills to help keep

you safe. It's up to you if and where you use them or not, but the greatest skill I can give you is control and the confidence to keep control."

"By giving me these things you are changing me."

"No, I don't think so. First, I'm not really giving you control, you already have it – sorry, wrong expression – I am teaching you how to use and keep control, helping you to have the confidence to use it so that it gives you the confidence to be who you want to be."

"OK, I think I understand that."

"Charlotte, you have grown over the past few days. You've already started to learn how to play some of the games, even if you don't realise it yet. You know when you are beat and when to give in and change the game. Mostly I'm in control but you are starting to take some back, with your body language and your smart-arse mouth. You're playing the games, you're getting more confident, you're telling me when you don't like something, even if you don't say."

"I don't think I do."

"OK, then, when you think you are going to do something you don't like or you've anticipated you are not going to like, your smart-arse mouth takes control. You know I won't tolerate it and you think a spanking will be better than whatever else will be on the menu."

"Oh."

"Yes, oh. So by you being smart-arse mouth I can assume you don't mind a spanking, in fact I think you quite like it. You didn't moan once yesterday about how many you were having, not once. You just took it."

Well, it was quite sensual the way he did it and it was nice, but I didn't want him to know I thought that.

"So I'm not hiding my thoughts?"

215

"No, you're not controlling them in the right way. You're not in control."

"Oh God, this is so complicated!"

"No, it's not. Lose control and you've lost the fight or argument."

"OK, I see that, but why do I have to be in control when I am with you, playing?"

"Because you might not always be with me and if you don't learn control you'll end up hurt again."

"So when's our next lesson then?"

Lloyd looked puzzled. "What?"

"When's our next lesson?"

"I know what you said. You just took me by surprise, that's all."

"I've surprised you? Why?"

"I thought you would need time to get your head around things."

"Look, my head has been screwed up for a long time. If I wait for it to unscrew I'll be in a Zimmer frame wondering what it could have been like. Anthony and I had a little chat too, you know, when he came into my bedroom as I'm sure he would have told you. He said a few things that have jumped into place as we've been talking. Now you're looking at a new me, I think, and I'll take the lead from you. I think I'm ready to put my trust in you."

"Charlotte, these are very brave words. Are you sure about this?"

"Yes, I am. Now or never. I'm willing to learn from you. My life has been a mess, but since Anthony found me my life has started to change and open up for me for the first time, and that's down to Nats, Anthony and you. I've enjoyed what I've done and the journey I'm on, so why should I get off now?"

"OK, but first a cuddle," He came over to me, put his arms around me and held me tight. "So are you going to do as I ask, when I ask, from now on?"

"No promises," I said.

"Good."

"What do you mean, good?" I moved to look at his face.

"Where would the fun be? When would I get to throw buckets of ice over you if you were always good?"

"Oh, so you want me naughty so you can be mean to me."

"No, not at all. I want you to be a little naughty so we can have fun together. Big difference."

I rested my head on his chest.

"Do you still feel emotional?" he asked.

"I don't think I was feeling emotional in that sense of the word. I think I was feeling scared."

"Scared of what? Not me, I hope!" Lloyd sounded alarmed.

"No, not you. Scared of you leaving me behind, losing me."

"I don't think you have to worry about that. Anthony said he hasn't seen you like this for years."

"What, naked?"

"No, he said you seem increasingly like the Charlotte he used to know."

"Oh, had I changed that much then?"

"In Anthony's eyes, yes, you had, but he said this morning it was nice to see you nearly back to your old self." He held me tight. "Just out of interest, has Anthony seen you naked before?"

"Oh, loads of times! I was more embarrassed because you were here than I was of Anthony."

"What, you feel embarrassed when you're naked in front of me?"

"No…well, yes…oh here we go."

"Charlotte, I know what you mean. Calm down don't lose control now. You've done very well this morning and I feel like it's the first time you've spoken to me about your true feelings."

"Thank God for that. I thought you were going to analyse me again."

"No, I've never done that, or I try not to." He moved to the edge of the sofa. "Ready for some fun and games? Ready to see how brave you really are?"

"Yes," I said.

"Come on then, downstairs with you!" With that he leapt off the sofa, pulling me with him.

When we were downstairs he took me into the first room, the room with all the things behind the concealed panel. Whips and stuff.

"What are we doing in here? Aren't we going to the fire and ice room?"

"No, punishment room for you today. I've been far to soft on you." He leaned closer and said quietly, "And beside which you asked me a question yesterday so I am going to show you."

"Oh! Do I really want you to show me? What was the question I asked you?"

"Come, I want you to stand here."

He led me into the middle of the room. He walked round me and then stopped in front of me. He kissed me and while kissing he pushed one of his legs between mine, making me part them. It was nice. He held my hair at the nape and stopped kissing me.

"Now," he said, "I want you to do exactly as I say,

nothing more and nothing less. This room is not the room that you want to misbehave in, do you understand?"

"Yes, I understand."

He planted little kisses on my neck. "Good. Right, I want you to bend over and hold your ankles tight. I don't want you to move, talk, or look round. Do you understand?"

"Yes."

"Do you remember what your safe word is?"

"Yes, 'Time out'. We changed it."

"Right, good." He pulled my head down toward my knees. "Hold your ankles." I held them tight. He walked away to the panel and opened it. He went inside and came straight back out. Then he came up behind me and lifted my skirt.

"Good, I see you remembered not to put panties on." He rubbed my arse with his hand. Then I felt something else touch me. I moved forward slightly.

"Please keep still. This is a paddle. Feel it, feel how soft it is." He smoothed it softly over my arse, ran it down the back of my legs, and then back to my arse. He took hold of my hair and pulled my head up.

"How brave do you feel, Charlotte?" he whispered. He ran the paddle down to the inside of my thigh. It felt lovely, so sensual, nothing like I thought it would be. I loved the feel of the soft leather on my skin. He raised it up between my legs and it touched my button. Oh God, it was so sensitive at the moment! It must be because I had a wax yesterday. I moaned softly, lost in the moment.

"Charlotte, I asked you a question. Can you answer please?" He brought it back to my arse. Oh this wasn't a punishment. This was pleasure! Don't stop, I begged him silently, my arse moving slightly in time with the paddle.

"Charlotte, I wonder if you would move to the rhythm of the paddle if it was spanking you?"

"Mmm," I moaned.

"Is that a yes? Shall I find out, then?"

"Oh Lloyd, this is just so nice, I'm lost in the moment." Just carry on, I thought blissfully, do what you do best and this is one of them…

Swipe.

"Fuck! Shit! What the fuck was that for? Shit, that fucking hurt!"

Swipe.

"What the fuck…" I couldn't move. He had hold of me in such a way that I couldn't let go of my ankles. Fuck, that hurt.

"Shit, Lloyd, please! That hurt!"

"Oh, you are here. I thought you had left. I have been talking to you, waiting for your answer, and nothing from you."

"It was so nice."

"So it might have been, but you are supposed to be keeping control."

"I was keeping control of my feelings."

"No, Charlotte, you should have answered me. You were lost in the moment again."

Oh come on, who are you? Do you never get lost in the moment, for fuck's sake? I can't believe that, and how would you like it if I bit you or something just as you were lost in the moment, I thought.

"Charlotte, can I have your attention, please?"

"Yes, Lloyd. What now?"

"Pardon me?"

"Oh, I mean yes."

"Charlotte, it's quite simple. Answer me correctly when I speak to you."

"Yes, Lloyd."

220

"Thank you."

He started rubbing the paddle on my arse, my tingling arse. Mmm, it felt so nice even though he'd just whacked it.

"Charlotte, it seems to me you're feeling brave, by the way you got lost in the moment there."

"No. Not brave. You're very good at what you do."

"Why, thank you, Charlotte, that's nice of you, but we're not talking about my skills at the moment, we're talking about yours."

"Oh, OK."

"You're not trying to distract me, are you?"

"Me, Lloyd? Never!" Distract him? He was the one who distracted me then slapped or whacked my arse for being distracted.

"Do I detect a little sarcasm in your voice?"

Oh, bloody hell, this was heading for a whack. No matter what I say, I thought, I am going to be wrong. What the fuck. In for a penny and I'll end up with a pound of fucking bananas.

"Oh Lloyd, just fucking whack me! You know you want to, for fuck's sake!"

"Smart-arse mouth, Charlotte."

Swipe.

"Fucking Jesus! I said whack me, not take my fucking arse into the next fucking room without me! What the fuck!"

Swipe.

OK, OK! Time out! Now! Time fucking out! That fucking hurt! Nope, not playing this fucking game...what were the fucking words? Yes, I had it now.

"Time out! Time fucking out! Fucking stop! That was just too much."

He dropped the paddle, lifted me up into his arms and cuddled me closely into him, rubbing my arse as he did so.

"Not so brave after all, Charlotte, and a little confused over your safe word?" he said.

Not so brave! I let him do it twice, what the fuck did he mean, not so fucking brave? My arse felt like someone had hit it with a cricket bat, for Christ's sake. Hey, but the cuddling was nice, it was very nice. I would have to remember 'Time out'. Hah, I thought, if I say 'Time out' he'll cuddle me! That will get him.

"Are you OK?"

"Yes, I am. I think so. Rub a little lower, would you."

"Why did you time out?"

"Because I didn't think I could take any more, that's why."

"So you reached a limit?"

"No, it fucking hurt!"

He laughed. What was so fucking funny? Was he laughing because I was hurt?

"Yet again you lost control. You lost control of the game, but your arse is fine, maybe a little red. Come, kneel here beside me, and let's talk."

Kneel beside him? Who the fuck did he think I was, some sort of slave? He had already played that game and I did what he wanted then. Now I wanted a nice soft sofa to sit on. Kneel beside him? No fucking way.

"I want to sit on the sofa," I announced firmly.

"I think you'll find kneeling—"

Before he could say another word I said even more firmly, "I'll sit next to you. We don't have rules yet, you can't make me fucking kneel."

"As you wish."

I did wish. Hold on, though – there was no smart-arse mouth comment from him. What was that about? As I wish, indeed.

He held my hand and led me to the sofa. He sat down and I…and I…oh for God's sake, that is…shit, that bloody smarts! I twisted and turned, trying to find a spot on my arse that wasn't tender but it was impossible. He was the fucking Dom from hell; he bloody knew that sitting would be impossible. He was grinning at me as I tried to sit down. Eventually I gave up, clenching my teeth and mumbling under my breath, "It's all right for you, you didn't even hurt your fucking hand." I knelt on the floor with my arse positioned in such a way that it did not touch anything.

"Oh, so you decided to kneel, then?" He was still grinning. Decided? No, I didn't decide to do anything. I couldn't fucking sit down and well he knew it, or I would be on that fucking sofa. Oh, Mr I-Know-Everything-fucking-Dom, don't think I haven't noticed that you are not explaining these fucking games right, because I have.

"Although it's nice to see the sub kneeling before you. Sometimes they kneel for a very different reason, as you have just found out."

"Why does it hurt more than a spank from your hand?"

"Because the leather bites a little, but to tell you the truth, you look fine for someone that has just used the safe word, not as bad as I thought, and I hardly battered your arse at all."

Hardly battered it? If I was a piece of cod I would be in the fryer now, and it wouldn't be hurting like this. What the hell did he mean? He had hardly battered it?

"You did, it felt like you knocked it into next week."

"Because you lost control."

There was a knock on the door.

"Listen, I've invited someone over to talk with you. In this room she is sub and she loves spanking, are you OK with that?"

"Oh great! You've just battered my arse, then you tell me I am meeting someone."

"When we Doms are training or trying out things we usually borrow each other's subs for practice and demos," Lloyd said as he went to the door.

Well, I wouldn't be a sub, for fuck's sake, it was hard enough just being a pretend sub.

"Hi, Sophie, how's you?" Lloyd gave her a peck on the cheek as she entered.

Again a very beautiful woman, a redhead with her hair straight. A low-cut top that clung to all the right bits. Hey, too low! Where did Lloyd think he was looking? Get some clothes on, lady! Hello, over here! What's wrong with my puppies then? They came over to the sofa, Lloyd with his arm around her waist, guiding her. Er, hello? Another sub in the room and he was ignoring me. Oh, finally he looked at me; nice of him to remember I was here. Like, after all it was *my* arse, not hers, he had just fucking battered. How come she got the soft treatment?

"Sophie, this is Charlotte."

"Hi, Charlotte, nice to meet you!"

Yes, and it would be nice to meet her if my arse didn't fucking hurt so much.

"Hi." I bared my teeth at her.

Lloyd waved a hand toward the sofa for her to sit down, and she sat just in front of me. Oh, great! Now I was kneeling down at the feet of another sub. Would that be in the rules? What the fuck! I needed to get out of here, it just wasn't right. I didn't mind when I was just with Lloyd, but another sub, for Christ's sake! Why wasn't she on the fucking floor?

"Charlotte is finding it hard to keep in control," Lloyd said to Sophie. She looked at me.

"Oh I see. Paddle?" she asked, turning to Lloyd.

"Yes."

Oh, talking over me yet again! Why couldn't they include me in their coded conversations?

"She'll get used to it, it's hard, Lloyd, you know?"

Hey! I'm here! Here I am!

"So, what do you want me to do, Lloyd? Want me to demonstrate or just talk?"

Oh for fuck's sake! Lloyd glanced in my direction and then looked back at Sophie.

"I hadn't really decided. What do you think?"

OK... OK. He knew I didn't like people talking over me. He was doing it on purpose just to wind me up, which of course he was. Give a girl a break. Come on! I wanted TLC; my arse was smarting... I started picking at my fingernails as a sign of boredom. Lloyd turned to me as they clicked and flicked.

"Sorry, Charlotte, do you want to say something?"

Oh, he'd noticed I was here! Then yes, I would want to say something if I could fucking think of something to fucking say.

"No, no, I'm fine here, don't worry about me, you carry on." Oh fuck, that wasn't quite right, was it? I saw him raise his eyebrows, and a slight snigger came from Sophie.

"Can you try to not flick your nails then, please?" Turning back to Sophie, he said, "So what do you think, then?"

"Maybe a demo to break the ice?"

"Want a warm-up first?"

Warm-up...warm-up...what the hell were they going to do and why hadn't Lloyd asked me if I was warm enough?

"No, just go straight to it. Maybe a few little ones, then whack away!" she laughed. "Charlotte, why don't you kneel on the sofa, and lean on the back. I'll stand the other side and I can talk to you at the same time."

Oh, so at last she acknowledged I was there! She put her hand out to help me off the floor then she and Lloyd went round to the other side of the sofa. Sophie bent over with her head facing me and Lloyd picked up the paddle. Going around behind her, he started rubbing her arse. Hold on, hold on, I thought, he hadn't raised her skirt and had she got panties on? I bet she had, and probably half a tissue factory down them for padding. That wasn't right, was it?

"Ready, Sophie?" He'd never asked me if I was ready! Why the fuck did she get the special treatment?

Sophie raised her head and winked at me. "Game on!"

Swipe.

Oh shit, oh fuck! My bottom clenched with referred pain. How the fuck did that happen? He whacked her, and I felt the pain! Hold on...hold on! She hadn't even moved! She was smiling at me! She gave her little bottom a wiggle and...

Swipe.

My eyes watered. And still nothing. Sophie repositioned her hands on her ankles.

"Usual word, Sophie." Usual word? What did he mean? Did he usually paddle her arse? What the fuck – I knew nothing about his life.

"Game on!" Again she winked.

He couldn't be whacking her as hard as he whacked me. That must be how they were doing it.

Swipe.

Oh fuck, where did he get that? Shit, lady, I would be on my knees by now. It had to be what I thought – she had padding under her skirt.

Swipe.

OK, enough is enough. "How the fuck do you take that and not fucking move?" I asked.

"Charlotte, please!" Lloyd snapped at me.

Sophie laughed. "Practice, Charlotte."

Swipe.

"No, no, no, no one can take that, for fuck's sake, no one!" I got off the sofa and walked round to where Lloyd was standing.

"Smart-arse mouth, Charlotte. Take that as a warning."

"You giving warnings now, Lloyd? You turning soft?"

Swipe.

"That was for your cheek." They both laughed.

"You'll have to do better than that, Lloyd, if you want to make an impact."

I looked at her arse. What the fuck, her skirt was so short you could see everything, practically what she'd eaten for breakfast. I glared at Lloyd.

"Problem, Charlotte?" He waved the paddle in the air.

"Er, no. No problem."

"Good."

I looked back at Sophie. Nope, no padding, only a red arse. She looked at me through her legs.

"Charlotte, this is fun. I love it and, trust me before he ever gets to hurting me I'll stop him. As long as I stay focused, I'm in control as well as him."

I bent right down so I could see her face.

"You weren't here when he paddled the crap out of my arse."

Swipe.

Oh shit! Oh fuck, I felt that one! He just swiped my fucking arse again. Fucking hell that hurt! I crumbled onto my knees.

"Smart-arse mouth, Charlotte."

I looked up at him as I rubbed my arse to take the sting out of it. "That was below the fucking belt!"

"What? Feeling brave now, Charlotte, are we?" he waved the paddle casually.

Sophie laughed. "That's the Lloyd I know!"

What the fuck did she mean by that, the Lloyd she knows? Leave off, Lady, I thought, I'm here now.

"Lloyd, this was supposed to be a demo for me to see how it's done, not for you to smash the shit out of my arse!"

"You changed the game, Charlotte, you'll learn how it's done," Sophie said as she stood up. She held out her hand to help me up.

"Look, if you change a game you have to prepare yourself for what's coming, Lloyd told you he wasn't going to tolerate a smart-arse mouth and the very next words out of your mouth were smart-arse. And with such a tempting arse sticking up in the air, what did you expect? Of course he's going to smack it, to a Dom it's an invitation."

"Couldn't have put it better myself," Lloyd said.

"No one hurts me, Charlotte," Sophie went on, "and no one does anything I don't like or enjoy. I keep control always and in return I do what the Dom wants me to do."

"But the pain?"

"I very rarely have pain now I've learnt to control it. I get more pleasure out of what I do and the pain just doesn't register because I'm having a good time."

"It fucking hurts me."

"Charlotte, *please.*"

"Lloyd, Charlotte is talking with me for a minute. Leave her be, go get a bullwhip, we'll play with that next."

A bullwhip? That would rip the skin off her back, surely.

"Now I've changed the game with Lloyd I must expect

him to pick up the pace, or he won't be happy with me at all."

Lloyd returned with a bullwhip. God he looked sexy! Almost Indiana Jones. I wiggled my hips. Sophie saw me wiggle.

"Tut tut, Charlotte, you are changing the game. I like that signal!"

"Right," said Lloyd, "if you two have finished I need to explain to the airhead sub. If she can keep herself under control for five minutes. Here, Charlotte, sit. You don't move, you don't talk, you do nothing or you'll get hurt even worse. Do you understand? I am not playing."

"Yes." I fidgeted on the sofa. My bottom still smarting.

"Be still, Charlotte, or you'll have something to fidget about." Lloyd's mood had changed. He looked very serious. He went over to the door, glancing back to make sure I was still sitting.

Why did he think I couldn't do this? All right, I would show him. You watch all you like, perfect Dom, I thought. He locked the door and nodded to Sophie to stand facing the window on the other side of the room. God, she isn't even going to face him! I wouldn't stand with my back to anyone with a fucking bullwhip in their fucking hand! How fucking stupid is that, for fuck's sake?

"You know what's going to happen here, don't you Sophie?"

"Yup, I think so, Lloyd." She took a deep breath.

Lloyd released the whip and gave it a few flicks.

"Sophie, move your hair forward over your shoulders, please."

She put her hand up and brought her hair to the front.

"Are you ready, and sure about this?" Lloyd flicked the whip again.

"Game on!" She lowered her arms by her side and stood stock-still.

A few hard flicks and… *Crack*!

The sound pierced through me.

"Oh fuck! What the fuck have you done to her?" I got up and rushed over to Sophie.

"Charlotte, what the hell are you doing?" Lloyd shouted at me.

"I don't care! What the fuck, I am not going to sit still and let you bullwhip her! That's the fucking pits, Lloyd!"

Sophie turned round, laughing.

"Charlotte, I'm fine! He hasn't made contact – look!" She turned and showed me her back. Not a mark. Nothing. "Charlotte, this is a test of ultimate trust and control. Come, let me explain."

My mouth had dropped to Australia. I felt numb. How could they play such a cruel trick on me, for fuck's sake? Sophie sat me on the sofa, I was just glaring into space. I didn't even register that my arse was still on fire.

"Lloyd, some coffee, I think."

"On its way."

Sophie took my hand. "Ultimate trust and control on both sides, that's what that was, Charlotte. I trusted Lloyd not to hit me. I had to control my body so I didn't move, not one little bit. The slightest movement could result in me getting hurt. Lloyd trusts me to say if I don't feel confident. He trusts me not to move, he doesn't want to hurt me at all, and he has to have the control to gauge the whip. There are only two people I trust to do this with. Lloyd is one and my Dom is the other."

"So why do it?" I asked.

"It's like an adrenaline rush, like bungee jumping. Why do they do that?"

"Oh." I was still staring into space.

Lloyd sat down opposite me after bringing the coffee to the table.

"Charlotte, you all right?" he asked, his eyes softening.

"How the hell can I be all right after that?"

I looked at him and then at Sophie. Did they think it was funny, what they had just done to me? My heart was in my mouth, fucking racing faster than Red Rum. I really didn't know what to think. Sophie handed me my coffee. I stared at her and then at him.

"Why the fuck didn't you explain to me first what the fuck you were going to do?"

"Charlotte, I know you are in shock, but please try to control yourself," Lloyd said.

"Charlotte, Hon, we had a very good idea what *you* were going to do," said Sophie. "Lloyd gave you very firm instructions. He said to me 'You know what's going to happen', talking about you, not about what we were doing. He locked the door so that no one would come in and distract him. The instructions he gave you were for safety, so that you wouldn't distract Lloyd or me. We had built you into the equation, so everything was safe. You were far enough away not to get in the way before the whip had stopped. The situation was always under control, even with a loose cannon, namely you, Charlotte."

Lloyd had his serious look again. "Charlotte, when I give you instructions you must follow them to the letter. I am going to give you instructions now, so listen. Concentrate. Right, if ever you are in this room without me and someone has a bullwhip, make sure you are always a good distance away from them. The whips here are just under a room's length. Always keep your eye on the end of the whip so you know what's going to happen with it. Never turn your back on anyone holding a whip unless it's me." He smiled briefly. "If at any time you feel in danger, get out when you can. Never talk and never move when someone is using a whip. Not everyone is as experienced as Sophie and me, do you understand?"

Did he really think I would sit here again watching someone with a whip? When it appeared I would be out of that fucking door before they could lock me in.

"Yes, I understand," I said.

"Good. Always do as I or any other Dom tells you. Here endeth the lesson."

What? Was he going to fucking hire me out now? Any other Dom? No way. Never.

"Charlotte, you will be OK with this lifestyle, just give it time, slowly. You have a good teacher – trust him. Keep in control, and you'll be surprised just what you can do, and what you can get out of it. Remember, it's a game. Stay one step ahead of the Dom!" she grinned.

"Charlotte, do you have any questions?" Lloyd asked.

"No, I don't think so. I am still trying to get my head around what I have just witnessed."

Sophie put her coffee cup back on the table. "Lloyd I've got to go. Nice to have met you, Charlotte, and hopefully I'll see you around if we haven't scared you too much."

"Yes, likewise, Sophie" I said.

"I'll see you to the door, Sophie." Lloyd went to open the door. "Thanks for today."

"That's OK, any time. She's lovely, she'll be fine and she'll give you a run for your money! Feisty, isn't she?"

"She is." He kissed Sophie's cheek and shut the door. I heard the lock click back on. No, that wasn't right. If he thought he was going to get out that whip thing he had another think coming... I spun round on the sofa and watched him as he came over. Resting his arms on the back of the sofa he leaned down and planted a kiss on my forehead.

"How are you feeling, Charlotte, my little smart-arse mouth?" Not knowing what he had in mind, but knowing he has something, I just squinted up at him, trying to read his thoughts.

"Ah, feeling brave are we?"

Oh no, not me, I am not a brave person. He'd obviously gone blind. I wasn't Sophie sitting here. I shook my head, my mouth widening slightly in fear of him bringing out the whip.

"Is that a no? You were feeling brave when you disobeyed me and used your smart-arse mouth."

The thought of him getting that whip out and cracking it with me in the room was just doing my fucking head in, and if he wasn't going to get it out why would he lock the door? I tried to speak but my mouth seemed to be empty. Fuck, where had all my words gone? He dropped his head onto his hands as he watched me, amused. He was enjoying my agony! What the fuck? I tried to speak again. A squeak. Where did that come from? Hello, brain. Please engage with my mouth! I want to say no, fuck off. Please help me, brain.

Lloyd raised his eyebrows at my squeak. "Oh, Charlotte, what was that? Surely you can do better than that? You did earlier, what's changed?"

What's changed? What's changed? He needed to ask that whip thing. That was what had fucking changed! I put my hands over my face to try to recompose myself. Maybe if I didn't look at him I could pretend he wasn't there. I covered my eyes. He wasn't there.

"Charlotte, if you want to be blindfolded it can be arranged, you know."

What? Blindfold me in here with you and that...that...

I dropped my hands and looked at him again. He was loving all this. Shit, come on, brain. Don't let me down now.

"May I assume that a blindfold isn't needed?" Yes… no…yes…oh, was it yes or no to that question? I don't want a fucking blindfold, thank you, I said silently. Now stop playing with my mind. I know…my mouth opened. My mouth was working, it was just words that didn't work. That was it! Kiss him! Kiss him long and hard. There was his mouth in line with mine. All I had to do was move forward to reach it. I looked at his mouth. As I did so he licked his lips. Oh shit, he knew what I was thinking! How the fuck could he know that? His lips looked so tempting when he did that. Hold on…what was it Sophie said? 'Stay one step ahead of the Dom'. Right. So he was expecting me to kiss him. Well, I wasn't going to – ha, Dommy boy, got you there haven't I? I looked back into his eyes. Keep eye contact, he'd told me. Match point to me, I thought.

"Still not feeling brave, Charlotte?"

No, I wasn't. I was squirming from the inside out. I raised my hands to my head and peeked through my fingers at his face.

"Oh yes, my smart-arse little Charlotte, engage brain with mouth might save you a raw arse before bedtime."

I was still glaring at him through my fingers, waiting for him to move, but nothing. He was still the same. I lowered my hands, shrugged my shoulders and gave him a cheeky, nervous grin. Stay one step ahead, that was all I had to do. He leaned forward and looked deep into my eyes. Ah, he was coming for a kiss…

"Boo!" My head jerked back. No kiss? Where was my fucking kiss?

"Oh, you are still in there, my empty, airhead, smart-arse mouth."

Right, that was it. Enough with the insults. Who the fuck did he think he was talking to?

"What game are we playing, Charlotte?"

Well if I could talk, it would be to say 'fuck your games'.

"I don't want to play." Yes, yes, I got that out all right. If I didn't want to play he would surely stop this.

"I thought that this game was one of yours. For someone who doesn't want to play, you seem to be playing very well."

What? I hadn't done anything or even said very much. Why did he think I was playing?

"You're the one who thought you were playing. You locked the door. You thought you were going to play with that whip thing. Well, you're not."

"I never play with whip things. It is an art and not to be used as play."

"Why lock the door then? You've never locked a door before except after waxing when you threatened to spank me there. Never once here have you locked a fucking door."

"Smart-arse mouth."

"No, no, I didn't!" Shit, I did. "It's you...you make me do it. You wind me up."

"Why do I make you do it? I'm trying to make you stop saying it, to keep in control of all situations. To use your words, engage brain, Charlotte. Suggestion is just as powerful as action sometimes, and that's the game I've been playing. All I did was lock the door and ask you how you were feeling and if you were feeling brave. Your brain has done the rest and it has been very amusing and entertaining watching you trying to work out what I'm doing or what I might do, and how you might get out of it. And trying to be one step ahead of me." He was laughing. Oh shit was I that obvious? I lowered my head.

"Eye contact!" he snapped. "The room is locked and

there is a whip in here. Don't you ever take your eye off the ball, Charlotte, when you are in such a vulnerable position. Not in this lifestyle or a vanilla one."

"Shit, Lloyd, I'm trying, don't shout at me!" I snapped back.

"No, Charlotte, I mean it. If you are in a vulnerable situation never lose eye contact, and right here, right now, you are vulnerable even with me."

"Why? You aren't going to hurt me, are you?"

"How do you know? I might pick something up that you haven't seen. I might use it and you walk straight in front of it."

"Lloyd, I think I know you well enough to know you would never do anything without telling me that I would be in danger."

"Oh, so you are taking something in at long last! But that isn't the point. When you're in a room alone with anyone, vanilla or lifestyle, don't lose eye contact with them. Look them in the eye whenever you can."

"Lloyd, when Sophie stood at the window she didn't have eye contact with you."

"No, that's different. We both know what we're doing, and we've spent years building up trust for such games. As yet, you don't have that sort of trust or control, but by God you'll get it and I don't care how many smart-arse mouth tantrums you throw and I don't care how shitty you think I am. At the end of the day your safety is all I care about, whatever you choose."

He stood up; his eyes fixed on mine, took his phone out of his pocket and speed-dialed a number.

"Hi, Anthony... Yes, fine thank you. I need you to do me a contract... Usual thing, but with the difference that Charlotte is going to sleep, eat and breathe me for six months. She isn't to do anything unless I say, when I say, and how I say...yes, she will...and I won't...if she ends up hating me so be it."

Fuck, he was pissed! I'd never heard him talk like that. What should I do? Lloyd hung up the phone, came back and stood over me.

"Six months, Charlotte. You have six months to sort your head out, six months of me playing with your mind, because your mind is so easily manipulated, and that's what your ex used against you and others will too, if you don't start sorting it out. I thought it was amusing watching you squirm just now. Your paranoia took control of you to the degree that you physically couldn't speak, leaving you in such a vulnerable state your fear was oozing from every pore of your body. Kissing someone when you are like that is suicide in my eyes. It's ultimate submission. But the sheer fact that you didn't kiss me was a relief. It meant there was something in there that was working, because, trust me, ultimate submission is very dangerous in any lifestyle and I really don't do that. Right, any questions?"

"I need time to process what you have just said."

"No you don't. I ask a question, you answer. It's a yes, Lloyd or a no, Lloyd, quite simple really."

"By the very nature of what you said to Anthony, you want me to totally submit to you? That's what you've asked him to put in your contract?"

"No, not quite. What I asked for was that you live, sleep, eat and breathe me. In other words, I am going to be in your face. There are going to be consequences to your actions. You won't always be warned, but you can still be you. You'll no longer be a pathetic wreck when you don't know what to do. You'll learn what to do and in six months' time you'll be a strong, controlled woman, someone who knows what she wants. At the end of six months you can choose what you want, so what is it to be?"

"Lloyd why are you being like this, laying down the law?"

"Because I never want to see you black or blue ever again. Or dead." He shuddered.

"This all seems so harsh."

"Not as harsh as your face black or blue, or worse." He had a look of pity in his eyes.

"Yes, Lloyd."

"Is that a yes to the contract?"

"Yes, Lloyd."

He walked to the door and opened it. "Upstairs, please."

Chapter Fourteen

We went upstairs in complete silence. When we were in the suite he said, "Bedroom now, and stay there. Anthony is on his way and I want to talk with him first."

"Yes, Lloyd" I said meekly, and went to the bedroom. Oh shit, he was really pissed with me, but I guessed he was right. I lay on the bed trying to digest all he had said, asking myself how I had found myself here. What had I done but try and play his games? That had been my choice – up until now, that was, but if I didn't want to change why had I tried to play his games? Most of them I had enjoyed. Maybe I'd wanted to change and not even known it, maybe I was looking that morning that Anthony bumped into me. I hadn't protested in any of this. I could have done many times but I hadn't. I hadn't got out. I heard Anthony come in. Oh shit, I hadn't closed the door. I got up to shut it. I could hear them talking.

"Bit harsh, Lloyd? I haven't ever known you have anything other than standard and you said that you weren't bothered until she had made up her mind," Anthony said.

"I know, but she'll end up either beaten to a pulp or dead. You know what I had planned for today. All the things went as you would expect, but afterwards she was a mess. She couldn't even talk, or move. She even thought about kissing me at one stage – ultimate submission when she was panicking. The thing I worry about is that she has a taste for this now and if she leaves she might look elsewhere and end up out of her depth big time."

"That bad? Jeez, I didn't realise."

"No, I didn't either, but I have a responsibility to her. I can't just let this go. Anthony."

"I can understand that, but you know you might lose her altogether."

"Don't you think I know that? I love her too much to let her go back out there in that state, panicking and so subservient, unable to handle situations. I fell in love with her from the first time I met her when we were at uni. It's only turns of events that have stopped me from doing anything about it. I now have the chance to have her, but I'd rather she be safe than with me."

"That's deep, Lloyd. Are you sure?"

"Never been more sure of anything in my life."

I stood, stunned. Then I carefully closed the door. I didn't want them to know I'd heard anything. I got back on the bed and lay down. I never realised, I never knew. Why hadn't I seen it? Shit.

A while later there was a knock on the door and Anthony peered round it.

"Can I come in, Charlotte?"

"Of course."

He came in and sat down on the bed. "Quite an eventful day, Charlotte."

"I've pissed Lloyd off big time."

Anthony laughed. "No you haven't, not at all."

"Oh, you haven't seen him – heard him."

"Yes I have. I've been talking with him outside. He's explained everything to me about what has happened. You haven't pissed him off. He's worried, so worried about you, you have no idea. Tell me what was going through your head when he put the bolt back on the door after Sophie left?"

"Oh Anthony, it was horrible! I thought he was going to use that whip on me. Then he asked me if I was feeling brave, which just accentuated the fear I had in my head. I can understand what happened to me now, but at the time I was terrified, absolutely terrified. I couldn't talk, I couldn't do anything."

"Did he explain the rules about the whip to you?"

"Yes, he did."

"So if you'd stopped and thought for a minute, you would have known exactly what to do. So why didn't you do it?"

"I just told you. I was petrified of what was going to happen."

"So instead of you taking control, you panicked and lost control."

"Yes, I suppose so." Then the penny dropped. "So you're saying what I should have done was get up and keep eye contact with him, and keep a safe distance."

"Yes, Charlotte, that's exactly what you should have done. Always look for an advantage. Don't give others the opportunity to take advantage of you. You can make other people do what you want them to do."

"Crap, that's what the game was, and I missed it!"

"Lloyd is right in what he says. You know that, don't you?"

"I can see it clearer now, yes."

"About things you have done with Lloyd – are you comfortable with him and what you're doing with him?"

"Oh yes, I've had loads of fun. In fact, I'm growing fonder and fonder of the lifestyle."

"OK, right. Wait here, I need to talk to Lloyd again. You sure you're OK?"

"Yes, I'm fine."

Anthony went out and I lay back down on the bed. Why hadn't I seen that before? Shit, it was so fucking obvious! Take control, use the situation to my own advantage, but I'd let others in to take advantage of me. It was there all the time, the fucking answer was there all the time, that was why I always ended up with total arseholes – because I gave them the advantage. Now the question I had to ask myself was whether I was brave enough to change into who and what I wanted to be, was I brave enough to take this journey? To hell with it – it was *my* choice, not Lloyd's.

I got up and put my hand on the door handle. A shiver ran through me. Come on, girl, I said to myself, you can do this. Head up, look him in the eye, and take control. This is your choice, not his.

I opened the door and marched into the room. Oh fuck, what had I done? Brave – I was fucking brave; I would show them how brave I was. Eye contact. There, over on the couch, there he was. Right, I mustn't fall down now. I was there. Keep the eye contact. No whips, only my tongue.

"Charlotte, do you want something?" Lloyd asked.

Oh yes, I want something all right, just you wait, I thought. Keep eye contact. I walked toward him, telling myself to stay brave. Lloyd stood up. Anthony remained seated. Keeping an eye on everything that might be helpful to me, I went up to him, looking him in the eyes. About three feet away I stopped.

"Anthony, you have something for me to sign, I believe?" I mustn't look at him. I had to keep focused.

"Yes, Charlotte, I have."

Don't look round, Girl. Stay where you are. I mustn't lose it now. "May I have it please?"

242

"Yes it's there on the table."

Don't look. Stay where you are. "Anthony, I thought you were a gentleman."

"I am, Charlotte."

"Would a gentleman not pass it to me?" Good one! Yes, match point to me, I thought. Anthony moved off the sofa.

"Charlotte, what game are you playing?" Lloyd asked, looking straight at me.

Don't look away. Don't get distracted. "This game, Lloyd, don't you know it?"

Anthony handed over the contract.

"What's in this contract? Anthony?"

"Read it," Anthony replied.

Lloyd was looking puzzled, I thought. Yes! I had him on the ropes now, didn't I?

"Let's put it another way, then. Is there anything in this contract that you think I should be aware of?"

"No, Charlotte, but as your friend I would advise that you read anything before signing it."

"Charlotte—" put in Lloyd.

I swiftly cut him off. "Yes Lloyd, what can I do for you?"

"Impressive, Charlotte, very impressive," Lloyd said.

I had to keep looking. I mustn't lose it. He folded his arms, and I took one step back, suddenly aware that if he put them down again I wouldn't see them without looking down and I mustn't do that. Eye contact all the time.

"Now, Anthony, the next question is do I trust you as his friend or mine?"

No reaction from Lloyd. Good, keep eye contact.

"Charlotte, what a question to ask me!"

"Yes, Charlotte, what a question. And even if he says he's your friend, can you really trust him, ultimately trust him to be telling you the truth, because if you trust him that much you would be very comfortable for him to use that bullwhip in his hand."

I mustn't look. I knew Anthony was sitting down, and besides, Lloyd was trying to unsettle me. I had to keep eye contact. Lloyd was the threat.

"Very good, Lloyd, but I looked around the room before I came in. Anthony, aren't you going to answer me?"

"Charlotte, I don't know where you're going with this."

"Please answer me, Anthony." hurry Anthony please! Let me get this over and done with

"Agitated, Charlotte? Was that a little whimper I heard?"

"No, Lloyd, not at all." and lets face it Lloyd even if I was I wouldn't tell you, would I?

Anthony said, "Charlotte, I am your friend and Lloyd's. I'll always see you both all right, whatever the circumstances. You know that anyway. You are both like brother and sister to me."

"Thank you," I said. I mustn't look away yet, I mustn't move yet. I waited to see what he would do, if anything. Giving myself a chance to think what to do next, I quickly felt the edges of the contract. Good, four pages. Last page was usually the one you had to sign and Anthony didn't do it differently. Was I sure about this? Yes, right. There was a pen on the table to the left of the contract when I walked in, it must still be there. What was Lloyd thinking? I must keep eye contact all the time. If he moved I would move. I was in control. Right, let's see if he would panic. "Anthony, if I sign this contract would you think me foolish?"

"No, Charlotte, I wouldn't." No reaction. Lloyd was still looking into my eyes. Just what I wanted him to do. His facial expression hadn't changed either, how does he do that. My expression must have changed about a 1000 times, since I came in here.

"If I don't sign—" I must keep calm and not give anything away. I was almost there. Eye contact, straight into his eyes.

"Are you asking me would I think you foolish if you didn't sign, Charlotte?"

"Yes, Anthony, exactly that." Oh my God, this was hard! Keep watching. Don't look away. I didn't know what Anthony was going to say. I could feel my legs starting to wobble at the knees.

"I wouldn't find you foolish whatever you decided, and again, Charlotte, I trust and respect that whatever you choose the choice would be the right one for you at this moment. I would also respect your choice if later you changed your mind."

Good, he was saying I had a get-out clause. Still no change. Lloyd didn't appear to be fazed at all. I told myself to stand still, wait, and compose myself.

I would have to take my eyes off him when I looked at the last page to see where the dotted line was. That was when he would react. OK, I'd got it right: three steps to the side kneel at the coffee table. The pen would be at my left hand. I had to pick the pen up and at the same time flip the contract over on the table, lift the last page and open it, take the pen in my right hand. That was the moment when I would have to look away from him, that was when he would have the advantage, if he was going to do anything, that would be when he was going to do it. I mustn't let him know when I was going to move. I had to keep looking at his eyes all the time.

Don't blow it, I told myself, one shot and one shot only. I heard Anthony slide back on the sofa. That was good, he wouldn't say or do any more now, he was sitting back to watch the show. OK, now or never. Three sideways steps.

I took the first one. Lloyd unfolded his arms and put them down by his side. Why did he do that? Keep calm, think. OK, got it! He thinks I am thinking he's going to make his move. Two more steps. Lloyd shifted his position slightly as I took the two steps. OK, now I must kneel down. This was going to be tricky. I felt for the table with my leg and took a small step back. Lloyd raised an eyebrow, trying to change the game, I thought. I must stay composed: before kneeling, keep eye contact all the time, oh his big blue eyes! No, Charlotte, I urged myself, keep with it, don't let him distract you now. I saw that he was closer to the table. He must have moved forward as well as changing position, so he must be going to make his move any minute now, either if I stopped looking at him when I knelt down, or when I looked at the contract to sign it. OK. I bent my knees, without losing eye contact. I reached for the pen, flipped the contract over and opened the back page. I passed the pen over to my right hand. Lucky I was a woman: a man would have struggled with all of that in one go. I held the contract down with my left hand. OK, this was it. He was going to do something. I knew he was. On one, eyes down. Three… two…one. I looked down at the contract for the dotted line. Lifting the pen, I set it on the line. Oh crap, brain, don't do this to me now. Don't panic me! Could I fucking really do this? Oh fuck my brain was losing control.

Lloyd slammed his hand down on the table.

BANG!

To be continued!

Acknowledgements

I would like to thank Helen Hart and all her team at SilverWood Books, for their help in publishing this book and for their patience. And my sister for talking me into writing and bringing Charlotte's story to life. Thanks, sis. I love you.